'A detective, a dog, and some major league prose. *Dog On It* is a genuine joy' Robert B. Parker

'Nothing short of masterful. Sequels are a given – and a must' *Los Angeles Times*

'Bernie and Chet may be the most appealing detective duo since Watson and Holmes' Sharon Kay Penman

'A winning debut ... that fans of classic mysteries are sure to appreciate' *Publishers Weekly*

'Spencer Quinn speaks two languages – suspense and dog – very fluently. Sometimes funny, sometimes touching, and in a few places terrifying, *Dog On It* has got more going for it than fifty of those cat cozies' Stephen King

'At last, a dog lover's mystery that portrays dogs as they really are ... Quinn's characters are endearing, and his narrative is intriguing, fast moving, and well written ... [*Dog On It*] is highly recommended' *Library Journal*

'This fast-moving and fun series entry will certainly please Chet and Bernie fans as well as gain new readers with its all-ages appeal. Expect this series to become the hot new thing in animal mysteries' Jessica Moyer

Spencer Quinn lives on Cape Cod with his dog Audrey.
He is currently working on the next Chet and Bernie
adventure. Keep up with him – and with Chet and
Bernie – by visiting ChetTheDog.com

Also by Spencer Quinn

Dog on It
Thereby Hangs a Tail
To Fetch a Thief

THE DOG WHO KNEW TOO MUCH

A CHET AND BERNIE MYSTERY

SPENCER QUINN

**SIMON &
SCHUSTER**

London · New York · Sydney · Toronto · New Delhi

A CBS COMPANY

First published in the USA by Atria Books, 2011
First published in Great Britain by Simon & Schuster UK Ltd, 2011
An imprint of Simon & Schuster UK Ltd
A CBS COMPANY

1 3 5 7 9 10 8 6 4 2

Simon & Schuster UK Ltd
1st Floor
222 Gray's Inn Road
London
WC1X 8HB

www.simonandschuster.co.uk

Simon & Schuster Australia, Sydney
Simon & Schuster India, New Delhi

A CIP catalogue record for this book is available from the British Library

ISBN 978-0-85720-850-7

Printed and bound by CPI Group (UK) Ltd, Croydon, CR0 4YY

For all the friends of the nation
within the nation

ACKNOWLEDGMENTS

Many thanks to Molly Friedrich, Lucy Carson, and Sylvie Rabineau.

ONE

Was I proud of Bernie or what?

True, he'd been pretty nervous going into this gig. I can always tell when Bernie's nervous—which hardly ever happens, and never when we're in action—because his smell sharpens a bit, although it's still the best human smell there is: apples, bourbon, salt and pepper. But now, up on the stage, he was doing great.

"Which, um," he was saying, "reminds me of a joke. "Sort of. Maybe not a joke," he went on, turning a page, "more like a—" and at that moment the whole wad of papers somehow jumped out of his hands, all the pages gliding down in different directions. He bent and started gathering them up. That gave me a chance, sitting a few rows back, to recoy or recon—or something like that—the joint, always important in our line of work, as Bernie often said.

We were in a conference room at a hotel near the airport, and everyone in the audience—maybe not quite as big as it had been at the beginning, when Bernie had tapped the microphone, a painful sound for me, pounding like drums right next to my ears, although no one else seemed to mind, cleared his throat, and said,

"Can, uh, you hear me all right?" a terrific start, in my opinion—
was a private eye, on account of this was the Great Western Private
Eye Convention. We're partners in the Little Detective Agency,
me and Bernie, Bernie's last name being Little. I'm Chet, pure and
simple, and we'd been in business for almost as long as I could
remember, although we'd never been to a convention before. "Not
our thing," Bernie said, so that was that, until Georgie Malhouf,
president of the Great Western Private Eye Association, offered
Bernie five hundred bucks to give a speech.

"A speech?" Bernie had said.

"Twenty minutes, tops," Georgie Malhouf told him. "Plus
questions."

"I've never given a speech in my life."

"So what?" said Georgie Malhouf. "There was also a time in
your life when you hadn't had sex. Did that stop you?"

That one zipped right by me, but the point was: five hundred
bucks. Our finances were a mess. We hadn't worked an actual
case—not even divorce, which we hated—in I didn't know how
long, plus there was the hit we'd taken from the tin futures thing,
and don't get me started on the stacks and stacks of Hawaiian
pants, locked away at our self-storage in Pedroia; we hadn't sold
a single pair. Why they hadn't caught on was a mystery to me:
didn't everybody love Hawaiian shirts? Bernie had lots of them,
was wearing one of my favorites right now up on that stage, the
blue number with the gold trumpets.

He picked up the pages, or most of them, and tried to get
them back into some kind of order. Meanwhile, I heard feet shuffling out of the room behind me, and across the aisle I was sitting in both Mirabelli brothers seemed to be asleep, their mouths
hanging open. On my other side sat Georgie Malhouf, a real
skinny guy with sunken cheeks and a thick black mustache.

There's something about mustaches that makes it hard for me to look away, so I didn't. After some time, I noticed that Georgie was looking at me, too.

"On the ball, aren't you?" he said. "Just like they say."

Ball? I'm just about always in the mood to play ball. A very faint thought arose in my mind, something about this maybe not being a good time for playing ball; but it sank quickly away, and I kept my eyes on Georgie Malhouf, waiting for him to produce a ball from somewhere. No ball appeared. Georgie Malhouf was keeping his eyes, small and dark, on me.

"Ten grand sound about right?" he said.

Numbers aren't my best thing—I stop at two, a perfect number in my opinion—but when it came to money anything with grand in it got us excited, me and Bernie. He was bumping us up to ten grand? Bernie's speech was going even better than I'd thought.

BAM BAM BAM. Bernie was tapping the microphone again. "Hear me all right?" He glanced up at the audience, from which came no response, and then quickly down to the papers in his hand. For some reason, he was holding them kind of close to his face, and they weren't quite steady.

"This, uh, joke—maybe more like a . . ." He lapsed into silence, a silence that seemed rather long—although the room was getting noisier, with more movement toward the doors behind me—then cleared his throat again, so forcefully it had to hurt, and said very loudly, almost a shout: "Riddle!" He toned it down a bit. "Riddle. That's it. Here comes the riddle: What did the duck say to the horse?" He glanced up in an abrupt sort of way and scanned the audience, what was left of it.

What did the duck say to the horse? Was that what Bernie had just said?

"Anybody?" Bernie said. "Duck? Horse?"

No response. I knew horses, of course, prima donnas each and every one. I'd also had an encounter with a duck, in the middle of a lake in the border country on our way back from a case we'd been working down Mexico way. Nipped me right on the nose, which came as a big surprise. But horses and ducks together? I had nothing to offer.

Up on stage, Bernie opened his mouth, closed it, opened it again. "'Why the long face?'" he said.

Silence.

Bernie reached out, maybe thinking of tapping the microphone again, but did not. "Duck?" he said. "Noting the horse's different physiognomy, which was the topic of my speech, facial classifications? A funny little approach to the subject at hand?"

More silence.

Bernie shuffled through the papers. "And I guess that more or less . . . brings us to the end of the prepared remarks." What was the word for when humans talk but you can't understand a thing? Muttering? Yeah. Bernie was muttering now. "Happy to take any questions," he went on, or something like that.

There were no questions.

"Well, then, it's time to, uh . . . thanks. Yeah. Thanks. You've been a great, um." Bernie raised his hand in a funny sort of wave, a page or two flying free, and started walking off the stage. Then came the applause. I heard it for sure, but my sense of hearing's probably better than yours, no offense.

"Fantastic, Bernie," Georgie Malhouf was saying. We were at a corner table in the bar of the airport hotel, and by now Bernie had stopped sweating. "You're a natural-born public speaker."

"I am?"

"Never seen anything like it." A fresh round of drinks came, beer for Bernie and Georgie Malhouf, water in a nice big soup bowl for me. Georgie clinked Bernie's glass. "Why the long face," he said. "Priceless. When did you make that one up?"

"Make it up?" said Bernie. "Can't really say I—"

"Not just a natural-born public speaker," Georgie said, "but a natural-born communicator in general." He handed Bernie a check. "Here you go, pal. Earned every penny."

I watched carefully till Bernie folded the check and put it in his pocket, not his shirt pocket, where we'd run into problems before, or his back pants pocket, also unreliable once or twice in the past, but the front pants pocket, safe and sound with the car keys.

"Bourbon still your drink, Bernie?" Georgie said. "How about a shot of something to go along with that beer?"

"A little early for—"

"Miss!"

Two shots of bourbon arrived. Glasses got clinked again.

"Communicators aren't exactly thick on the ground in this business," Georgie said. I could make out a stretch of ground through the window, saw nothing but a parking lot with a red car pulling in. "So why don't I cut to the chase?"

That was the kind of thing I liked to hear. I got my back paws up under me, ready to move.

Bernie lowered his glass, tilted his head slightly to one side. That was a sign of his brain clicking into gear, and Bernie's brain was one of the best things we had going for us at the Little Detective Agency. His brain and my nose: plenty of perps now wearing orange jump suits can tell you about that combo.

"Life's not fair," Georgie went on, losing me right away. "Man of your ability." He shook his head.

"No complaints," Bernie said.

"See, right there—the quality factor," said Georgie. He took out a pack of cigarettes, offered one to Bernie. Bernie had quit smoking lots of times, but right now we were in the middle of one of his best efforts.

"Don't think there's smoking in here," Bernie said.

"Hotel's a client," said Georgie. "Live a little."

They lit up. Bernie took a deep drag, let the smoke out with a sigh. Poor Bernie. Smoke drifted over toward me. I was smelling how pleasant it smelled when I noticed the red car parking right beside our ride. Our ride's a Porsche, but not the new fancy kind. It's brown with yellow doors, very old, and the top went missing back when we were working the Hobbs case, a story for another time. A woman sat behind the wheel of the red car; she didn't seem in a hurry to get out.

Georgie sipped his drink. "Like this bourbon?" he said.

"Very nice," Bernie said.

"Tell you the truth, Bern," Georgie began, and I missed some of what came next, on account of: *Bern*. Bernie hated that! In fact, the last guy who'd tried it, a carjacker from the East Valley, name escaping me at the moment, was now breaking rocks in the hot sun. Were we about to take down Georgie Malhouf? His mustache was really starting to bother me.

". . . whole chain's a client," Georgie was saying, "including the Arbuckle Palace in LA. Check out the world around us. Security—my kind—is only going to get bigger."

"What's the other kind?" Bernie said.

Georgie made a motion with his hand, like he was waving away flying insects, although there were none around. I always know when insects are around: they're very noisy. Birds are much quieter when they fly, kind of crazy.

"The other kind," Georgie said, "is the lone wolf." He leaned forward, wagged his finger at Bernie. "Headed for rapid extinction, Bern." Sometimes things go by so fast you can't keep up. For example, Georgie's wagging finger had curly black hair on the back, always interesting, but there was no time to dwell on it, not if wolves were suddenly in the picture. I knew wolves, but only from Animal Planet. I glanced around the bar: no wolves, no creatures of any kind, except humans and me. But the fur on my neck was up and stiff.

"I'm offering you a job," Georgie said. He looked over at me. "You and Chet, of course."

"You mean you want to subcontract a case out to us?" Bernie said.

"Nope," said Georgie. "I'm talking about a real permanent-type job, assistant VP Operations, Malhouf International Investigations, eighty-five K to start, plus benefits and two weeks' paid vacation."

Bernie shook his head, a very quick side-to-side. Charlie—that's Bernie's kid, who we don't see nearly enough since the divorce—has the exact same headshake. All of a sudden Bernie looked younger.

Georgie sat back in his chair. His eyes, dark to begin with, darkened some more. "Not even going to think about it?" he said.

"I appreciate the offer," Bernie said. "But it wouldn't be a good fit."

"I'll be the judge of that," Georgie said.

"See?" said Bernie, and he laughed.

Bernie has a great laugh, so much fun to listen to—the way it comes from deep down—but Georgie didn't seem to be enjoying it. "Always considered you a serious individual, Bern," he said. "Must be some reason you're not taking me seriously."

Bernie shrugged.

Georgie leaned forward. "I do my research. That means I know what you've been making. Or not making, to put it more accurately. Christ, I know about the tin futures. And even the goddamn pants. What else? You're late on your kid's tuition and you're upside down on your house."

Upside down on our house? I gave up on understanding Georgie. But whatever he was talking about seemed to have gotten to Bernie. When Bernie's angry, a little jaw muscle starts clenching, and it was clenching now. He put down his drink and started to rise. "Thanks for the drink," he said. "The answer's no."

Georgie shrugged; I always watch for that one. "Gotta do what you gotta do," he said, rising too. He took something from his pocket, something that looked like another check, and held it out to Bernie.

"What's this?" Bernie said, not taking it.

"Ten grand," Georgie said.

"What the hell?"

"Not for you."

"What are you talking about?"

"It's for Chet."

"I don't understand," Bernie said. Ten grand! Maybe it was a prize or something. I'd once won a whole box of Slim Jims at an agility contest, but no time to go into that now. All I thought was: take the money!

"I want to buy Chet," Georgie said. "Have him come work for us."

What was this? Something without Bernie?

"Chet's not for sale," Bernie said. His face had gone pale, practically white. "Not now, not ever."

"Fifteen grand," Georgie said. "Final offer."

Bernie didn't touch the ten-grand check. And as for the five-hundred-dollar check—this was getting pretty complicated, with two checks in play—Bernie dug it out of his pocket and dropped it on the table. I was sorry to see it go, but only a bit. We walked out of the bar, me and Bernie. Was I proud of him or what?

TWO

"Next time," said Bernie, "what if I lead with the joke?"

Sounded good to me, although if there'd been a joke I'd forgotten it. We went down a long line of cars, the Porsche near the end. It's hard not to get excited when the Porsche comes into view. What beats riding shotgun? Nothing in this dude's life, amigo. But I'm pretty good at controlling myself at times like this, a professional through and through, and—

"Chet? Easy, big guy."

Oops. Racing around the parking lot in tight little circles, ears flat back from the breeze? That might have been me. I got a grip, walked in a dead-straight line at Bernie's side, head up, tail up, beyond reproach, whatever that meant exactly. We were close enough to see our bumper sticker from Max's Memphis Ribs, our favorite restaurant in the whole Valley—hadn't been there in way too long—and the bullet hole in our license plate, can't go into that now, when the door of the red car opened and the woman stepped out.

"Bernie Little?" she said.

Women of a certain type have an effect on Bernie. This was

that type of woman, easy to see just from the way Bernie's mouth fell slightly open. Curvy shape: check. Big blue eyes: check. Face tilted up in his direction: check. Poor Bernie: that was all it took.

"That's me," Bernie said. "And this is Chet."

She backed away. "He's so big. I'm not comfortable around dogs."

Not comfortable around me? True, I'm a hundred-plus-pounder, but she had nothing to be uncomfortable about, unless she pulled a gun or something like that. I watched her hands, square-shaped, a little plump, with bright red nails.

"You can be comfortable around Chet," Bernie said.

"Why is he looking at me like that?"

Bernie glanced over at me. "Uh, not sure, actually. But he means well."

Of course I did! But I kept my eyes on her hands, just in case. Funny how the mind works: mine was making some kind of connection between red nails and guns. Then I started thinking about the way women paint their nails—I'd seen Leda, Bernie's ex-wife, do it many times—and men never did. Next I thought about what human nails were for, so small and dull-edged. And after that I lost the thread.

"My name's Anya Vereen," the woman was saying. "I heard of you from a friend."

"Who?" said Bernie.

"You might not know her by her real name," Anya said.

"No?" said Bernie. "What name would I know her by?"

"Autumn."

Autumn! I knew Autumn. She worked for Livia Moon at Livia's Friendly Coffee and More, over in Pottsdale—not in the coffee part out front but in the house of ill-repute part out back. Autumn was one of those humans who really liked me and my kind—the nation within the nation, Bernie calls us—and she's also a world-class patter. We'd interviewed her not too long ago, but the details of the case weren't coming to me at the moment.

"Ah," said Bernie. Then came a silence. Silences like that often happened when Bernie was getting to know women of a certain type.

"Ah?" said Anya. "Meaning what?"

"Nothing," Bernie said. "Nothing at all—just that, yes, I've met Autumn."

"And you've jumped to the conclusion that I'm in the same line of work."

"No," said Bernie.

He was right about that. I love Bernie, and he can do just about anything—you should see him in a fight!—but jumping is not one of them. That's on account of his war wound. Bernie went to war in the desert—not our desert, but some other desert far away, and this was before we got together—and came back with his leg wound. He never talks about it, but he limps sometimes when he's tired. When that happens I slow down a bit so he can keep up.

"Because I'm not in her line of work," Anya said. "Although sometimes I wish I was."

"Oh?"

"She's making real good money. I should know—I do her taxes."

"You're an accountant, Anya?"

"Correct. And you're not pronouncing my name right."

"No?"

"It's like On Ya."

"Um," said Bernie.

"Autumn says you're the best private detective in the Valley."

Bernie nodded. He's a great nodder, has all sorts of nods that mean this and that. This particular nod meant he disagreed about being the best in the Valley but didn't mind hearing it. But that was just Bernie being Bernie: he is the best in the Valley, ask any perp.

"I'd like to hire you for two days," Anya said.

"To do what?" Bernie said.

"Security."

"What kind of security?"

"Bodyguard work, I guess you could say."

"Bodyguarding who?"

"Me," said Anya. "More or less."

"Are you in danger?" Bernie said.

I glanced around. The sun beat down on us—we were still in the hot time of year—and glared off windshields in the parking lot, making little suns all over the place, but I saw no signs of any danger. There was only one human in sight, a man looking in our direction from a balcony about halfway up the side of the hotel: Georgie Malhouf, in fact, easy to recognize with that black mustache of his. He raised a pair of binoculars.

"Not real physical danger, I don't think," Anya said. "But just your very presence should prevent any unpleasantness."

"Unpleasantness from whom?" Bernie said.

"That would be Guy Wenders," said Anya. "My ex."

"How long have you been divorced?"

"Six months. We were separated for two years before that. Pretty much." She looked Bernie up and down. "Maybe I should give you some background."

"That would be nice," Bernie said.

"Autumn didn't mention your sense of humor." Anya gave him a not-very-friendly look when she said that, but at the same

time I picked up a scent coming off her—faint but unmistakable—that meant she was starting to like Bernie. Nothing about
humans is simple: I've learned that lots of times in my career.

"Could we get out of the heat?" she said. A tiny drop of sweat
had appeared on her upper lip; I noticed that Bernie was watching it, too.

"The divorce was my idea," Anya said. We were out of the heat
sitting under a tree in a little park across the street from the hotel,
Bernie and Anya on the bench and me beside it, sitting up nice
and straight, a pro from nose to tail. "Guy has had trouble dealing
with it," Anya said.

"What kind of trouble?" Bernie said.

Anya's big blue eyes got an inward look. "Conceptual, I guess
you'd say. We were so young when we met. He doesn't realize how
much we've gone off in different directions."

"What directions?" Bernie said.

"I wanted to make something of myself," Anya said, "which
was why I started taking accounting at Valley CC's night school,
working temp jobs during the day. Guy wanted to make something of himself, too. But he had his own ideas about how."

"Like?" said Bernie.

"He runs a sort of investment firm," said Anya. "Some of his
associates aren't the kind of people I want around Devin."

"Who's Devin?"

"Our kid, mine and Guy's. That's sort of what this is all about,
me hiring you."

"Are you in a custody fight?" Bernie said.

"No," said Anya. "I have custody. But it's parents' weekend
at Big Bear Wilderness Camp—that's where Devin is for the
month—and Guy's going to be there. He made some remark

about rekindling things under big western skies. I don't want that to happen."

"What do you expect us to do?" Bernie said.

"Us?" said Anya.

"Chet and I," Bernie said.

Anya glanced in my direction. Interesting: I was no longer sitting by the bench but seemed to have shifted over toward the base of the tree, where I was now sniffing out lots of smells, mostly from a bunch of my guys who'd left their marks on the trunk. I raised my leg—you always want to be on top, mark-wise—eyes on Anya at the same time, which involved sort of twisting my head around to look backward, no problem at all for me. Strong no-nonsense splashing sounds came from behind me, or in front—things can get confusing sometimes.

Anya turned to Bernie. "What I'd like you to do," she said, "is just be my friend."

It's hard to surprise Bernie, so the look on his face at that moment was not one I saw often. "I'm sorry?" he said.

"Pretend-friend, I meant to say," Anya said. "If I show up with a male friend, Guy will get the message."

"You want to hire me to masquerade as your boyfriend?" Bernie said.

"We don't have to define anything—just your being around should do the trick."

"You said that before," Bernie said. "But I didn't understand the context. The answer's no."

"No?" Anya sat back. "Why not?"

I picked up a twig—more like a small branch, really—and wandered back to the bench.

"We don't do that kind of work," Bernie said, "and even if you find someone who does, you'd be wasting your money."

"Why do you say that?"

"Because this doesn't sound like something you couldn't take care of on your own."

"Shouldn't I be the judge of that?" Anya said.

Bernie gazed at her for a moment or two and then said, "Maybe."

"All right, then. What's your fee structure?"

"Eight hundred a day plus expenses, if that's what fee structure means," said Bernie. "But the answer's still no."

"I'll double that," Anya said. "Thirty-two hundred for the weekend." Bernie sat motionless. A look came into his eyes, a look I'd seen before, and meant *no* was coming. All I knew was that our finances were a mess. That worried me, and when I get worried, I like to be closer to Bernie. I went closer to Bernie, maybe a little too abruptly, and possibly forgetting the branch in my mouth. Did the end of the branch—perhaps not so small after all, and also somewhat pointy—catch Bernie on the side of the elbow?

"Ow," he said. The elbow: one of those sensitive human body parts; still there tends to be an overreaction at times like this, if you want my opinion. "Chet, what the hell?"

But even if he was overreacting, I'd never want to hurt Bernie. I dropped the branch—which turned out to be on the largish side—immediately. Did it land on his foot? Oops. But if so, he didn't say "ow" again, or at least not very loudly. I did notice he was wearing his flip-flops. Was that what humans wore for giving talks? I wasn't sure.

Meanwhile, Anya's eyes were on me. "He's actually kind of good-looking," she said. "What's his name again?"

"Chet."

"That's a nice name. Short for Chester?"

Short for Chester? What was that supposed to mean?

"Just Chet," Bernie said.

"How did you pick the name?"

"I didn't. He was already Chet when I met him."

I remembered that day, a bad day—flunking out of K-9 school just before the leaping test, my very best thing! Was a cat involved? Blood? Those parts were pretty hazy. But a real good day, too, on account of that was when I got together with Bernie.

"Who picked his name?" Anya said.

"Funny you should ask," Bernie said. "I've been looking into that. Chet was rescued from some rough circumstances as a puppy, but evidently he already had the name."

"Good coming from bad," Anya said.

Bernie glanced at her, said nothing.

"I was never a dog person," Anya said. She reached out, gave me a quick pat on the side, very light. More, was my thought.

Bernie seemed to be thinking, too. He took a deep breath. "All right," he said. "We'll do it."

That breeze starting up behind me? Had to be my tail. We were back in business.

On the way home we stopped by Suzie Sanchez's office. Suzie's a reporter for the *Valley Tribune*. She has bright dark eyes that gleam like the countertops in our kitchen, that one time Bernie polished them, and she smells like soap and lemons. I liked Suzie and so did Bernie; in fact, they were kind of boyfriend and girlfriend, especially now that Dylan McKnight—Suzie's old boyfriend, possibly a burglar or drug dealer, I couldn't remember, although that time I chased him up a tree was very clear in my mind—seemed to be out of the picture.

Suzie's office was in a strip mall, a nice strip mall with nothing boarded up. We went in. There were a bunch of workstations, all empty except for Suzie's at the back. She looked up from her computer and smiled.

"How did the speech go?" she said. She has one of those nice voices, easy on the ears. Leda's voice isn't like that.

"Pretty good," Bernie said. "Or okay. Not a complete failure. Almost certainly."

Suzie glanced down at Bernie's feet, kind of pale in the flip-flops. "These things always go better than you think," she said. "The audience wants you to do well."

"Wish I'd known that before," Bernie said.

Suzie laughed and rose. She gave Bernie a kiss. He gave her a kiss back. I squeezed between them, just being friendly.

"Dinner at my place?" Bernie said. "I'll pick up steaks on the way home."

Suzie shook her head. "I'm covering the debate tonight."

"A debate? Friday night?"

"There's an election coming, Bernie, like it or not."

"Which one's for protecting the aquifer?" Poor Bernie. The aquifer, whatever it was, preyed on Bernie's mind. Something about water, but we had water out the yingyang: drive by any golf course—and we've got them out the yingyang, too—and you'll see sprinklers working early and late every day.

"Both in theory," Suzie said. "Neither in fact. Rain check for tomorrow?"

Rain? Was this still about the aquifer? It hardly ever rains in the Valley, not a drop in ages. Hey! Yet still we had water out the yingyang! How cool was that? What a country, as Bernie likes to say.

". . . bodyguarding," Bernie was telling Suzie. "So we'll have to shoot for Monday."

"Bodyguarding who?" said Suzie.

"Um, kind of complicated," Bernie said. "It's sort of like—"

Suzie's phone rang. She went to her desk, answered it, listened, said, "But I'm already—" and listened some more. After a while, she glanced over and gave us a little wave good-bye.

We left Suzie's office, me and Bernie. Sometimes big questions pop up in life. For example: was steak still on the menu or not?

THREE

I woke up early the next morning—always easy to tell early from the faintness of the light coming through the window, a light that reminded me of Leda's pearl necklace, which I still feel badly about whenever it pops into my mind. But it didn't quite pop into my mind now, and I rose, feeling tip-top. First, I had a nice stretch, butt way up, front paws way forward: can't tell you how good that feels. Next, I glanced over at the bed. Bernie was asleep on his back, one arm over his face, chest rising and falling in a slow, even rhythm. I watched him breathe for a while. Sometimes Bernie calls out in his sleep—"Hit the ground, hit the ground": I've heard that one a few times—but now he seemed quiet and peaceful. I left the bedroom—once Bernie and Leda's, now just Bernie's—and went into the hall.

Nothing like being at home, except when we're on some adventure, when it turns out there's nothing like that, too. Home is our place on Mesquite Road. That's in the Valley, which goes on just about forever in all directions. We've got two bedrooms—the second one's Charlie's, the bed all made for whenever the next every-second-weekend rolls around—plus the office and other rooms I'll have to describe later, because right now I was sniffing at the crack under the front door, which I do every morning, part of my job.

A squirrel had been by, and not long ago. That bothered me. I hurried to the long window beside the door and gazed out. We've got three trees in front of the house. The middle one's my favorite for lying under, and that was where the squirrel, chubby and gray, tail raised in a very annoying way, was busy burying something. The next thing I knew I was standing straight up, front paws on the glass, barking my head off. The squirrel shot up the tree without a backward glance: burying things under that tree is my department, little pal.

"Chet! What's all the fuss?"

Bernie was up? I hadn't even heard him. That was bad. I slid down off the window real fast and smooth, like I'd never been up there at all. Bernie came over and gazed out, giving me a pat at the same time. His hair was standing out in clumps here and there; one eyebrow was crooked; he wore what Leda had always called his ratty robe, although there wasn't a single rat on it, just a pattern of martini glasses with long-legged women sitting in them. In short, he looked great.

Bernie peered out the window. "I don't see anything," he said.

He couldn't see that bushy gray tail hanging down from a high branch?

"Was old man Heydrich up to something?"

I fixed my gaze right on that bushy tail and barked. All Bernie had to do was glance in the same direction. But instead he said, "Take it easy, big guy," and went back down the hall.

Old man Heydrich's our neighbor on one side. He likes to sweep stuff from his part of the sidewalk onto our part of the sidewalk when he thinks nobody's looking, and that's just one of his tricks. Iggy lives in the house on the other side with this old couple called the Parsons. Iggy's my best pal, but the Parsons aren't doing so well these days, plus there's some confusion with their electric fence, and now Iggy doesn't get out much. I went over to our side window. And there he was at his side window!

Iggy stared at me. I stared at Iggy. After a bit of that, he turned and trotted away, wagging that stubby little tail of his. A few moments later, he returned. Now he had something in his mouth. It looked like . . . oh, no, was that possible? Iggy had a whole package of bacon? And I didn't?

Iggy stared at me. I stared at Iggy. I recognized that wrapping, mostly see-through, with a gold band at the top: we had the same kind—excellent bacon, farm-fresh and organic, according to Bernie—in the fridge. I wanted bacon real bad, and not just any bacon, but Iggy's bacon. He just stood there, the package in his mouth. Mr. Parsons appeared in the background, approaching Iggy slowly, on account of his walker. Iggy didn't seem to be aware of Mr. Parsons at all: he was too busy making sure I got a nice long look at that bacon. And now Mr. Parsons was right behind him. Grab that bacon, Mr. Parsons, quick! Mr. Parsons reached down to grab the bacon, but not quick. Iggy saw his hand at the last moment and booked; also not quick, but quick enough. Mr. Parsons stumped after him, both of them vanishing from my sight.

I went into the kitchen and stood in front of the fridge. We'd worked on doors, me Bernie, and there were now some I could open, but fridge doors weren't among them. So I just stood there. I could hear Bernie singing in the shower, some of his old favorites: "Born to Lose," "Crying Time," "Death Don't Have No Mercy in This Land." He was in a good mood.

* * *

We ended up having a quick breakfast, toast and coffee for Bernie, kibble and water for me—the fridge not even getting opened once. But no complaints. "Let's go earn our money, big guy."

I reached the door first, got outside first, hopped into the Porsche first. Bernie was opening the door—he doesn't do much hopping, on account of his leg—when a big black SUV pulled into the driveway behind us. The driver, a neckless shaved-headed dude, stayed behind the wheel, maybe a good thing because that neckless look in a human sometimes got me going. The passenger, Georgie Malhouf, climbed out, some papers in his hand.

"Morning, Bernie," he said.

"What's up?" said Bernie.

"Looks like I just caught you," Georgie said. "Headed anywhere interesting?"

"No," Bernie said.

Georgie laughed. "Always loved your sense of humor," he said.

"Yeah?" said Bernie. "We haven't really spent much time together."

"Maybe I'm a quick study."

Bernie gave him one of those second looks. "Maybe you are."

"Why I'm here," Georgie said, "is to make sure we get past that little hiccup yesterday."

Hiccups! I had them once. So weird. Bernie clapped his hands real loud, right in my face, and they went away. But hiccups yesterday? I had no memory of that.

"Already past it," Bernie said.

I watched him closely. Was Georgie saying Bernie had the hiccups? I'd never seen him hiccup before, hoped he had no plans to start now.

"What I'd like is for you to accept the speaker's check," Georgie said.

Bernie shook his head.

"In that case, my lawyer wants you to sign this waiver." He handed Bernie the papers.

Bernie riffled through them. "Saying I agree to accept no fee for the speech?"

"Legal verbiage to that effect."

"This is a lot of bullshit, Georgie."

"You know lawyers."

Bernie dug in his pockets, failed to come up with a pen. Georgie gave him one.

"Sign there," he said.

Bernie signed.

"And initial here. And here. And here."

"For Christ sake."

Georgie shuffled the paper. "And one last signature right there." He stabbed his finger at the bottom of a page. Bernie signed, not even looking. "Much obliged," said Georgie. He got in the SUV. The driver backed onto the street, turning his head. That gave me a real good view of his necklessness. I barked.

"What's on your mind, Chet?" Bernie said, and then a nice pat pat.

Nothing really, besides wanting to give that driver a quick nip.

Bernie climbed in the car. "Know what I'm thinking?" I waited to hear. "Lawyers are an easy target." I waited some more. "Do you want a nation of laws?" I didn't know. "Then you're going to have lawyers." The only lawyer I could think of was Rex Lippican Jr., whom we'd brought down for doing something or other and was now sporting an orange jumpsuit up at Northern State. But if lawyers were okay in Bernie's book they were okay in mine.

* * *

Anya Vereen lived in the North Valley. It was one of those developments Bernie hated where all the streets were cul de sacs and all the houses look the same. "How can this be sustainable?" he said as we pulled into her driveway. I wasn't sure about that, but there was no doubt in my mind that someone was frying bacon, and not far away. Some days—has this ever happened to you?—bacon crops up over and over.

The door opened and out came Anya, wearing jeans, a tank top, and a small backpack. She hurried over to the car and paused, her eyes maybe on me, riding shotgun.

"Oh," she said.

"Oh?"

"I'd forgotten he was part of this."

"Chet?" Bernie looked confused. "He's part of . . ." He glanced over at me. ". . . everything."

Of course. We're partners, me and Bernie, in the Little Detective Agency, if I haven't made that clear already.

"Okey-doke," said Anya. "I'll just squeeze in behind."

"Oh, no," Bernie said. "That's not necessary. Into the back, Chet."

The back was this tiny little sort of bench. I'd sat there before, but only when Charlie or Suzie was coming along for the ride.

"Chet?"

I have this ability to make my whole body very stiff and immovable, but I hardly ever use it.

"That's all right," Anya said. "He's bigger than I am anyway." She sprang into the back and wedged her backpack between the front seats, all in one easy motion.

Bernie's eyebrows rose. They were straightened out now after his shower, but Bernie's eyebrows were always expressive, spoke a language of their own. Right now they were saying he was impressed.

"I weigh ninety-nine pounds," Anya said. "Soaking wet."

Bernie looked thoughtful. I was thinking, too, along the lines of: I'm a hundred-plus-pounder. More or less than Anya? I'll let you be the judge of that.

"How much do you weigh, Bernie?" Anya said as we pulled away from the curb.

Bernie's weight: had that ever come up before? Not that I remembered. I waited to hear.

"Not actually sure," Bernie said.

"Don't be shy."

"Haven't stepped on a scale in a while," Bernie said.

"How about at your last checkup?"

"That's been a while, too."

She gave him a long look, but he didn't see it, now that we were on the road. We drove out of Anya's development, went by some strip malls packed with fast-food joints. Humans come up with great ideas sometimes, fast-food joints being one of the very best.

Maybe Bernie was thinking the same sort of thing—not the first time that had happened to us—because he said, "Want to pick up something to eat along the way?"

"I packed some sandwiches," Anya said, tapping her backpack.

Tuna, peanut butter, egg salad: old news.

"Hey, thanks," said Bernie.

We took a ramp, hit the freeway.

"Too breezy?" Bernie said, glancing at Anya in the rearview mirror. The wind was blowing back her hair—short and kind of reddish. Women often looked different with their hair sort of out of the picture like that. Anya, for example, looked older.

"I love the wind," she said.

Me, too. Then I had a strange thought: so did Suzie. Where had that come from? What did it mean? No idea. I pushed the whole thing out of my mind. That was easy. Nothing sets you up better for the day than a clear mind.

"Good thing," Bernie said, "because the top's gone."

"What happened to it?" Anya said.

We merged into light traffic, got in the fast lane. We like the fast lane best, me and Bernie. He started telling the story of how we lost the top, a long story I'd heard many times, involving a perp named Fishhead Hobbs, a heist he was planning at the jewelry store in the Downtown Ritz—this was the same case where I ran into trouble at the fountain in their lobby—and a bee sting, which was when Fishhead's whole plan started coming apart. Bernie's words streamed by in a very pleasant way. City smells grew weaker; country smells grew stronger; and at last we were out of the Valley and into the desert. Hills rose in the distance, the zigzag foot trails up their slopes shining like silver in the morning light. I've been on trails like that before, wanted to be on them again, like right now, and real bad.

"Easy, big guy," Bernie said.

"What got into him?" said Anya.

"He likes open country, that's all," said Bernie.

Doesn't everyone?

We left the freeway, took two-lane blacktop, rose higher, the air getting fresher and cooler. Did Bernie say something about crossing a state line? Maybe, but that was around the time I spotted a roadrunner. This little bugger, like all roadrunners, thought he was fast. Well, get ready, amigo, to see what real speed—

"Chet?"

Soon after that, we took a lunch break. Bernie parked by a long flat-topped rock at the side of the road, just like a bench. Peanut butter for Bernie; egg salad for Anya; tuna for me—the chunky kind, my favorite. Mountains rose, not too far away, greener than the mountains I was used to.

"Tell me about your ex-husband," Bernie said.

"What do you want to know?" Anya said.

"Start with the investment business."

Anya gazed at the distant green mountains. A cloud or two hung over them, not dark clouds, but the fat, golden kind.

"This used to happen to me a lot as a kid," Anya said.

"What's that?" said Bernie.

"Wishing that time would stop."

Whoa. She was wishing time would stop right now, leaving us with the crusts of one egg salad sandwich? At that moment I knew one thing for sure: Anya was a risk taker.

She turned to Bernie. "Do you ever think that?"

"No," said Bernie. Phew. We were on the same page, meaning dinner was still in the plans, and possibly a snack before that.

Anya's face flushed. That's something I look for. You see it in kids and in women, hardly ever in men. It has something to do with feelings inside; I haven't gotten farther than that—every time I try I come up against the thought: does that mean kids and women have more feelings than men? And stop right there, on account of knowing Bernie the way I do.

"Sorry," she said. "Didn't mean to—"

"Nothing to be sorry about," Bernie said. "Back to the investment business."

Anya took a deep breath, her color returning to normal. "Guy handles money for some private investors," she said.

"Are these the people you don't want around Devin?"

"Maybe that wasn't fair," Anya said. "I don't really know them."

FOUR

Back in the car. So quiet, except for the wind, and even the wind was sort of quiet. There are lots of different quiets: this one was all about everybody thinking to themselves. No idea what was on Bernie's mind or Anya's, but I was thinking: we're dealing with a guy named Guy on this job? That couldn't be good.

We drove into green mountains, tall trees unlike any I'd known standing by the side of the road. A fast-flowing creek also appeared at times, the water frothing over shining rocks and looking delicious.

"Has Guy ever been violent with you?" Bernie said after a while.

"Not really," Anya said.

"I'll take that for a yes," said Bernie.

Anya gazed at the back of his head. From the way I was sitting in the shotgun seat—where I belonged—angled and facing Bernie, I could easily watch both of them without turning my head. Humans have to turn their heads much more than we do, in the nation within, to keep their eye on things.

"You're a smart man," Anya said. "Autumn mentioned that."

Bernie looked surprised but didn't say anything.

"He pushed me, but just once," Anya said. "That was the night I made up my mind to separate. There's a line, you know? Especially with someone the size of Guy."

"Does he carry a gun?" Bernie said.

"I don't know about now, but back when we were together, no," Anya said. After a silence she said, "I notice you didn't ask how big he is."

Bernie shrugged.

"Wouldn't most men in your position?"

"What position is that?"

"My—air quotes—friend," said Anya, kind of losing me.

Bernie shrugged again. This was about the size of the guy named Guy? Who cared about stuff like that? Not me and Bernie.

"Are you armed, Bernie?" Anya said.

"Nope."

Oh, too bad. A little gunplay is always exciting, and the .38 Special is often in the glove box. So: this wasn't a real job, more like a vacation trip. All of a sudden my eyelids got real heavy. Does that ever happen to you, so fast that you barely have time to get comfortable before they slam shut?

". . . actually a pretty good father," Anya was saying. A dream I was having—all about chasing a chubby javelina in the canyon behind our place on Mesquite Road, a chubby javelina that from out of nowhere sprouted a rattlesnake rattle on its twisted little tail in that way dreams have of abruptly getting away from you—broke in tiny pieces that zoomed away and vanished, like spaceships in those sci-fi movies when Bernie and I went through a period of watching sci-fi movies, over pretty quickly, one good thing about it.

"Not that he sees much of Devin," Anya went on, "but he's never missed a child support payment and he's paying the whole shot for the camp—it was even his idea."

We weren't moving. I poked my head up over the door. We were parked at the side of a narrow road, flowers everywhere and a creek bubbling by. Hey! It was still a dream!

Then I saw Bernie and Anya. She was on the near side of the creek, dipping her bare foot in the water. Bernie was on the other side, sort of wandering around at the edge of a forest—the first forest I'd seen in real life, although I knew them from the Discovery Channel—like he was looking for something.

"It's not a fat camp, exactly," Anya was saying. "More of a build-you-into-a-man wilderness thing."

"Uh-huh," said Bernie, a sort of uh-huh he had for when he wasn't really listening.

"Not that Devin doesn't have a weight problem," Anya said. "It breaks my heart sometimes. Kids can be so cruel." She took a pack of cigarettes—uh-oh, Anya smoked cigarettes?—from the pocket of her jeans—how they fit in there was hard to say, her jeans being so tight—and lit up, flinging the match in the stream. "Tell me why that is?"

"Ah," said Bernie, suddenly stooping by a tree trunk and pulling something out of the ground. "I thought this might . . ."

"What's that?" said Anya.

Bernie held it up. *"Boletus edulis,"* he said.

"A mushroom?"

"Yup."

"Edible?"

"Delicious."

I hopped out of the car, no particular reason.

"Are you sure?" Anya said. "When I was a kid my dad told me never to eat wild mushrooms."

"Yeah?" said Bernie. "My dad showed me how to find the good ones."

Bernie's dad was suddenly in the picture? He never talks about his dad, who died a long time ago. His mom, a real piece of work, lives in Florida with the husband who came after the husband after Bernie's dad, with possibly one more husband in there somewhere. I met her once: she called Bernie Kiddo! But I know now that wasn't enough reason to do what I did, and it will never happen again, supposing she pays us another visit.

"He sounds like a cool guy," Anya said.

Bernie didn't say anything.

"Your dad, I'm talking about," Anya said. "Are you still close?"

Bernie shook his head.

"That's too bad," Anya said.

"Yeah," said Bernie. He looked over at me. "C'mon, Chet, grab a drink of this nice mountain water."

Exactly what I was thinking, or just about to think. The next thing I knew I was standing midstream up to my shoulders, lapping up just about the best water I'd ever tasted—fresh and cold, with just a little hint of something stony from the water flowing over smooth clean rocks.

"Amazing," said Anya.

"What is?" said Bernie.

"The way he really seems to understand you."

Bernie gave her a funny look, like he didn't quite get what she was talking about. Neither did I. He took a long step onto one of those smooth rocks in the stream—careful, Bernie!—and another, maybe slipping a bit on the second one, but he lowered his hand to my back and kept his balance, and then he was on the near-side bank.

"Who wants to try this mushroom?" Bernie said. He and I were the only takers. What can I tell you? Delish. About that time, kind of late in the game, Bernie noticed the cigarette in Anya's hand. "You smoke?"

"I'm trying to quit," Anya said.

"Me, too," said Bernie.

"Sorry," Anya said and spun the cigarette into the stream. It fell in with a tiny hiss—I love sounds like that!—and bobbed away in the current.

"Hey," said Bernie, giving her another one of those second looks of his. "Thanks."

Not long after, back in the car, we entered a long rising canyon with mountains on both sides, tall green trees growing on their lower slopes but all rocky and steep above that. The air smelled different from any other air I'd ever smelled in my life, all the scents—of trees and grass and flowers, and the toothpaste Bernie had used that morning, and the smoke on Anya's every breath even though she hadn't lit up again—so much stronger and also each one more spread out, with more room for itself, sort of more smells and less air. Made no sense, I know, and I drove the whole complicated business out of my mind just as we turned onto a dirt road and passed under a sign that hung beneath a huge set of horns nailed to a thick wooden beam. Who needs complications?

"Big Bear Wilderness Camp," Bernie read. "Eight thousand and ninety-nine feet."

Did he say *bear*? We didn't have bears in the Valley, or anywhere in our desert, but I knew all I needed to know about them from Animal Planet, which was that I had no desire to meet one.

"This is exactly where my altitude headache kicked in when I drove Devin up here," Anya said.

"And now?" Bernie said.

"Nope. I feel fine."

So did I. I'd had a headache once, after this time when a perp name of Jocko hit me with a baseball bat, a Willie McCovey model, Bernie said, which we later sold to a collector for a "tidy sum"—"for once, how about a sum so big it's untidy?" Bernie had said to our buddy Sergeant Rick Torres from Missing Persons in the Valley PD, a joke Rick didn't get, me neither, and anyway, Bernie invested the money in something or other that soon went belly up, and Jocko's now breaking rocks in the hot sun, so nothing to worry about there, but the point was that unless I'm dinged on the head I don't get headaches, which is different for humans. Bernie, for example, wakes up with a headache if he drinks too much bourbon the night before—half a bottle always does the trick—and as for Leda, headaches could strike at any time for any reason, although most often when they were about to go to bed, she and Bernie.

But enough of that. We crossed a narrow wooden bridge. A stream flowed underneath, wider and faster than the creek I'd drunk from. Not thirsty at all, but I wouldn't have minded a quick sample. What was going on with all this water? Nothing like travel: you got to see new things.

We went through a grove of trees—did I spot something dark and shadowy moving deep in there?—and followed the road on a long curve toward the sunny side of the canyon. Up ahead a large, flat clearing backed into the mountainside, and in the clearing stood a few big log cabins—smoke rising from the chimney of the biggest one, eggs and sausages in the air—and across from them at the top of a little rise, two rows of blue tents. Camp!

Of course! Everything clicked together in my mind, a lovely feel-ing that hadn't happened since the Furillo divorce when I caught the scent of Mr. Furillo's aftershave on the flight attendant who turned out to be his girlfriend. Case closed, although I didn't grab her by the pant leg: that's a no-no in divorce work, a lesson I'd learned early on, and then relearned a few times. But the point was we had a tent, me and Bernie, and had been on lots of camp-ing trips, bringing Charlie along, plus Suzie, once or twice. Some-times our camping trips took us out into the desert, but mostly we camped in the backyard. My job was to carry the mallet for banging in the tent pegs, and soon after that we'd be roasting all sorts of things over a fire, and Bernie would haul out the ukulele and singing would start up, all our favorite camp songs like "Para-chute Woman," "The Sky Is Crying," "Arrivederci, Roma." Had we brought the ukulele now? I didn't remember seeing it, but nobody's memory is perfect, as Bernie had said to Leda during one of their last fights.

We parked between two dusty pickups in a dirt lot. "I don't see Guy's car," Anya said.

"What's his ride?" said Bernie.

"A black Mercedes," said Anya. "License plate PAYME."

"So he has a sense of humor."

"He always thought so."

We walked toward the nearest cabin. Some people stood out-side, grouped around a tall dude in a cowboy hat. He pointed toward a trail leading up the mountain. The people started trudg-ing off in that direction just as we came up.

"Ranger Rob?" Anya said. "Anya Vereen, Devin's mom."

"Welcome to parents' weekend," Ranger Rob said. He had a leathery face with little eyes lost in all the wrinkles.

"My friend, Bernie Little."

"Rob Townshend, camp director," said Ranger Rob.

"Hey," Bernie said.

He and Ranger Rob shook hands. Ranger Rob didn't look at me, even though I was right there. Some humans are like that.

"Where's Devin?" Anya said.

Ranger Rob glanced at the people on their way to the trail. "As I was explaining to those folks, the campers from tent seven aren't back quite yet from their three-day."

"When are they expected?" Anya said.

Ranger Rob shifted from one leg to another. "In actual fact, last night," he said.

"Last night?" said Anya.

"Had some rain," Ranger Rob said. "Makes that last long climb up the Big Bear gorge a mite slippery. Most likely Turk Rendell—he's the trip leader—had 'em bed down near Whiskey Lake. Six or seven miles from this spot, as the crow flies." He checked his watch. "So I'm expecting them any time. You can join those others at the trailhead, if you like. There's some nice benches, ten-minute walk from here."

Anya turned to go.

"One moment," Bernie said. "Has this trip leader of yours called in?"

Ranger Rob shook his head. "Cell coverage is real spotty up here, have to go down to the town of Big Bear before it's reliable. But as a matter of philosophy, we prohibit cell phones on our wilderness hikes."

"Philosophy?" said Bernie.

"Preserving authentic Western self-reliance," Ranger Rob said. "That's what we're about."

Bernie opened his mouth to say something, then closed it, remaining silent. Ranger Rob walked toward the cabin. Bernie and I started for the trailhead, a little behind Anya. He spoke in this low voice he has sometimes for just talking to him and me. "The Donner party was as self-reliant as it gets," he said.

Bernie and I have been to lots of parties, which is maybe why I didn't remember that specific one. I checked the sky for crows and saw none; saw no birds of any kind, just some low dark clouds moving fast over the blue.

FIVE

There were a few benches at the trailhead, all taken by the time we arrived. I didn't feel like sitting anyway, especially when a woman asked the man beside her to pass the bug spray. I hate bug spray—both the smell and how it feels on my coat—and always keep my distance. Lots of humans have a strange thing about bugs, are always spraying themselves or swatting at the air. What's so bad about bugs? Some are even quite tasty.

Anya took a few steps onto the trail—nice smooth packed-down trail, the way trails usually were at the start—and gazed up a gentle rise. Not too far along, the path took a curve and vanished in the trees. I went over to Bernie. He was leaning against a split-rail fence, cell phone in hand.

"Suzie?" he said. "Hear me all right?" He listened for a moment, then spoke again. "Any chance you can get away on Monday? This job's in primo hiking territory, but it'll be all wrapped up by Sunday, and—"

And then came some more chitchat, but a light breeze had risen and it carried a very interesting scent, completely new to me, but the scent of a creature, for sure, and I lost track of the conversation. Who wouldn't have, picking up a smell like that: strong, sharp, penetrating, musky. Once on a case—something do with the football coach at Valley College getting blackmailed, or maybe he was doing the blackmailing, hard to keep all the cases straight—Bernie and I were in the locker room after a game when the equipment dude was picking up the dirty uniforms and T-shirts and jockstraps and tossing them in a hamper. This new smell at the trailhead kind of reminded me of that hamper, but wilder, if that made any sense.

The breeze died down, taking the scent with it. Bernie was saying, "Great, see you then." He clicked off, gave me a smile. "How're you doin'?"

Me? Tip-top. I pressed against Bernie, not too hard.

"Easy, big guy." He gave me a pat. Then we walked up the path and joined Anya. She was gazing at that curve where the trail disappeared.

"It's so quiet here," she said, turning to Bernie.

"Sure is," said Bernie.

"Doesn't it creep you out?" Anya said.

"Far from it," Bernie said.

"I guess I'm a city girl," Anya said. She checked the trail again. "Devin's kind of like me in that respect. He didn't want to come here at all. I had to bribe him."

"With what?" Bernie said.

"Guy's putting up the actual prize—some new video game player, I don't even know the name."

"Devin likes video games?"

"That's pretty much his whole life these days. I've tried to get him to cut down, but he's alone at home a lot and . . . well, you know the story."

"Does he play any sports?" Bernie said.

Anya gave him a look. "You sound just like Guy."

They were talking about sports? Sports: maybe the best idea humans ever came up with, in my opinion. Back when we were on the football case, I actually got into a real game! Bernie and I were right on the sideline, on account of we had to stay close to the blackmailer—it's all coming back to me now, love when that happens—who turned out to be the assistant coach, yes, right on the sideline, close up to the action, when a punt happened, one of those punts down deep, whatever that means, but it's the expression Bernie uses and he really knows football—played in high school, but dropped it when he went to West Point so he could concentrate on baseball—but forget that part, the point being that on the down deep punt the receiver stays away from the ball in the hope that it goes into the end zone, wherever that is, and meanwhile the other team tries to corral the ball, and footballs bounce in a crazy way, and when I see something crazy like that—

Whoa. I went still, ears up. Sounds came from behind the trees where the trail disappeared: snap of a twig, skittering of gravel, a human voice, either a woman's or a child's.

Meanwhile, Anya was looking at her watch. "How much longer do you think we'll have to wait?" she said.

Bernie checked his watch, too. This was the cheapo watch. Bernie's grandfather's watch, our most precious possession, was back at Mr. Singh's pawnshop. Great guy, Mr. Singh, and I can listen to him talk forever, almost like music, and there's often lamb curry on the stove. Even goat, once or twice! A treat on top of a treat, if you see what I mean, although actually I don't quite. Not important. The important thing was Bernie studying his watch and saying, "Six or seven miles, call it seven, likely on the move an hour after first light, averaging maybe . . ." He looked up. "Probably should have been here by now." Anya got a worried expression on her face, and Bernie quickly added, "But the trail may be rougher than it looks from here, and they could have stopped for a snack—twelve-year-old boys, and all."

"So I won't worry," Anya said.

"Nothing to worry about."

Total agreement on my part. By this time I could feel approaching footsteps under my paws, and also heard a boy say, "This rise?" and a man answer, "The next one. Almost there." I glanced at Bernie and Anya: no reaction. Then I looked back at the trailhead benches: no reaction there, either. The bug woman was spraying herself again. The rest of them seemed bored. The human ear is a funny little thing—sometimes not so little: one of the dudes at the trailhead had the real big stick-out kind—but what were they for, exactly? I lay down and waited. My ear to the ground, of course, hearing lots of *thump thump thump,* heavy-footed sounds of humans when they're tired. I took a nice stretch, getting my front paws way out front. Hey! That thing where they start vibrating happened. So weird. I tried to make it keep happening, too late remembering that that always stops it, which is what went down. Sometimes not trying is the way to go, Bernie says. He calls that the Zen way, why I'm not sure. We took down an identity thief—no clue what that was about—name of Howard Zen sometime back, but he tried—tried real hard, in fact, all grunting and pouring sweat, especially when I had him by the pant leg, which was how we always knew the case was closed, me and Bernie.

Time passed. After a while, Anya cocked her head to one side. We do the same thing in the nation within, but much, much sooner, as I hope I've made clear. "Do you hear something?" she said.

Bernie cocked his head, too. A very nice sight, Bernie with his head cocked like that. Had to love Bernie. "Nope," he said. "It's just the wind."

Wind? I raised my head. There wasn't a breath. But while my head was up, I saw a kid come around the curve up the trail, a dusty sort of kid, baseball cap on sideways and carrying a backpack. I rose.

"Hey!" said Anya. "They're here!"

She started walking toward the boy, but not fast, so it probably wasn't her boy. Bernie trailed behind her; I got myself right beside Bernie. Now another kid rounded the curve, and another and another and another, me losing count, and then a man with a bandanna wrapped around his head, and after that nobody. None of them, not the kids or the man, seemed to be at all in a hurry: they were kind of dragging their feet, not so much the way people do when they're wiped, more like when they don't want to go where they're going, Charlie for a haircut, say. So: they wanted to stay on the hike longer? That was my only thought.

Now, from behind, down at the trailhead, came voices: "There they are." "Is that Tommy?" "I see Preston. Preston! Preston! Hi!" That sort of thing. The distance between us and the hikers kept shrinking. Now I could make out their faces. None of them looked happy.

"Which one's Devin?" Bernie said.

"I don't see him," Anya said.

"How many are in his tent?"

"Five, I think."

"One two three four," said Bernie, counting with his finger; Bernie's hands are beautifully shaped, the nails clean and shining. "He must be lagging behind."

The first kid approached.

"How was the hike?" Bernie said.

The kid didn't say anything, just kept going. The other kids passed by, all silent. Then came the man in the bandanna. By that time, there was plenty of distance between us and the top of the rise, but no one else had appeared.

The man reached us, slowed down. He was a small, muscular dude, carrying a heavy-looking pack like it weighed nothing.

"Where's Devin?" Anya said.

He turned toward her, but not quite meeting her gaze. "I, um, better talk to Ranger Rob first."

"Oh my God," Anya said. "Has something happened to Devin?"

The muscular dude licked his lips; that's something I always look for. Perps do it just before they're about to screw up, but was this guy a perp? Wasn't he a hiking guide? Maybe I'd missed something. "I don't think I'm authorized to say anything," he said, and turned to go.

Bernie stepped in front of him. "You're the trip leader?" he said.

"Yeah."

"Brock something or other?"

The dude's face turned red. "Turk Rendell," he said.

"Well, Turk," said Bernie, saying the name Turk real, real clear. "This is Devin's mom. Where is her son?"

Turk's eyes went to Anya, back to Bernie, then toward the ground. "He, uh, seems to have, like, wandered off."

"Wandered off?" Anya said, her voice rising, high and sharp. "What are you saying?"

Turk licked his lips again.

"You lost him?" Bernie said.

Turk nodded.

Anya's eyes opened wide. She covered her mouth with her hand: women do that sometimes, the reasons not clear in my mind. Then her face went white, just as white as corpses you see if you work a job like mine. Bernie took her arm. She would have screamed otherwise: you could feel it coming.

Ranger Rob had an office in the biggest cabin. Huge steer horns over the door and lots of wood smells: a real nice office. There was a big map on one wall and Bernie, Anya, Ranger Rob, and Turk Rendell stood in front of it.

"We were makin' pretty good time," Turk said. "Camped thereabouts Thursday, not long after six." He jabbed a finger someplace on the map; he had stubby fingers, not at all like Bernie's, and the nails were dirty.

Ranger Rob leaned closer to the map. "The clearing east of Stiller's Creek?"

"Yeah," Turk said. "Set up, got a fire goin', chowed down, everyone sacked out by nine. Roused 'em at dawn"—he turned to Bernie—"boys in the tent, me in the open 'less it's raining, and they filed out. No Devin. First, I thought he'd gone off to take a—you know, relieve himself, but after a few minutes we started callin' and lookin' around. Long story short, we spent the whole day searchin' both sides of the creek, all the way down to the Slides and all the way up to the old mine, and, uh . . ." He shrugged.

"So Devin's been missing for over a day and a half," Bernie said.

Turk gazed at the floor. "See, what I figured was he'd gotten up sometime in the night—the relievin' himself theory, just changed a little bit—and then lost his way back. So he couldn't have gone far, which is why we kept lookin', stead of hikin' right out and raising a more general, you know . . . alarm. Plus we didn't meet anyone the whole time, no one I could send back with a message. Can't leave the kids, of course—that's rule one."

Turk, eyes down, missed the look Bernie was giving him, maybe a good thing. "Suppose you're right," Bernie said, "and Devin got lost in the night. Wouldn't he have called out for help?"

"You'd think," said Turk.

"You would," Bernie said. "But no one heard anything?"

Turk shook his head.

Ranger Rob cleared his throat. "I'm sorry about your boy, sir. But I think Turk did fine in a difficult situation. Once he realized they weren't finding him, he got back fast as he could. Those kids were dead on their feet."

"Devin's not my boy," Bernie said. "I'm a friend."

"Oh," said Ranger Rob. "On the list it said parents."

"Devin's dad is coming," Anya said. She glanced at her watch.

"I'm also a private detective," Bernie said.

Ranger Rob took a step back, his eyes still on Bernie, but in a new way.

Bernie didn't seem to pay attention to any of that. "Chet here is one of the best trackers in the West," he said. Ranger Rob looked at me. I looked at him. "I assume you're calling in the authorities," Bernie said, "but I'd like to get started right away."

"Started on a search?" Ranger Rob said.

"Correct," said Bernie.

"Appreciate your willingness to help," Ranger Rob said, "but our budget—"

"Right now you have bigger worries than your budget," Bernie said.

There was a silence. Then Ranger Rob nodded, a tiny move-ment: any tinier wouldn't have been noticeable at all.

Bernie said, "We need Turk, supplies for three days, and a satellite phone if cell service really doesn't reach out there."

"It doesn't," Ranger Rob said. "We're right on the edge here in camp, as I mentioned. And I'm afraid we don't have a satellite phone. It's never been necessary, if you see what I mean."

Bernie didn't: I could tell from his face.

SIX

We walked out of the cabin, me, Bernie, Anya. "This is so horrible," Anya said.

Bernie didn't say anything.

"I was against the whole idea right from the start," she said.

Bernie nodded.

"Everything Guy does turns out so—" She made an angry gesture with her hand, sort of like smacking the air. Then her eyes got damp and a tear or two came spilling over her lower lids. "Just tell me it's going to be all right," she said.

Bernie shifted on his feet, looked real uncomfortable. Even though I knew she was a bit uneasy around me and my kind, I moved closer to Anya and stood beside her, just touching. I felt her hand on my back. Sometimes humans pat you without knowing they're doing it. This had the feeling of one of those, as though the hand was acting on its own. Nothing crazy about that: my tail does the same thing.

Anya wiped away her tears on her sleeve. "I'm sorry," she said. "I know it's stupid to ask that."

"It's not stupid," Bernie said. "And we've got a lot going for us." He glanced at the sky. "Weather's good. And it's unlikely Devin's far from the campsite—when they get lost in the woods, most people end up walking in circles."

Anya perked up a little. "Is that true?"

Bernie nodded, but was there a slight hesitation? We'd been on plenty of search-and-rescues, and I didn't remember that walking-in-circles thing. "Plus we've got Chet," he added. And we had Bernie, too. His brain was one of our most important assets. So maybe I had heard the walking-in-circles thing before.

Anya looked down at me. Our gazes met. Her eyes dampened again. "Please," she said, so softly I almost didn't hear, meaning real softly. No worries: that was my thought. We'd bring her boy back and that was that. I gave myself a good shake. What were we waiting for?

"Have you got a picture of Devin?" Bernie said.

"Why do you want that?" said Anya.

"Standard procedure."

"But aren't I coming with you?"

"The picture's to show any hikers we might run into," Bernie said.

"I want to come."

"Do you have any backcountry experience?"

"None."

"Then you'd only slow us down," Bernie said.

"But—" Anya began.

Bernie interrupted her. "And wouldn't it be better if you're here when your ex-husband arrives?"

Anya gave him a long look. "That's pretty acute of you," she said.

Didn't quite get that one. Bernie shrugged. Maybe he didn't get it either.

Anya took out her cell phone, pressed some buttons, held up the screen. "Here's Devin," she said.

Hard to see from my angle, but I glimpsed a long-haired, round-faced, unsmiling kid. What else? One of those snub noses. I knew that expression from a snubnose .32 I'd taken off some perp, name escaping me at the moment, but we've still got that little gun in the office safe.

"A nice-looking kid," Bernie said. Anya's lower lip trembled. "The camp will have a computer and a printer."

Anya nodded and walked toward the office.

Bernie and I went the other way, toward the tents, big tents, and each one flying a flag. We stopped in front of one of them, stood before the closed flap. Bernie checked the flag, and then called out, "Number seven? Anybody home?"

No answer. But I could hear breathing inside. I moved closer to the flap. Bernie raised it, letting in a flood of daylight. The boys inside—same ones who'd returned with Turk—looked at us, all of them squinting against the light.

"Boys?" said Bernie. "I'm Bernie Little, and this is Chet. We're headed out to find Devin, but first we could use some help from you."

The tent was real messy, clothes and gear all over the place. The boys lay on cots. One cot was empty. None of them spoke.

We stepped inside. Bernie smiled. "What are your names?" he said.

They remained silent. Humans have a right to remain silent. You hear a lot of talk about it in my job. No offense, but this is a right humans hardly ever take advantage of.

The smile stayed on Bernie's face. "Well, let's see. We know we've got Tommy and Preston." We did? But that was Bernie for you, every time. "So which one's Tommy?" Bernie scanned their faces. "That would be you," he said, pointing with his chin at a dark-haired kid with braces on his teeth. The other kids might have had braces, too, but Tommy was the only one with his mouth open.

The kid nodded.

"Nice meeting you, Tommy," Bernie said. "And Preston?" His gaze swept over the others, stopped on a red-haired kid with a sharp-featured face. "Hey, there, Preston," he said. How did he know that? Not my concern: if Bernie said this red-haired kid was Preston, then question period was over.

No nod from Preston. No reaction of any kind.

"So that just leaves you two," Bernie said, turning to the remaining boys. Bernie was still smiling, but not as broadly. The two boys sat up.

"Keith," said one.

"Luke," said the other.

"Hi, guys," Bernie said. He moved toward the empty cot. "This one Devin's?" he said.

There was a pause. The boys exchanged glances. Then Tommy sat up—now I could see he was a pretty big kid—and said, "Yeah." Preston's eyes narrowed.

Bernie sat on Devin's cot. I took a spot on the floor beside him. They all checked me out for a moment. Tommy and Keith were comfortable with me and my kind; Preston and Luke were not. Never hurts to be aware of that.

"You guys made good time today," Bernie said. "Must be wiped."

They all shrugged, Tommy, Keith, and Luke sitting up, Preston still lying down.

"I understand you tried real hard to find Devin," Bernie said. Tommy nodded. Then Keith, then Luke. Not Preston.

"How did that go, exactly?" Bernie said.

Tommy, Keith, and Luke all turned to Preston. No one answered.

"My guess is you just followed Turk's orders," Bernie said.

Preston sat up. "Yeah," he said. Hey! Preston wasn't Tommy's size, but he had the voice of a man. The others still talked like boys. Did I already know about that whole thing? Couldn't remember. Then a strange thought zipped in: was Charlie's voice going to change one day? Wow! I wasn't used to having thoughts like that.

"And what were Turk's orders?" Bernie said.

"Fan out with him in the middle, calling out every minute, then listening," Preston said. "Kind of obvious."

"You said it," said Bernie. "Calling out what?"

"Deh-viiin, Deh-viiin," Preston said. Something in the way he said the name bothered me.

"But no response of any kind?" Bernie said. "Wouldn't have to be his voice, could be just the sound of a rock being thrown, for example."

"Why wouldn't it have to be his voice?" Tommy said.

"Punctured lung, windpipe damaged in a fall, lots of possibilities."

Silence. Then Tommy said, "Turk didn't mention any of that."

"So what?" said Preston. "Did we hear any rocks or stuff? Not me."

The other boys shook their heads.

Another silence. Bernie gave the cot a little pat. "What do you think happened to Devin?" he said.

They all shrugged.

"Tommy? Got a theory?"

"Um, theory?" said Tommy.

"Like where he is right now," Bernie said. "And how he got there."

"Where he is right now?" Tommy said.

"Yeah," Bernie said.

"Lost," said Tommy. "He's lost."

"And how did that happen?" Bernie said.

"Um," said Tommy. "I don't, uh . . ." He slowly turned toward Preston. They all did.

"He went out in the night to take a piss," Preston said. "Then he got lost."

"Did you hear him get up, Preston?"

Preston met Bernie's gaze. "Who are you, again?"

Bernie still wore a bit of a smile on his face. He was the kind of guy who likes kids. But this particular smile was one I'd never want to see aimed at me. "Bernie Little," he said. "I'm a friend of Devin's family. I'm also a private detective, and Chet here is a great tracker. So we're going to bring Devin back, and of course when we do we'll hear his side of the story, too." I thought he was going to say more, but he stopped right there, leaving a strange emptiness in the air, like someone just had to say something to fill it. Bernie was a great interviewer, if I haven't mentioned that already. I bring other things to the table. We're a team, me and Bernie.

Preston kept his eyes on Bernie. "I didn't hear anything," he said. "When I woke up the kid was gone."

"And when you went to sleep?" Bernie said.

"When I went to sleep?" Preston said. "I don't get it."

"Where was Devin when you went to sleep?" Bernie said. "A simple question—especially for a smart kid like you."

Preston's eyes—very light colored, although I can't be trusted when it comes to color, according to Bernie—narrowed. "He was asleep when I went to sleep. And gone in the morning."

"Couldn't be clearer," Bernie said. He turned to the others. "Same story with you guys?" he said.

"Yup," said Luke.

"Yeah," said Keith.

Tommy nodded, just the tiniest movement.

Bernie started to rise, then sat back down as though he'd had a new thought. "What kind of kid is Devin, anyway?" he said.

"You know," Tommy said. "A kid."

"Normal?"

Tommy glanced at Preston. "Yeah, sure."

"Was—is he enjoying camp?"

"I guess," Tommy said.

"How about you guys—like it here?"

More shrugging.

"First time for all of you?"

They all shook their heads.

"For any of you?"

More head shaking.

"So you knew each other from past summers?"

Nods.

Bernie got up. "All we'll need now—what Chet needs, actually—is something of Devin's, something with his scent on it."

Laughter is the best human sound except for a kind of laugh that's called the snicker. The snicker is one of the worst. Preston snickered and said, "Like his dirty underwear?"

Luke and Keith laughed—more like the nice kind, but far from the nicest I'd heard—and then tried to stop, their faces swelling up and reddening. What was funny? They were all wearing dirty underwear, a fact I'd known the moment we'd stepped inside the tent.

"A T-shirt will do," Bernie said.

Luke and Keith went on another laughing spasm. Preston watched them, looking amused. Tommy didn't look amused.

"Devin's laundry sack is under the cot," he said.

Preston turned to Tommy. Tommy looked away. The tent was pretty big—way bigger than the tent we had at home—but I was beginning to feel closed in. Bernie reached under the cot, pulled out a canvas bag, fished around inside and found a sock. One of those white sports socks: perfect.

"Perfect," Bernie said. "With a name tag, no less. Chet?"

I moved closer. Bernie held out the sock. I took a quick sniff or two. It's really quite easy. From that moment I had Devin's smell locked in forever.

Bernie took a plastic bag from his pocket and sealed the sock inside. He always did that, in case I needed a refresher somewhere along the way. I never did, but Bernie didn't know that.

"Chet's smart, huh?" said Tommy.

Bernie smiled. "Do you have a dog at home?" he said.

"My mom's allergic."

Allergic: I'd heard that one before. Once at a party this woman had wanted me to go wait in the car. Bernie and I left immediately, of course: parties are supposed to be fun. But what was up with the allergy thing? Humans could be funny inside.

"Too bad," Bernie said. We turned to go. "Thanks, guys," he said. "You've been a big help."

Luke and Keith seemed surprised to hear that. The expression on Preston's face was complicated. Only Tommy looked pleased.

Bernie and I went back to the parking lot. He took the small backpack he'd brought for the trip out of the trunk and then unlocked the glove box. There was the .38 Special, always a pleasant sight. Did I have a faint memory of Bernie telling Anya we weren't carrying this weekend? Bernie could still surprise me sometimes. He tucked the .38 Special in his backpack and was slinging the backpack over his shoulder when Anya came up.

"Here are the prints," she said, handing them over. I caught another sight of that unsmiling, round-faced, long-haired kid. The smell on the white sports sock fit him nicely, hard to explain.

"The SAR team'll want copies, too," Bernie said.

"When are they getting here?" Anya's voice was high and tight, like she was trying to keep something inside from bursting out.

"As soon as they can," Bernie said. "They'll have a satellite phone, so I'll be able to report back to you when they reach us."

"And I haven't been able to contact Guy." Her face was strange, almost like it was frozen stiff. I got the feeling she wasn't listening.

"The service is spotty," Bernie told her.

"But Guy said he'd be here by midmorning at the latest."

Bernie put a hand on Anya's shoulder. "What you can do," he said, "is study the maps, get familiar with the whole area, so you'll be up to speed when I call you."

Anya nodded, one of those puzzled kinds of nods. What was Bernie saying? I didn't get it either.

Up in the clearing where the cabins stood, Turk appeared, carrying a pack. He saw us and made the waving motion for *come*.

"Got to go," Bernie said, slipping his hand from her shoulder. Anya grabbed Bernie's hand in both of hers and squeezed tight.

"He means everything to me," she said. "He's the only decent thing I've done in my—" Her face unfroze and she began sobbing.

Bernie tugged his hand free. "Um," he said. "Just, ah, familiarize yourself with . . ." He gazed down at her. Bernie can handle just about anything. Of the things he can't handle, sobbing women probably come first.

We headed up toward the cabins. "Waiting is the hardest

The Dog Who Knew Too Much

part," Bernie said quietly. "You always give them something to do, even if it's bogus."

Bogus? Didn't know that one. But did I let it worry me? Not for a second or even shorter, and I know a second's a short time. Missing persons was our specialty at the Little Detective Agency, kids especially. This was what we did, me and Bernie. We were on the job.

SEVEN

At first the trail was wide enough for all of us to walk side by side, me, Bernie, Turk. Then it narrowed and steepened, and Turk took the lead, with Bernie following. As for me, I sometimes handled the leading part, also sometimes I did the following, and sometimes I kind of did both, hard to explain how, exactly. Being outdoors in the wide open spaces: this was the life.

Turk was a fast hiker for a human, maybe the fastest I'd seen. A smaller guy than Bernie, and carrying a bigger pack, but as the trail got gnarlier—that was hiking lingo—the distance between the two of them grew and grew. Turk wore shorts, the muscles in his strong legs swelling with every step. Bernie had strong legs, too, except one of them had gotten wounded in the war. The wounded leg looked just about as strong as the other one, unless you happened to see the scarred part. Bernie didn't wear shorts much, mostly just around the house; right now he wore jeans, the real faded pair, his favorite. He wasn't limping—I checked every now and then—but he kept falling farther back. Maybe we should all just slow down? That was my thought.

No slowing down happened. Trees with whitish trunks

appeared: I'd never seen that before. They smelled great, a bit like the red bark mulch Leda had made Bernie return to the garden store, back in the day, but with a hint of something close to lemon. One or two had been marked by coyotes. I laid my own mark on top, just sending a message.

Meanwhile we were switchbacking up and up, and also sometimes down and down, just part of the fun of hiking. Love switchbacks, myself, although once or twice I didn't bother, and tore straight through. A big black bird circled high up in the sky, not over us but way ahead. Birds bother me, I admit it. I dropped back to be with Bernie. "How're you doing, big guy?" he said.

Tip-top, of course. Bernie himself was huffing and puffing a bit, and even though the air was pretty cool and getting cooler, there were sweat beads on his forehead. I wanted to lick them off, but this probably wasn't the time. He stepped over a big rock poking up through the ground and said, "Our buddy Turk's really motoring." Huff puff. "Feeling guilty, or just showing us how good he is?" Huff puff.

I didn't know the answer, didn't really understand the question. I hopped over a thick tree root that crossed the trail and rounded a corner. No sign of Turk—unless you included his scent, of which there was plenty, that very penetrating scent given off by a human male who has broken a fresh sweat after he was already coated in dried-up sweat—but up ahead lay a pool of golden light, meaning we were about to leave the woods and enter some open country. I sped up.

And soon came to a beautiful meadow, full of tall golden grass, with brightly colored flowers poking up here and there in all that gold. Bernie says we're all together on this planet, fact one. There's also a fact two, slipping my mind at the moment, but going back to fact one, the point is I wouldn't be anywhere else for the world. Maybe a bit confusing, now that I thought about it, which I didn't do for long. Instead I raced into the meadow, the trail widening and flattening out, and soon caught up to Turk.

He was sitting on a rock at the top of an easy rise. What else? I smelled water, lots of it. And Turk was smoking a joint. Turk looked at me. I looked at him. A lot of humans will say something to you at a time like that, just being friendly. Turk did not. He took one last drag, then dropped the butt and ground it into the earth. You run into potheads in this business—Bernie's had fun conversations with some of them—but Turk was way more energetic than any pothead I'd ever met. I went over and sniffed at the remains of the joint, then got to work on digging it up out of the little hole Turk's heel had made.

"What the hell?" Turk said and sort of kicked out at me. Whoa. I backed away and barked. At that moment Bernie came in sight, moving much better now on the flat ground, that tall golden grass waving slightly, and Bernie looking sort of golden himself. He strode up the rise and stopped beside us.

"You two getting acquainted?" he said.

Turk glanced at me. "I guess."

I barked again, not my real scary bark, but lower and more rumbly, the bark that lets you know the real scary one is on the way, unless something you're up to or not up to changes pretty damn quick. Why I was doing it now was a bit of a mystery. But the next moment, Bernie shot a real quick look directly at the ground-up butt of Turk's joint, more like his gaze sweeping right over it, so if you didn't know Bernie, you would have missed the whole thing. But I knew Bernie.

"Been meaning to ask you something, Turk," he said, leaning against a tree. "You're going so fast I thought I'd never get the chance."

Turk glanced at the sun. Hey! It had sunk pretty low in the sky when I hadn't been watching. "This ain't fast," he said. "What's your question?"

"Devin must have had a pack," Bernie said.

"Sure," said Turk.

"Where is it?"

"I left it at the campsite in case he came back." Turk rose. "With food and water inside, plus a note telling him to stay put."

"That was smart," Bernie said.

"I know my job," Turk said. He gave Bernie one of those down-the-nose looks. "Had enough rest?"

Bernie pushed himself away from the tree. We moved on.

The smell of water got stronger and stronger and then the sight itself came into view, a lovely smooth sheet of blue, darker than the sky.

"Whiskey Lake," said Turk.

Wasn't whiskey a kind of bourbon, or bourbon a kind of whiskey? I tried to remember the details of a discussion—if that's what it was, with all the yelling and shouting and broken glass—about this very subject at the last Police Athletic League social. But the point: whiskey was a kind of golden brown, not dark blue. So was this lake full of whiskey or not? I sniffed the air for whiskey, detected none.

Bernie has some beliefs. One is you don't bring a spoon to a knife fight. Another is don't overthink. We're on the same page about that one, me and Bernie. The next thing I knew I was swimming in Whiskey Lake. Not whiskey at all, but cool, delicious water. Turk and Bernie followed the path around it, appearing and disappearing through a screen of tall cattails. I'd seen cattails once before on a riverbank down on the border. The name bothered me, but I tried and succeeded in not thinking about it as I swam straight across the lake. Love swimming—it's just like trotting, only in the water—which I don't get to do nearly enough in the Valley, where we have aquifer problems, a bit of a mystery but one of Bernie's biggest worries.

The far shore was steep and rocky. I scrambled out, ran onto the trail just ahead of Turk and Bernie, and gave myself a good shake, the kind that starts at my head, ripples down to my tail and all the way back again—can't tell you how good that feels—maybe spraying them just the slightest bit. Bernie laughed. Turk raised his hands to block the tiny water drops and said, "Christ almighty."

Bernie stopped laughing.

We climbed a steep ridge, saw rocky mountaintops streaked with white in the distance. The sun sank behind those peaks and the sky turned purple. I'd never smelled air like this, so fresh and pure. A funny kind of air: I wasn't panting or anything—how could hiking with a couple of humans bring on panting?—but I seemed to need more of it. Bernie was huffing and puffing again, but now he didn't fall behind, even seemed about to go into the lead once or twice. That was Bernie: there's something inside him.

Time passed. We were in the trees again, not those white-bark trees: these looked more like Christmas trees. The going got rougher, the trail almost disappearing as we worked our way along a narrow crest. I was in the lead now, and starting to pick up human scents, faint but there: by a tall spiny bush, I found Preston's smell, for sure. Not long after that, I glanced back. Hey! Bernie and Turk had put on headlamps. I checked the sky: dark, with twinkling stars. No headlamp for me: night or day doesn't make much difference. I turned and trotted on, not my fast trot, but the go-to trot, as Bernie calls it, the trot I can keep up as long as I have to. More scents now: Preston's again, Tommy's, and Turk's. Plus just a trace of that strange locker-room-laundry-hamper scent I'd first picked up at the trailhead. Locker room laundry hamper, yes; human, no.

Kind of puzzling, but then I caught sight of the white streaks on the mountaintop. I couldn't see the mountain, just the white streaks, a new and beautiful sight, and I forgot all about whatever had been puzzling me. Other questions arose, like: Was the moon coming tonight? Stars came out every clear night, which was just about every night in the Valley. The moon was trickier, appearing some nights but not others, and often changing its shape. Bernie had explained the whole thing to Charlie at the dinner table, and I'd gotten that feeling in my head when I come very, very close to understanding; a nice feeling, almost as good as actually understanding. What a life!

Up and up I went, and then the ground leveled out, and I heard trickling water. A few more steps and I could see a gurgling little stream, sparkling with starlight. The great outdoors—that's what humans call it, a perfect name—and at night: hard to beat. I leaped onto a broad flat rock in the middle of the stream and lapped up more delicious cold water. I wasn't thirsty, but what a treat, all this tasty water around. We'd have to cross the state line more often, if that was in fact what we'd done.

The two headlamp beams bobbed up in the distance, moved closer and closer in a jerky kind of way, and then shone on me. I heard their voices.

"There's your dog," said Turk.

"Uh-huh," said Bernie.

"Stiller's Creek," Turk said. "Weird how it ended up here—the camp can't be more'n a hundred yards away, just on the other side."

"Not it," Bernie said. "He."

The headlamp beams both swung around, turning on each other. Light shone on both their faces, Bernie's and Turk's. They looked squinty, tired, annoyed. That was a bit of a surprise. I couldn't remember feeling better, myself. Okay, there was the time Bernie and I went on vacation to San Diego, and I surfed. But other than that.

I hopped over to the far side. Bernie and Turk crossed the stream, both stepping on rocks to keep their feet dry. That's not something I worry about.

Turk walked up a little slope toward a shadowy grove of low trees. Bernie and I followed, side by side. Bernie has a kind of walk for when his leg hurts but he's trying not to show it; he was doing it now.

We reached the top, moved into the grove. I smelled ashes, plus chocolate, the way it smells when hot chocolate gets burned in the pot, and then Turk's headlamp beam illuminated a small circle of stones: the remains of a not-too-long-ago campfire. I knew fire pits, of course, went over and took some closer sniffs. Burned hot chocolate, yes. There'd also been Spam and something eggy. I stuck my nose just about right into the ashes. They were cold.

"Where did you leave the pack?" Bernie said.

"Huh?" Turk said.

"Devin's pack."

"Oh. Yeah."

Turk took off his headlamp and shone the light carefully around a tree stump outside the circle of stones.

"That's funny," he said.

"What is?" said Bernie.

"This is where I left his pack—leaning against the stump."

I sniffed at the stump, didn't pick up Devin's smell, although I did detect the scent of burned marshmallow. Marshmallows: you can have them—just way too sticky. Same for cotton candy.

We walked around the clearing, the two light beams poking at trees, rocks, bushes. No pack in sight. "Tent was over here," Turk said.

Bernie looked around. "And where did you sleep?" he said.

"Under the stars, like I told you," said Turk.

"I asked where," said Bernie.

Turk pointed with his thumb, back toward the fire pit. I'd slept next to fire pits, too; if you make a roaring fire, those stones stay warm almost till dawn.

"Maybe the kid came back and headed out with the pack," Turk said.

"But your note said to stay put," Bernie said. Meanwhile, he was crouched down, sweeping his light slowly back and forth over the place where the tent had been. I crouched beside him, picked up the scents of Preston and Tommy, plus those two other boys, their names escaping me.

"Maybe he didn't read it," Turk said.

Bernie rose. "Turk?" he said.

"Yeah?"

"That's enough theory. Have you got any facts for us?"

Turk gave Bernie a hard look, said nothing.

Bernie turned away from him. Then he cupped his hands around his mouth and shouted, "Devin! Devin!" louder than I'd ever heard him. Turk jumped right off the ground. So did I, kind of, even though it was Bernie.

"Devin! Devin!"

The night was silent.

EIGHT

We sat around the fire pit in the darkness. No one seemed to be making a fire. That was a first in my camping experience. Did no campfire wipe out the possibility of nibbling on roasted things in the near future? I feared that from the get-go and turned out to be right. Turk and Bernie ate sandwiches—peanut butter and jelly, the smell so much better than the taste, a strange disappointment I'd tested out more than once—and I had kibble. I was just about finished licking out the bowl—our traveling bowl, a little smaller than the kitchen bowl but nice and round at the bottom, the way I like—when Bernie said, "Tell me about the kids."

"What kids?" said Turk, wiping his mouth on his sleeve.

"The kids in tent seven," Bernie said. "The ones in your charge."

Turk shrugged. "I take what they give me."

"Meaning?"

"I've guided hundreds of kids into the backcountry," Turk said. "Maybe thousands. They all blur together after a while."

"Understood," said Bernie. "You're only human."

Hey! One of my favorite expressions—it made so much sense to me.

"Damn straight," Turk said.

"But," said Bernie, and he paused—Bernie's a real good pauser, all part of his interviewing technique; I bring other things to the table, in case I haven't mentioned that already—"of all these hundreds, maybe thousands, Turk, did you ever lose one before now?"

"Fucking well didn't. And you're startin' to push me, pal."

Uh-oh. Turk had a temper. I got my back paws under me. I've seen lots of trouble, comes with the job, and it often starts right about now.

"See, Turk," Bernie said, "you just admitted you've never been in a situation like this. Chet and I have, more than once. The goal is to bring Devin back alive. Nothing else counts."

Turk sat there, a dark shadow but sort of bulging, like a muscle loading up.

"So let's talk about the kids in tent seven," Bernie said. "How did they get along?"

I heard Turk taking a deep breath. The violence that had been building inside him escaped into the air; I could sort of feel it. "Didn't give me problems," he said.

"Glad to hear that," said Bernie. "But it's not what I asked."

"Lost me," Turk said.

"Yeah?" said Bernie.

When he said "yeah" like that it always meant he didn't believe what had just been said, not one bit. Love Bernie's little ways! We were on the job!

"Let's narrow it down," he went on. "How did the boys—meaning Preston, Tommy, Luke, and Keith—get along with Devin?"

"Pretty good, I guess."

"Guess harder," Bernie said.

"Huh?"

"The four boys are all returning campers. Devin's new. That can be tough."

"Tough? None of them know shit about tough. They're all rich kids from the city."

"Bullies can be rich or poor, city or country," Bernie said. "Preston's a bully. Luke and Keith are followers. Tommy's stand-up, but he's still too young to know it. What about Devin? Is he the victim type?"

"Where are you getting all this info?" Turk said.

"Doesn't matter."

"Ranger Rob? I didn't think—" Turk cut himself off. Sometimes the mouth gets ahead of the mind in humans. I watch for that one.

"You didn't think what?"

"Nothin'," Turk said.

There was a silence, except for the breeze rustling the trees, and an owl doing that hooting thing, but very distant, right at the edge of what I could hear.

"What kind of a kid were you?" Bernie said. "Bully, victim, follower, or stand-up?"

"Hell, stand-up for sure. Ask anyone who knew me."

"If it comes to that, I will," Bernie said. "The question now is did you stand up for Devin?"

"Don't know what you're talkin' about."

"Preston was bullying Devin. At the very least the others stood by. That left it up to you."

"Didn't notice any of what you're talkin' about."

"No?" Bernie said. "You missed the fact that Devin wasn't sleeping in the tent with the others?"

Turk leaned back, almost like he'd been pushed in the chest.

Bernie pointed back to where the kids' tent had stood. "Four rectangular impressions on the ground, Turk. Faint, but there. The fifth one's a good thirty feet from the others, way outside the tent. Means Devin slept in the open. Just like you—making it hard to miss."

Another deep breath from Turk. "Yeah," he said. "Maybe they ragged on him some. Preston's a fuckin' monster."

"I don't doubt it," Bernie said. "But see what this does to your theory."

"What theory?" said Turk, a question I was glad to hear, a little lost myself.

"The theory we've been operating on," Bernie said. "Devin leaves the tent to take a piss and can't find his way back."

That was the theory? Theories, whatever they happened to be, I always left to Bernie. But something about this particular theory made me leave our little circle for a moment or two, all the time it took to lift my leg against a nearby rock. When I returned, Turk was saying, "I'm a real heavy sleeper. Is that a crime?"

"Depending on the circumstances," Bernie said. "A sentry who falls asleep on duty, for example. Or an airline pilot—maybe a closer analogy."

"You threatening me?" Turk said. "Like I'm some criminal?"

"Why would there be any need for that?" said Bernie. "We're on the same side. If you feel threatened, it's just from the situation."

"What the hell are you talking about?"

"People—starting with Devin's parents—are going to find out you let the kid sleep in the open."

"That's what he wanted," Turk said.

"That's what Preston and the others made him want," Bernie

said, his voice growing sharper and quieter at the same time; we often get good results from that combo. "There's a difference."

Turk said nothing. The expression on his face, dark and shadowy, was hard to see. But a new smell was coming off him, a tangy smell a bit like this blue cheese Bernie likes, except mixed with pee: the smell of human fear.

"Did you light a fire that night?" Bernie said.

"Sure."

"Douse it out when you turned in, or just let it die down?"

"Die down," Turk said. "This fire pit's safe—you can see for yourself—and there was no wind."

"I trust your judgment on that," Bernie said. "What's puzzling me is that the coals would have glowed most of the night, so if Devin, already outside the tent, did get up for some reason, it's hard to imagine how he couldn't find his way back."

"Know something?" said Turk. "I'm gettin' tired of all your questions."

"That last one wasn't a question," Bernie said.

Turk rose. "The hell with you," he said. "Who says I need to take this shit? I was just doin' my job." He grabbed his pack.

I could feel Bernie about to say something but he did not.

We own two tents, the big one that fits Bernie, Charlie, and Suzie, and the little one Bernie set up on the edge of the shadowy grove of trees. The little one's called the pup tent. I've done a lot of thinking about that and pretty much gotten nowhere. Has a puppy ever been inside the little tent? No. So therefore? I just don't know: the way we have things arranged at the Little Detective Agency, Bernie handles the so therefores.

Bernie lay down in the pup tent. There was maybe just enough room for me to squeeze in, but I preferred to stretch out on the ground in front of the flap. By that time, Turk had already unrolled his sleeping bag by the fire pit and climbed in. His eyes were silvery and open in the starlight. I kept my own eyes open until his closed. Then I closed mine and listened to Bernie's breathing from inside the tent as it got slower and more peaceful, if that makes any sense, and soon I knew he was asleep. For a while I just lay on the ground—mossy ground, very comfortable—and enjoyed the feeling of being the only one awake in the night, one of my favorite feelings. Then a delicious kind of fuzziness came rolling into my mind. I never fight that.

Some humans—Charlie's amazing at this!—are totally zonked out when they're asleep, almost impossible to wake. That's not the way it works in the nation within the nation. I get plenty of rest, no complaints, but I'm never totally zonked out, which was why sometime later I was suddenly wide awake.

The breeze had strengthened, blowing from the direction of the white-streaked mountaintop, now just a jagged lightless shape blocking out the stars. I got the impression that the stars had moved, weren't where they'd been when I'd gone to sleep. That was a little trick of the night that I'd noticed before but almost forgotten. But that wasn't the important part. Eye on the ball: that was an expression of Bernie's and I loved playing ball, goes without mentioning; but better to mention, just in case. There are many kinds of balls in the world: tennis balls, soccer balls, baseballs—will I ever forget the first time I discovered how complicated they were inside?—but lacrosse balls are my favorite, what with their crazy bounces, and especially the way they felt in my mouth when—

Eye on the ball, Chet. Something was not right. The night was silent, except for the breeze, but it was one of those strange silences you get after something has just happened, if you know what I mean, and I'm actually not sure I even do. First thing, I listened for Bernie, heard his slow, regular breathing right away, meaning he was safe, so if something had in fact just happened, it couldn't have been all that bad.

I rose. Nighttime security was part of my job. Grabbing perps by the pant leg is another. That's how we know the case is closed here at the Little Detective Agency, but this case didn't feel closed. Was it even a case? I didn't know. A case meant someone was paying. Anya was paying Bernie to be her friend. Now her kid was missing. I couldn't take it past that, so I started sniffing around. When it comes to nighttime security, you can't go wrong by sniffing around.

Nothing new to pick up, the scents of the boys still all over the place—although growing fainter—plus Bernie's scent, Turk's, and my own, the most familiar smell in the world: old leather, salt and pepper, mink coats, and just a soupçon of tomato; and to be honest, a healthy dash of something male and funky. My smell: yes, sir. Chet the Jet was in the vicinity, wherever that was, exactly.

Bernie: safe in the tent. Me: on the job, checking things out. That left no one to check out except Turk. I moved toward the fire pit, picked up a faint smell of mold coming from Turk's sleeping bag. That happened with sleeping bags, nothing unusual. The only unusual thing was the way Turk's bag seemed kind of flat.

I went closer, didn't see Turk's head sticking through the opening at the top. I pawed at the sleeping bag, felt the ground underneath. Turk wasn't inside.

I looked around, saw a few dark forms around the campsite that had vaguely human shapes, and examined every one, finding only rocks and bushes. Lots of Turk's scent around, some of it old, some fresh. I followed a few scent trails, all of them leading round and round in circles. Whenever that happens I start getting frustrated, just can't help it. I went over to the tent and barked this soft muffled bark meant not to attract attention from anyone except Bernie.

"Chet?" he said, his voice soft, just like mine. Bernie's a deep sleeper, but when it's important he's wide awake right away. You could always rely on Bernie.

He crawled out of the tent with the headlamp in his hand, switched it on, and followed me over to Turk's sleeping bag. The beam moved back and forth over the empty bag, then swept around the campsite.

"I screwed up the whole goddamn case, big guy," he said.

So it was a case, after all. As for Bernie screwing it up: impossible.

NINE

Bernie strapped on the headlamp. I growled at him and felt bad right away, but I couldn't help it: that headlamp on his forehead makes him look like some kind of machine, and there's more than enough machine in humans to begin with, no offense.

"For God's sake, Chet—you do that every time."

I do? News to me. But I got most of my news from Bernie, so no problem.

We took a recon or recoy or whatever it was of the whole campsite, ended back at the fire pit. Bernie sniffed the air. That caught my attention: Bernie has a nice big nose for a human, but what's that saying? Not much.

"Smell anything, big guy?" he said.

Did I smell anything? Was that the question? Where was I supposed to begin?

"I do," he said, "and it stinks."

Wow. That Bernie! I smelled so many things at the moment—the boys, Turk, Bernie, me, a female coyote, some squirrels, different flowers, tree sap, another mushroom like the one Bernie had pulled out of the ground, name gone from my mind, the dirty-locker-room-hamper thing, and lots more if I took the time to sort them all out—but nothing that qualified as actual stinking. I waited to hear.

"For example," said Bernie, "his backpack's gone but not the sleeping bag."

The sleeping bag? Was Bernie saying it stank? I went over and gave it a sniff or two. It smelled strongly of Turk, no surprise, but did it stink? Not to my way of thinking.

Bernie started taking down the tent. I helped by pawing at it a bit. Soon we had it all folded up and stuck inside the pack. Bernie hoisted it on his back.

"Okay, Chet, where did he go?"

That was the problem. There was so much of Turk's scent around, old and new, that I started going in circles again, frustration building inside me. Had to produce in this business, Bernie said so.

"Take your time," Bernie said. "No rush."

Bernie had the nicest voice, if I haven't made that clear by now. I felt calmer right away, and just then picked up a new trail, a little fresher than any of the others. It led over a mossy patch, so soft under my paws, and down to the stream, where it kind of petered out. I crossed over, sniffed around on the other side, came up with zip.

"He walked in the stream," Bernie said.

I knew that one. A perp name of Flyhead Malone had tried to lose me once by doing the same thing; he was now wearing an orange jumpsuit up at Northern State. The warden, a pal of ours, invited us to the inmate rodeo a while back. What a day! It ended a bit early, but if we're ever invited again I'll handle the excitement much better. Those bulls, snorting and pawing! What got into me? But perhaps a story for another day.

Bernie gazed at the flowing water, mostly black but a little silvery here and there. I glanced at the sky, and over in one direction it was turning milky. Bernie switched off the headlamp and put it away. Way better.

"The question is," he said, "upstream or down?"

Bernie thought. Upstream or down, a tough one: I could tell by the look on his face. I sat beside him. We did our best thinking that way. When Bernie's brain is really working, you can feel it, like breezes springing up in the air, dying down, springing up again—not a bad feeling at all. The milky part of the sky turned red and then orange, and day spread around us.

"Upstream's the contrarian answer," Bernie said. "But that's the way I'm feeling right now." He gave me a pat. "How about you?"

Me? I felt tip-top.

We walked beside Stiller's Creek. Sometimes there was a path, sometimes not, and once or twice we had to make inland detours when the going by the stream got too rocky. Too rocky for Bernie is what I meant: too rocky for me is hard to find. As for whether this was the right direction, I was picking up just faint scents of the kids—although never Devin—but there were stronger whiffs of Turk, plus the odd weak one, too. So, were we right or wrong? I didn't know. Did I worry about that? Not a bit.

I hadn't spent much time around creeks—we have them, too, in the Valley, and even rivers, but they all run dry, although back in Indian times, Bernie says, things were different. Donny O'Donnell, an Indian pal of ours who heads up security at the Little Bighorn Casino, always tells Bernie his tribe is hiding all the water until the palefaces go back where they came from, and Bernie gets a big kick out of it every time, but who the palefaces are and what Donny's talking about is anybody's guess. And it doesn't even matter—what matters was how much fun creeks with water in them turned out to be. I even saw a fish that jumped right into the air! I was after him in a flash, of course, almost got a paw on the little bugger, but he dove back in and sped away with a flick of his tail.

"For God's sake," Bernie said from the side of the creek, his clothes kind of wet for some reason, "you don't even like fish."

True, but only on account of this bad incident with a fish bone—that's what they're called despite not looking at all like bones. I climbed onto the bank, gave myself a good shake—"Chet!"—and headed up-country, focused, alert, professional.

The creek grew twistier and narrower and flowed faster; at the same time our path steepened. I came so close to making—what would you call it? a connection?—yes, a connection, between all those things. Was I cooking or what?

We passed through some woods—mostly more of those Christmas trees—and came to a small clearing, Bernie huffing and puffing a bit. He sat on a log. I sat beside him. The white-streaked mountain peak rose in the distance, maybe closer now. In between stood a series of ridges, growing bluish the farther away they got.

"Did he really bring the kids all this way?" Bernie said. "And we haven't even reached the mine yet." He pinched the bridge of his nose between his thumb and first finger. I never liked seeing that, not sure why. "But it's always possible that . . ." His voice trailed away, so I didn't find out what was possible. Fine with me: one thing I've learned in this business is that lots and lots of things are possible. "Either that," Bernie said, "or we're on a wild goose chase."

Whoa right there. Did Bernie just say we were on a wild goose chase? I'd waited so long for this moment, wanted to go on a wild goose chase more than anything.

"Chet! Knock it off!"

Oops. Was that me standing up, my front paws on Bernie's shoulders, almost pushing him off the log? Yes, my paws for sure, nice and big, one mostly black, one mostly white. A mistake, and I corrected it immediately.

"What's with you?" he said, tossing away a button that had somehow come loose from his shirt. "Did you hear something?"

As a matter of fact, I did hear something at that moment, the unmistakable *whap-whap-whap* of chopper blades. I'd even been up in a chopper once, so I knew the sound from the inside out. Hey! Does that make any sense? Probably not.

"You do hear something, don't you?" Bernie said. He cocked his head, ear to the sky. I love when he does that. Bernie has very nicely shaped ears, not that small, so even if they can't do much, they're still nice to look at. "Don't hear a thing, myself. There's the creek of course, and maybe a bird was singing a minute ago, but—"

WHAP-WHAP-WHAP. A chopper roared in at treetop level, zoomed over us, tilted a bit, and circled. *WHAP-WHAP-WHAP.* Bernie heard it now, no doubt about that. The human face does a sort of cringing thing when real loud noises start up, like someone's going to hit them. Not that Bernie would ever cringe—and anyone who ever did hit him, and we've had a few who tried, got paid back good—but I could tell. He waved at the chopper. It tilted the other way and flew off.

"Rescue," Bernie said, "probably dropping a team at the campsite." He checked his watch. "Should be more coming on foot, all experienced people. Plus other positives, like clear weather and plenty of drinking water. So why don't I feel good about this?"

Bernie didn't feel good? That was a surprise. I gave him a little bump. We moved on.

The sun was high overhead when we reached a slope where there were no more trees. The footing was all broken-up flat rocks, kind of tricky for Bernie. Also that strangeness about the air, like I couldn't fill up even with my deepest breath, was getting stronger. What else? The creek had thinned out to a trickle. We followed it to the base of a cliff where it disappeared, or maybe not completely, since it seemed to be bubbling right out of a hole in the rock.

"Pure spring water," Bernie said, in between huffs and puffs. He gathered a double-handful and splashed his face. "Ah." He looked around. "Imagine what life was like back then."

I didn't quite get that. What about right now? Life was pretty good, no? But Bernie had reasons for everything, so I tried to imagine some other life. No other life came to mind. Bernie made a little shrugging motion, adjusting the pack. We started working our way along the base of the cliff, and soon, in a shadowy spot under an overhang, spotted some white stuff, white stuff that reminded me of the white streaks on the mountain.

"Snow, big guy."

Snow? I'd heard of it, of course, seen it lots of times on TV during the divorce, when for some reason Bernie had really gotten into skiing videos. The snow sent coldness up into the air. I sniffed at it. Snow went right up my nose! I sneezed. Bernie laughed. I licked at the snow. It turned into water on my tongue, although not much water. Bernie picked some up and patted it—hey!—patted it into the shape of a ball. Yes! One thing about Bernie: just when you think he's done with amazing you, he amazes you again. Now, after all this time, I was just finding out he could turn snow into a ball. I knew what was coming next, one of my favorite feelings.

Bernie reared back to throw. He has a great arm—pitched for Army, in case that hasn't come up yet—and can fling a ball a long, long way. *Whoosh.* The snowball rose high in the sky. I took off after it, this bounding run I have when quick starts are needed. The snowball, sparkling against the blue sky, came arcing down. I caught up to it at the last instant and snatched it out of the air. But what was this? It broke apart and kind of vanished, leaving me with a cold nose; very different from any other ball I'd fetched.

I turned back toward Bernie, and as I did noticed a big dark hole in the face of the cliff. I could see some thick wooden beams inside, and beyond them just shadows and darkness. This was an old mine. We'd been in lots, me and Bernie. It was one of our hobbies, if hobbies meant things we did that made no money and annoyed Leda.

Bernie came up, gazed at the mine. "No way Turk took them inside, is there?"

Not sure where Bernie was coming from on that one, although I remembered Turk very well. In fact, his scent was strong at the moment; the scents of the kids were pretty much gone.

Bernie went to the mouth of the mine. "Devin," he shouted. "Devin."

No reply. I sniffed the air, smelled nothing of Devin at all. Bernie unslung the backpack and was taking out the headlamp when he spied something on the ground, maybe a tiny scrap of cloth. He picked it up. Yes, a tiny scrap of cloth. I'd seen something like it, and not long ago. It came to me: the name tag on Devin's sock.

I could see writing on this one, too. Bernie read it aloud. "Devin Vereen," he said. "Oh, Christ." He put on the headlamp. We entered the mine.

TEN

C areful, big guy," Bernie said.

That was rule one when it came to exploring old mines. There were other rules, too, but they didn't come to mind at the moment.

Bernie approached one of the support beams. "You just never know about these places." He gave the beam a little shake. "Seems solid enough." From somewhere up ahead came a thump, muffled but heavy, like part of the ceiling had collapsed. "Hmmm," said Bernie. Hmmm was always a sign of Bernie doing some serious thinking. He gave the beam another shake. No surprise there: Bernie was a great thinker, always came up with the exact right idea. We listened, heard nothing this time, and kept going. That's what being on the job's all about.

Some mines we'd explored were almost roomy, with rusted-out railroad tracks and lots of old equipment lying around. Others were so small we could barely squeeze through. This one was in between. We walked side by side, following the spreading light cone from Bernie's headlamp. Dust came swirling by, almost like it was flowing out of the mine, and turned golden in the light, a beautiful thing to see.

The floor, ceiling, and walls were solid rock, the surface rough, hacked-at, and reddish. I smelled copper, often the case in old mines, and some human scents, too, but faint and confused. Copper always made things difficult, one of the things you learn in this business. We passed the last support beam—Bernie stopped to read aloud something carved in wood: "Bonanza Bill, June seven, 1876, keep the hell out"—and right after that things began narrowing in around us. Bernie had to stoop a little, but not me, meaning I could go faster, which I did—always best to be in front, of course—and—

"Hey, Chet—where are you?"

Whoa. Had I gotten a little too far ahead of Bernie? I seemed to be beyond the cone of light. I waited. Beyond the cone of light, yes, but that didn't mean I'd stopped seeing. A little way up the line, for example, the tunnel split in two, one of the openings looking real small.

Light came wobbling up and found me. Bernie, stooping more on account of the ceiling getting lower, rested a hand on my back and peered ahead. "Left or right, big guy?"

Left or right: not the first time I'd heard that question, but I hadn't made much progress in figuring out the meaning. So, probably not important, our success rate being what it was at the Little Detective Agency. The cases we'd cleared! I could think of two without even trying.

We moved forward, reached the split. Bernie aimed the beam at both openings, and we looked down two tunnels, one big, one small. Bernie reached into his pocket, took out the baggie that contained Devin's sock and held it open for me. Like I needed reminding! But I took a sniff or two: I'd never want to hurt Bernie's feelings.

"Chet?" he said.

Sometimes I waited to see what Bernie would do. Sometimes he waited to see what I would do. This was one of those. The problem was the absence of Devin's scent in either direction. If Bernie thought Devin was in here, then he was, but I couldn't catch the slightest whiff. Coppery smells were stronger, confusing me more, plus there was now some watery smell, and on top of that, the way scents sometimes stacked up on one another, a real strange smell, kind of like the burned air thing you get after lightning strikes. All of a sudden my mind made itself up, just like that, and I ducked into the small tunnel.

"Chet? Wait—there's no way I can foll—"

I moved on. That was my job. Bernie shone the light behind me. I followed my shadow. It stretched out, getting longer and bigger. I was huge! Then it disappeared. Why? I glanced back—I can twist my head far around if I have to, a real advantage in a place like this tunnel, with no room to turn my whole body—and saw the light, now shining on a side wall. I'd gone around a kind of bend, and was now in darkness again. The lightning-strike smell got stronger. I slowed down, not liking that smell one bit, even thinking about curling up in a ball. Not that I was afraid or anything like that, but I knew something was about to happen.

And when it did, just a moment or two later, it turned out to be hardly anything at all. Just . . . what? A very tiny trembling of the ground under my feet? Something like that, here and gone in no time. Then, from not too far away, came a thud that reminded me of the time Bernie was building the patio out back and dropped one of the flagstones. He'd pulled his foot back in the nick of time—that expression comes from this real fleet-footed perp named Nick Beezer, but I really can't go into that now, except to point out he was fleet-footed for a human, not the same thing as being fleet-footed period, no offense—and the flagstone had broken and the pieces had bounced around. I heard some of those rocky, bouncing-around sounds here in the small tunnel. And then, farther along, a shaft of light appeared, very much like what you see when you're casing a house at night and some perp inside opens the door. Dust was boiling in that shaft of light. I closed in for a better look.

Well, well, well. A small section of the wall had caved in, and beyond it lay an open space. Not a very big open space, with hacked-at walls and piles of earth and rock, plus more boiling dust. This was a sort of chamber, with light coming in from a very small hole—no bigger than my head—in the rocky wall on the far side; not headlamp-type light, but the real daytime thing. I squeezed through the gap in the near wall, crossed the floor, climbed on top of a rubble pile and peered through the hole.

Hey! I saw the world outside, specifically a steep slope, and at its base an old falling-down cabin, way too ruined for anyone to live in, except that a pair of denim overalls hung on a line. I watched those overalls swaying in the breeze for a while, then turned back toward the little chamber. Light—this nice, strong daylight—was shining on the opposite wall, revealing a thick . . . seam? Was that the word? Yes, because when we explored old mines, Bernie often said, "Keep your eyes peeled for a seam of gold, big guy. We'll find it one day." Never mind that the peeling eyes thing had always made me feel uneasy; the point was I now had in my sight a thick seam that gleamed and glistened in a golden way. I moved off the rubble, my plan being to stand up real tall and lick that golden seam, just so I'd know for sure. I'd licked gold once before—a story all about a watch of Leda's that

I won't go into now—so I'd done my homework. But before I could get to the wall, I caught sight of something from the corner of my eye.

I knew a human skeleton when I saw one—we're not beginners, me and Bernie—but it always gets your heart racing. This particular skeleton, lying partly under the rubble, which was maybe why I'd missed it, had no flesh at all on it, or hair: a first for me. And also: no smell, not the faintest whiff. I went closer. The skull rested on its side. This was what lay behind the human face. I couldn't take my eyes off it. Laughter is one of the very best human things, and a kid's laughter the best of the best—you should hear Charlie when I take him for rides on my back—but there's a kind of nasty laughter that some humans use—never Bernie—just to be mean to other humans. And when they're getting ready to laugh that nasty laugh, the expression on their faces is just like the expression on the face of every human skull I've ever seen, including the one in front of me. That almost led me to another thought, but not quite, and this wasn't the time. I sniffed around the skeleton—still smelling zip—and came to the bony hand. Shaped like a hand, yes, but most of the bones weren't connected, and lying right in the middle was this small rock. A bumpy, golden rock, golf-ball size.

I licked it. Gold, no doubt at all. I picked it up. Was there a word for a little gold rock like this? I waited for it to come to me, and while I was waiting, I smelled that burned air smell again, and at the same time felt a tiny trembling under my paws, like something was going on deep, deep down. That disturbed me, I admit it: I like solid ground under my feet. Then—just when I was remembering the name of the little gold rock, funny how the mind works—the whole world shifted toward one side, the side where the daylight flowed in, and then shifted back, much harder, the other way.

KA-BOOM. The ceiling fell in, and the walls fell in, and the floor fell up, and also darkness fell, complete. I took off—rocks bouncing off me, dust filling my lungs—not toward where the light had been, but toward Bernie. Something huge and strong knocked me down. I rolled over, bumped against rocks that wouldn't give, bumped against more and more and more rock in every direction, solid rock but on the move at the same time, and started clawing, clawing, clawing, seeing nothing, smelling nothing, hearing nothing—except my heart, pounding like crazy—and feeling nothing but rock, closing in from all around.

Claw, big guy, claw. I heard Bernie's voice in my head. I clawed, clawed my very hardest with all my paws. And suddenly I popped out into open space, not a big space, but big enough for running. I ran, starting to see a bit, or at least sense where I was in the darkness: back in the small tunnel. Yes, because in the distance I glimpsed Bernie's light swinging back and forth.

"Chet! Chet! Where are you? Chet! Chet!"

Poor Bernie. He sounded so upset. I flew toward him.

From behind: *KA-BOOM*. And another *KA-BOOM*. I glanced back, saw there was no longer a tunnel behind me, just a wave of solid rock chasing my tail. I kicked it up a notch, hit top speed, raced into the cone of light and right smack into Bernie. We both went flying, the headlamp pointing wildly all over the place.

We picked ourselves up, me and Bernie. The headlamp lay on the ground, the light shining straight up. As Bernie bent down to grab it, everything went quiet, all of a sudden the quietest quiet I'd ever known, so quiet that the slight scrape of the headlamp on the rock as Bernie picked it up sounded sharp and clear, like sounds when I put my ear right against the speaker in the Porsche.

Bernie put on the headlamp. We looked around. I saw I was back at the junction where the big tunnel and the small tunnel—what was left of it, hardly any length at all, the rest filled in by the rock wave, finally at rest—came together. The ground was still, the air was still, Bernie and I were still.

He let out his breath. It sounded like a gentle breeze, and smelled good, too: toothpaste, coffee, and a touch of something sweet that was just Bernie. "Plate tectonics, big guy," he said. "Who'd think to factor that in?"

I missed that one completely. We turned and walked out of the mine. So good to be in the sunshine! Bernie gave me a pat. I dropped the nugget at his feet. That was the name: I'd learned it when we took down Nuggets Bolliterri, who always wore one—although not as big as this—around his neck.

"Chet?" he said, picking it up. "Where'd you get this?" He gazed at me. I gazed at him. Then he held the nugget up toward the sun and gazed at that, slowly turning it in his hand. I sat down beside him, looking at nothing in particular. The nugget was pretty. Nice to have it, no doubt about that. But how were we doing on the case? I wasn't sure.

Bernie tucked the nugget in his pocket. He turned toward the mine opening. From here it looked just the way it had looked before, all the support beams still in place, no sign of anything going on inside. "Safe to check out the big tunnel?" he said. I waited to hear. "There's Devin to think about."

Bernie was right, no surprise there. Finding Devin: that was the job, although wasn't Anya actually paying us to do something else? I couldn't remember. Once when Bernie's mother came to visit, she said, "What I can't remember can't be important." She's a piece of work—calls Bernie Kiddo, if I haven't mentioned that already—but I hoped she was right about the memory thing.

I rose. Bernie and I headed back toward the mine. We were just a few steps in when a man spoke behind us.

"Goin' someplace?" he said.

ELEVEN

We whipped around. A tall skinny dude with long stringy hair and a long stringy beard stood on the path leading to the mine. He wore overalls like the overalls I'd seen on the line, had a mule behind him carrying a heavy load, and also held a shotgun, not pointed at us, exactly, but not *not* pointed at us either, if that made any sense. That shotgun was important, of course, but I couldn't help being more interested in the mule. Hadn't dealt much with mules in my career, and new experiences kept you fresh. That was one of Bernie's core beliefs. I'd heard it the first time the night we got thrown in jail down in Mexico, a story for another time.

"That was our intention," Bernie said.

I got the impression he was answering some question, but I couldn't quite remember it.

"Like, say, goin' into the mine?" said the dude, his words not too clear on account of the fact that he was chewing on a straw; so was the mule.

"And if so?" said Bernie.

"Huh?" said the dude.

Bernie smiled. The shotgun barrel rose. Bernie's smile disappeared. "If we were planning on entering the mine," he said, "what's it to you?"

"No fuckin' way you're goin' in there," the dude said. "Simple as that."

"My understanding is we're on federal land," Bernie said.

"So?"

"So unless you're a ranger in disguise, you've got no authority here."

"You tryna be funny?" said the dude. He made another motion with the shotgun, kind of like the way humans sometimes talk with their hands. Those little hand gestures of theirs, always so much fun, but imagine what they could do if they had tails.

No time for imaginings, because at that moment I was sidling away. Some perps are surprisingly unaware of the nation within, hardly seem to see us. This dude—had to be a perp, what with that shotgun—turned out to be one of those. So I kept sidling with no real plan in mind, and as I sidled I caught my first whiff of the mule. Wow.

". . . that you've got some claim to the mineral rights?" Bernie was saying.

"Yeah. I got a claim. Been working this here mine for just about one whole year of my goddamn life. That's my claim."

"A claim without a permit," said Bernie.

The dude's eyes, kind of red and runny, narrowed. Still not pleasant, but better without the red runniness. "Know what?" he said. "I don't like you."

"Get in line," Bernie said.

"Huh?"

"Not important," Bernie said. "What's important is that there's a lost kid in the mine."

"Bullshit," said the dude. "Ain't no kids here."

I was pretty close to the mule by that time, circling around behind him. He had all sorts of stuff on his back—shovels, gas cans, a big duffel bag. Plus there were hot dogs in there somewhere; I never miss that. Also dynamite.

"That's where you're wrong," Bernie said. "Kids from Big Bear Wilderness Camp hiked through here on Friday."

"I warn't here on Friday."

"Which is why you couldn't know," Bernie said. "But time is crucial when it comes to finding missing kids, so let's get started. Any knowledge you've got about the mine will be useful."

The dude's voice rose. "Knowledge of the mine? What are you aimin' at, bud?"

"Nothing," Bernie said. "Just I'm sure you'll want to help us find—"

The dude's voice rose some more. "I'm not helpin' you do shit. Knowledge of the mine is my business. We clear on that?" He waved the shotgun. "Now beat it."

Hey! There were lots of tiny insects buzzing around the mule. He waved his tail at them, a stubby little tail for such a big guy, pretty much useless when it came to swatting bugs, and I was just about to feel sorry for him when he suddenly lashed out at me with one of his hind legs, real quick and nasty. I dodged to the side, just a bit quicker, but I felt the breeze from that big hoof flashing by. Close calls like that often get me barking. I barked, the short, sharp bark I have meaning, *Don't try that again, pal.*

Was that what made the mule suddenly bolt forward? No way of knowing, mule behavior being a gap in my education, as I already mentioned. But the mule's reasoning really didn't matter. What mattered was how he bolted forward—amazingly quick and powerful—and clobbered the dude with the shotgun square in the back, knocking him flat.

Things happened fast after that. The mule trotted off, clumsy but surprisingly speedy, banging into the side of the cliff on his way and splitting the big duffel bag. Out popped the package of hot dogs—Hebrew Nationals, the exact same kind Bernie and I bought, with the red packaging. The exact same kind, which happened to be the tastiest hot dogs out there—Bernie and I had tried them all. Just when you think life can't get any better, it does! The next thing I knew I'd snapped up that red package, practically before it even landed. I could taste the hot dogs through this tiny hole my teeth must have made by mistake, but I didn't take advantage of that to scarf them up. Somehow—hard to explain why, and it wasn't even like me—I knew that would be bad, and if not actually bad, then not good either. Anyway, far too much to think about. I hurried over to Bernie. By that time, he had the shotgun and everything was under control. That's how we do things at the Little Detective Agency.

The dude sat up. His nose was bleeding, but only a little. He wiped it on the back of his bare arm—he was the kind of overall wearer that didn't bother with a shirt underneath—and glared up at Bernie. Bernie broke open the shotgun, took out the shells and stuck them in his pocket. At that moment, he happened to glance at me.

"Chet?" he said. "Maybe not now."

Which I'd already known! Were Bernie and I on the same page or what? I let go of those Hebrew Nationals, no problem. The dude shifted that glare my way, maybe noticing me for the first time.

Bernie held out the shotgun. The dude, looking confused,

didn't take it. Bernie regarded him in a businesslike way, not smil-ing, as if to say I took your gun and now you're down and I'm up. That wasn't Bernie.

"What's your name?" he said.

The dude gazed up at Bernie. He licked his lips, something I always watch for in humans. He had a stiff, pointy tongue, kind of whitish at the tip. I made up my mind about the dude: bad news, period. Period means case closed. Our cases closed just about every time with me grabbing the perp by the pant leg. So if I snapped down with a nice toothy grip on one of those overalled legs at this very moment, did that mean the job was done and we could pick up our check and head for home?

I considered that question from many angles—actually, none—and while that was or was not going on, the dude said, "Everyone calls me Moondog."

Whoa right there. Sometimes with humans you can't be sure you heard right.

"Moondog?" said Bernie. Maybe he was having the same problem.

"Got an issue with that?"

"None at all," Bernie said. "It can get kind of isolated up here in the mountains."

"What's that sposta mean?"

"Just that I'm guessing you've done some baying at the moon in your time, possibly under the influence of this and that," Ber-nie said. "No big deal—so have I."

Damn straight. And me, too, although under the influence of nothing in my case.

"Yeah?" said Moondog. He looked up at Bernie in a new way, hard to describe, but something in it made me start to change my mind about him, and so soon after I'd just made it up. Funny how your own mind can surprise you. And if your own mind can surprise you, then think of . . . of a lot of big shadowy ideas that drifted just beyond my reach.

"Would I lie to you?" Bernie said. He smiled down at Moondog. Moondog looked confused again. Bernie lowered his hand. Bernie has beautifully shaped hands, in case that hasn't come up yet. Moondog stared at Bernie's hand for a moment and then took it. Bernie helped him up, gave him the shotgun. "What we're going to do now, with your help," he said, "is search this mine for the boy. His name's Devin, and he's all we're interested in. I couldn't care less about any other contents."

Moondog stepped back. "What the hell other contents?"

"Exactly," said Bernie.

"There ain't no other contents," said Moondog.

"Understood."

"And if there was, I'd be the first to know. Who the hell do you think's been diggin' his ass off in there and comin' up with diddley."

Oh, no. Bo Diddley was a big favorite of ours. Bernie can play "Hey Bo Diddley" on the ukulele in a way that always gets me going. Was Moondog saying that the skeleton I'd seen was Bo Diddley's? I couldn't figure out how that was possible, but strange things happened in this line of work, made it kind of frustrating at times.

"What the hell's he barkin' about?" said Moondog.

Bernie looked at me. "I think he wants to get moving."

"Moving on what?"

"The search."

"Huh? He don't know about no search. He's a goddamn dog."

Bernie's face darkened in a way you didn't often see; it tended to scare people. "Language," he said.

"Language?" said Moondog. "He's a g—he's a dog."

"True," said Bernie. "And he doesn't like to be kept waiting."

I didn't? Wasn't I a pretty good waiter? But if Bernie said I wasn't, then I wasn't. Still, a bit confusing, so I barked some more.

"See?" said Bernie.

"Guess so," said Moondog. He glanced around, fixed his gaze on the mule, now standing on a ledge above the cliff. "But what about Rummy? Can't just leave him up there."

Bernie looked up at the mule. "How about calling him?"

Rummy seemed to be watching us, too. Was he still chewing on that straw? Too far away to tell for sure.

"Like calling him works," said Moondog. "He's a mule, for Christ sake."

Bernie turned to me. "Chet?" he said.

What happened after that seemed to go on forever and was dusty, bloody, and noisy. Let's just get it on record that I went up onto the ledge and persuaded Rummy to come back down and leave it like that.

We left Rummy tied to one of the support beams and freed of his burden—Bernie insisted on that part—and entered the mine, Moondog first, holding a big lantern he'd taken from the duffel, then me and Bernie; he wore the headlamp although we didn't need it, the lantern being so bright.

"Who was Bonanza Bill?" Bernie said.

Moondog almost stumbled, like he'd missed a step. "What do you know about him?"

"Just that he carved his name on one of the beams," Bernie said.

Moondog resumed normal speed. "Yeah, that's what I know, too," he said.

"So that's that," Bernie said.

"Yup," said Moondog.

I got the feeling that something was on Bernie's mind and tried to figure out what. But not for long. Soon we came to the split, the big tunnel leading one way and what was left of the small one another.

Moondog shone the lantern in that direction. "Another goddamn cave-in," he said.

"Were you working that area?" Bernie said.

Moondog glanced back, doing his narrow-eyed thing again. "Whose business is that?"

"Not mine," Bernie said.

"Goddamn right," Moondog said, moving on.

"Just making conversation."

"Goddamn right," said Moondog again. "And for your information I worked that little tunnel the very first thing on account of what the map—on account of for reasons of my own. Wasted two months—nothin' there but rock—rock as hard as a witch's tit."

"Hmmm," said Bernie.

"What I'd do to that goddamn Bonanza Bill," Moondog said.

"But I take it he's long dead."

"Not long enough for me," said Moondog, losing me completely; even Bernie looked a little lost. "They say he's in here somewhere," Moondog went on.

"Yeah?" said Bernie.

"But here's all you need to know 'bout minin'—nobody knows nothin'."

"Easy to remember," Bernie said.

"Down thisaway's where I been working now," Moondog said, leading us into the big tunnel.

"How's it going?"

"Whose business is that?"

Bernie smiled at the back of Moondog's head. "Not mine," he said. Was something funny? Not that I could tell, but I always liked it when Bernie was enjoying himself.

We kept going. The tunnel started narrowing, and I got the feeling it was sloping down. We passed a broken pickax, a tipped-over wheelbarrow, a rubble pile in front of an opening that had been cut into the rock. After that came another rubble pile, and another, and another, all with hacked-out spaces in the solid rock on the other side.

"You've been working hard," Bernie said.

"Been accused of a lot of shit," Moondog said, "but not working hard's never been—" He cut himself off.

We stood before another rubble pile. This one was different from the others and we all saw how right away: poking out of the bottom was a human hand, covered in black dust, almost looking more like a glove than a hand.

"The kid?" Moondog said.

"Oh, God," said Bernie.

Then Bernie was down on his knees—and so was Moondog—both of them side by side, digging frantically at that rubble pile. I knew it wasn't Devin, of course, also knew who it actually was, and that we were too late to do anything for him. Otherwise I'd have been in there digging, myself; it's one of my specialties.

They got the face exposed. The eyes were open but covered in black dust. There was also a round red hole in the forehead. The digging stopped, Bernie's hands and Moondog's hands frozen in midmotion, black dust drifting in the lantern light.

"Turk," said Bernie, sitting back on his heels.

"Uh-huh," said Moondog.

Bernie turned Moondog.

"You knew him?"

Moondog nodded. "Hated the stupid son of a bitch."

TWELVE

Bernie closed Turk's eyes, gently, like Turk was still alive. One thing I've learned about life: when it stops, the smell starts changing right away.

Bernie turned to Moondog. "Did you hate him enough to kill him?"

"You some kind of a cop?" Moondog said. "I don't like cops."

"Tell me something I don't know," Bernie said.

The light flickered, like Moondog wasn't holding the lantern quite steady. I eased over a little closer to him, just in case. "I'm no killer," Moondog said.

Bernie nodded. He has all kinds of nods, part of his interviewing technique. That meant this was an interview, a fact I'd have to keep in mind. Sometimes whoever we were interviewing turned out to be the perp, sometimes not. It was always fun to find out which, just another reason this job is the best. But back to Bernie's nod. One of my favorites, and it meant: nothing in particular.

"You don't believe me?" Moondog said.

"I'm a private investigator," Bernie said. "It's not a faith-based job. I deal in facts, and you haven't been giving me any."

"Pegged you for a cop."

"I just told you—I'm not." Bernie made a little gesture with his chin in Turk's direction. "But real cops will be in your life soon. Call that fact one."

Moondog's eyes shifted. Sometimes that was a sign of a dude getting ready to do something not good. I moved still closer to him.

"Here's the difference between us and the law," Bernie said.

Moondog glanced around. "Who's us?"

"Chet and I, of course," Bernie said. Moondog gave me a funny look. I gave him a look back, not funny, just my standard look. "We're flexible," Bernie said. That was a new one: I'd try to remember it, although the meaning wasn't quite clear to me. "And the law is not," Bernie went on. "The law is a system, always grinding away. Smart people try not to get caught in its teeth."

"You're sayin' I'm not smart?" said Moondog.

"Still waiting to find out," Bernie said.

Moondog opened his mouth. At that moment, I felt one of those tiny tremors from way down in the earth. No sign Bernie noticed it, but Moondog flinched just the slightest bit, and I went back to thinking about his name again, not that I came up with anything new. This time no big jolt happened. Something about plates, Bernie had said. I've eaten off plates plenty of times, no problem, but prefer my bowl, hard to say why.

The earth stayed still. Moondog stopped flinching. He took a deep breath and said, "Meth is where I draw the line."

"Turk was in the meth business?" Bernie said.

The meth business? We've come up against it once or twice, here at the Little Detective Agency. There are nasty and powerful smells that go along with the meth business—I'd actually learned them long ago in K-9 school—and I detected not a trace now, standing over Turk's body, but what that meant I couldn't tell you.

"Meth killed Harley," Moondog said.

"Harley?"

"My brother."

"Sorry for your loss," Bernie said.

Moondog gave him a long look. His face softened. "Can't think what it's got to do with the kid you're lookin' for, but Turk's mother has a meth lab down by Jackrabbit Junction."

"Thanks," said Bernie.

"You didn't hear it from me," Moondog told him.

Did that mean jackrabbits were in our future? I'd had fun with rabbits more than once, but never jackrabbits, which sounded like even more fun. Maybe they'd be a little less shifty and I'd actually end up catching one.

We searched the rest of the tunnel—it didn't extend much farther—and found nothing. By the time we got outside, back in real light, that *WHAP-WHAP-WHAP* was coming from the sky again. The chopper appeared, circled a couple times, and then landed by the creek, the closest flat space around. We made our way down to it, past the overhang with the snow underneath, me and Bernie, Moondog, and Rummy. I took one quick lick at the snow in passing; and so did Rummy.

The chopper sat near the creek, blades still. A tall man in a Stetson climbed out and walked toward us.

"Laidlaw," said Moondog. "Biggest asshole in the county."

"What does he do?" Bernie said.

"Runs it," said Moondog. "He's the sheriff."

Sheriff Laidlaw came closer. He wore sunglasses, the mirrored kind. I hate all sunglasses, the mirrored kind the most. He also had a sandy-colored mustache and thick sandy-colored sideburns, none of which I was fond of. The stream was very narrow at this point, not even a single human stride across. The sheriff stopped on one side, us on the other.

He turned his mirrored eyes in Moondog's direction. "Surprised to see you still in these parts," he said.

"Free country, 'less something's changed," said Moondog.

"Forgot about that sense of humor," the sheriff said. "One of those family traits, like a harelip."

Moondog said nothing, but a vein in his forehead that I hadn't noticed before was now noticeable.

"Sheriff?" Bernie said. "I'm—"

"Know who you are," the sheriff said. "Boyfriend of the missing kid's mom."

"Friend is more accurate," Bernie said. "More relevant, in light of the situation unfolding, is that I'm also a private investigator."

The sheriff held out his hand, made one of those thumb and fingers rubbing gestures that meant: give. Bernie took out his wallet, flipped it open, held it up. The sheriff didn't appear to look at it, those mirrored eyes still on Bernie's face. I got the idea, maybe wrong, that he was waiting for Bernie to step across the stream and hand over the wallet. Bernie did not. Finally the sheriff did the stepping. He took the wallet, removed his sunglasses—hey, his eyes weren't interesting at all, flat, small, dull—and checked our license, not the first time Bernie and I had been through this.

Sheriff Laidlaw flipped the wallet closed and tossed it—in a casual sort of way, like he didn't care if it fell, and Bernie caught it in a way that was somehow even more casual: that Bernie!—and meanwhile the sheriff was saying, "Guess you are at that. But not in this state."

"Never made that claim," Bernie said. "But how about we bat

this around some other time?" I was all for that: we have a Pumpsie Green model back home, picked up in a case too complicated to go into now, and Bernie can hit baseballs so far with it that they turn into tiny black dots in the blue. "Right now we've got the trip guide lying dead in the mine and the kid still lost."

The sheriff's flat eyes got flatter. "Turk Rendell?"

"Shot in the head," Bernie said. "You'll want to take a look."

The sheriff turned, spat into the stream. Spitting always interests me—why men and not women, for example?—but it was important to concentrate so I tried my hardest not to watch that yellowish spit glob bobbing in the blue ripples, growing a tiny tail, then suddenly corkscrewing beneath the surface and disappearing.

". . . bona fides," the sheriff was saying. "I'm acquainted with a number of private operators down your way."

"Such as?" Bernie said.

"Georgie Malhouf, for one," said the sheriff.

"I know him," Bernie said.

"Does he know you—that's the question."

"I just spoke at his convention."

"Yeah?" said the sheriff. "About what?"

"Facial recognition techniques," Bernie said.

There was a pause. I thought Sheriff Laidlaw was about to spit again, but instead he said, "Let's see this body of yours."

Not long after that, we were gazing at Turk's body again, just the not-covered-up parts, meaning mostly the hand sticking out of the rubble, and the face with the round red hole in the forehead. We had Moondog's lantern, but not Moondog, who the sheriff had told to stay outside.

"Take that bullet hole away and he coulda died in a cave-in," the sheriff said. "We get a moron like that every year or two, searchin' for a pot of gold. Take Moondog—shoulda been dead years ago."

"The bullet hole's not going away," Bernie said.

The sheriff smiled at Bernie. He had very white teeth, almost glowing. Bernie always said that teeth like that weren't real. I had a strange thought, not my usual kind at all: did that mean the smile wasn't real either? What a thought! I hoped that none like it came again, at least not for a long time.

"Never do, do they?" the sheriff said. He pointed at Turk with the pointy toe of his cowboy boot. "Know anything about him?"

"A little," Bernie said.

"Like what?"

Bernie shrugged. He was a pretty good shrugger, although a much better nodder. "He was the trail guide for the kids' wilderness hikes."

"That it?"

"Should there be more?" Bernie said.

"Naw," said the sheriff. "But word of caution—Moondog and his ilk are piss poor sources of information around here."

Piss poor? That was a new one. I kind of liked it. I myself was piss rich, no doubt about that. I wandered out of the circle of light and lifted my leg against the tunnel wall. Chet the Jet!

Standing there in the darkness, one leg lifted, listening to the nice faint splashing sounds, I looked back toward the circle of light. The lantern sat on the ground, casting an unsteady light upward and making their faces strange, all the shadows leaning in the wrong direction. Not Bernie's face of course: how could there ever be anything strange about Bernie's face? But Sheriff Laidlaw looked like a Halloween version of himself, if that makes any sense. I love all the holidays, but not Halloween. If there's a party, I don't go: that was how we solved the problem, me and Bernie.

The sky was reddening when we got back outside, and Moondog and Rummy were gone. The sheriff and a uniformed guy stayed behind; Bernie and I piled into the chopper with the pilot—no big deal, I'd flown in a chopper before—and got taken back to the camp. At least that was where Bernie said we were going. Something about the motion made my eyelids get heavy right away. If you've logged any chopper time you probably know what I'm talking about.

I dreamed about gold nuggets, piles and piles of them. A lovely dream, on account of the state of our finances, until just before the end, when the piles of nuggets turned into piles of Hawaiian pants. Those Hawaiian pants were real, in case I haven't made that clear. I opened my eyes. We were on the ground and Bernie was looking at me closely.

"You all right, big guy?"

All right? Way better than that. I was rested, refreshed, rarin' to go.

"Maybe just a bad dream," he said, patting my head. "You were whimpering there for a bit."

Oh, no. How embarrassing. Up in the cockpit, the pilot was busy with the switches, maybe hadn't heard me. Bernie popped open the door. We hopped out, Bernie not exactly hopping, and stayed low, those blades still *whap-whap-whapping*. Solid ground felt good under my paws. Had I just been worrying about something? I tried, not hard, to remember, and couldn't.

The pilot opened a side window and shouted over the noise of blades, "Good-looking dog."

What a nice pilot!

"Does he like Slim Jims? Got half of one left."

In fact, the greatest pilot in the world. And quite good-looking himself, with a bald shiny head and a jowly round face, a little bit greasy. I got hit by this crazy notion of licking off that grease. Maybe later.

We moved away from the chopper. It took off, veered in a big curve and soared up the mountain. I looked around, got my bearings. We were in the parking lot at Big Bear Wilderness Camp. The sun, all fat and red, was perched right on a big round mountaintop, but no time to take in the way it was about to wobble and sink from view—a sight I'd seen before, although it never got old—because Anya was running toward us along the path that led down from the main cabin, running so fast and out of control I thought she might fall at any moment. And also—what was this? A yellow Beetle was driving up the canyon road? Car identification wasn't my best thing, but Beetles were easy and this yellow one easiest of all, on account of the fact that it belonged to Suzie and I'd ridden in it many times.

Anya tore up to us, grabbed both of Bernie's hands. "Oh my God—you didn't find him?"

"No," Bernie said. "But there's still hope."

Her big blue eyes opened wider; they had a wild look. "There's still hope? What do you mean, still? Still? Still? Oh my God."

"Well," said Bernie, "the facts are—"

Anya started beating on Bernie's chest with her fists. "Make me hear it," she said, her voice rising and rising. "Make me hear hope."

Uh-oh. A bad situation, and it got worse in a hurry. First, the yellow Beetle drove up and parked. Then Anya, her back to the Beetle, collapsed sobbing into Bernie's arms. Bernie, looking real uncomfortable, gazed up at the sky, like he wanted help to come down and bail him out. Right about then was when Suzie got out of the car. She had a big smile on her face. It faded fast. Bernie patted Anya on her back, maybe even rubbed it a little. Anya calmed down but still clung to Bernie, kind of wrapped all over him, her hands now clasping the back of his head. Suzie got in her car. At that moment, Bernie's gaze came down and he noticed the Beetle for the first time.

"Suzie!" he said, trying to free himself from Anya. "Suzie!"

Through the windshield, Suzie's face looked hard. She fishtailed around in a tight turn and sped off down the canyon road.

THIRTEEN

Bernie ran a few steps after Suzie's car and then stopped. Me, too. Do I have to mention I'd been running with him? If Bernie starts running, then so do I—it just happens.

I'd caught up with the odd car in my time, but this was a long shot, and with Bernie not a shot at all, which is maybe what he'd just realized. Bernie can surprise you by running quite long distances; still, you'd never call him fast, not even for a human. That's on account of his war wound; I'm sure he ran like the wind before it happened.

The yellow Beetle disappeared, leaving nothing but a dusty sort of tail, reddened by the sinking sun. A pretty sight, but all this reddishness in the light was making me a little uneasy. Did I remember that ever happening before? No. Then I thought of Turk back in the mine, and that round red hole, and kind of understood. The next moment, I realized my tail was drooping. That was a shocker. I got it back up, high and stiff, and pretty damn quick.

We walked back into the parking lot. Anya was wiping away her tears. "Who was that?" she said.

Bernie gave her an annoyed look. There was annoyance in his voice, too. "Nothing to do with the case," he said. Was he annoyed with Anya? I couldn't think why.

"Sorry," Anya said. "I'm just so . . . I'm going crazy. My whole life is—" Her voice broke. She started crying again and turned away.

Bernie gazed at her shaking back. "It's all right. You didn't do . . ."

We all just stood there. The sun dropped behind the mountaintop and the air cooled down right away. Anya turned to us, tear tracks on her face but no longer crying. "What am I going to do?" she said.

"What we're going to do," Bernie said, "is start approaching things from a different angle."

"What do you mean?" Anya said, and I was with her on that.

Bernie glanced at the mountain. We'd been up there, but none of what we'd seen, like the mine or the place where the kids had camped, was visible from here. "The story won't hold up," he said.

"What story?" said Anya.

"Devin wandering off in the night and getting lost," Bernie said. "The facts we've been developing just don't support it."

Anya rubbed the side of her head. "What facts? I don't understand anything you're saying."

"Do you know Turk Rendell in any other context?"

"Who's he?"

Bernie's voice, which had been getting a bit impatient, at least for him, meaning still pretty nice, softened. "The guide."

"Oh, God, of course," Anya said. "I can't think straight. But no, he was a complete stranger."

"What about your ex-husband? Any relationship with Turk?"

"Guy never mentioned him, not that I heard."

"You said this camp was Guy's idea," Bernie said. "How did he know about it?"

"He's from up this way originally," Anya said.

"Yeah?" said Bernie. He ran his gaze over the cars in the parking lot. "I'd like to talk to him."

Anya bit her lip, almost chewing on it. That's something I can't take my eyes off. "He's not here yet."

"How come?" Bernie said. "Haven't you told him what's going on?"

Anya shook her head. "I haven't been able to reach him. I drove down to where the service is better and left messages at all his numbers, but he hasn't called back."

"Wasn't he supposed to be here Saturday morning?" Bernie said.

Anya nodded, bit her lip again.

"Anya?" Bernie said. "What's the story?"

"Story?" she said.

"With Guy," said Bernie. "Why isn't he here?"

"I have no idea. Even when we were married, I didn't get much information about his comings and goings."

"You told us he runs an investment firm," Bernie said.

"That's right."

"You also said some of his associates aren't the kind of people you want around Devin—I believe those were your exact words."

I loved when Bernie did the exact words thing, hadn't heard it in way too long. Had we ever blown a case when the exact words thing happened? Not that I remembered.

". . . but I also said I didn't really know them," Anya was saying, "so it wasn't really fair."

"What are the names of these investors?" Bernie said.

"I don't know any names," Anya said.

"What's the company called?"

I knew from the looks on their faces that this was an important conversation, but that was it as far as I was concerned.

"Wenders Associates, but you're way off base," Anya was saying. I knew that one, of course: it meant you were about to get picked off. "None of them could ever be involved in hurting Devin in any way. Guy would kill them, for one thing."

"How much killing has he done?"

"I didn't mean literally."

"Think carefully about that," Bernie said. "Because real killing is happening."

"What are you talking about? Is Devin—" Anya covered her mouth. Women sometimes did that, men never, just one of the differences between them. There were lots, something we can get into maybe later.

"I told you there's still hope for Devin," Bernie said. "Not so for Turk—someone put a bullet in his head."

Anya, mouth still covered, shook her head from side to side, kind of wildly. I saw fear in her eyes, smelled it, of course, and even thought I heard her heart pounding, but that last part might have been my imagination. Bernie says the imagination can play tricks on you. Leave it to Bernie to figure out something as big as that.

"Any idea who might have done that?" Bernie said.

Anya kept shaking her head. Bernie surprised me a bit just then: he took her chin in his hand—not rough, but not namby-pamby either—and held her face still. I went still myself.

"Got to step up now, Anya," Bernie said. "Ever comes a time you have to look back at this, you'll want to know you did your best."

Tears welled up in her eyes but didn't overflow. She uncovered her mouth. "Tell me what to do," she said.

"Point us in the right direction."

Whoa. Pointing was my job. I was sitting at the moment, and I stayed sitting, but I moved kind of between them the littlest bit, dragging my butt along the ground.

"I have no idea what that is," Anya said. "I dropped Devin off in this godforsaken place and now he's gone. That's all I know."

Bernie stared at her. There was something in his eyes that I'd never want aimed at me, and of course it never would be.

"You don't believe me," Anya said.

Bernie was silent.

"You think Guy not being here has something to do with this?" Anya said.

"You said you had custody?"

"Guy didn't even contest it—whatever else he may be, he's a good father and knows what's best for Devin, meaning living in my house."

"But you said he wanted to rekindle things with you," Bernie said. "The ostensible reason for my being here in the first place."

"Ostensible?" Anya said.

I was right with her on that one, too. Anya and I were turning out to think along the same lines. A good sign? I had no idea.

"It didn't sound kosher from the get-go," Bernie said, and then he added something I missed, on account of: kosher! That took me back in a flash to the Teitelbaum divorce and the chicken at the celebration dinner, best I've ever tasted, although the celebration might have been a little premature, coming just before Mrs. Teitelbaum drove the earthmover into the garage where Mr. Teitelbaum kept his antique car collection. He had a bunch of Porsches, all of them way nicer than ours, and then not.

". . . ulterior motive," Anya was saying, "none whatsoever. I told you the truth."

"Some of it, maybe," Bernie said. "What was Guy's motive for wanting to get back with you?"

"Is it so hard to imagine he might still be interested?" Anya said.

Bernie got this expression I hadn't seen on his face since the Leda days. "Don't know him, so I can't answer that," Bernie said. "What I'm searching for is something that will lead us to Devin. Maybe Guy decided he wasn't happy with the custody arrangement, for example."

"He never said a word about it, and he's not the kind to stew in silence."

A distant look appeared in Bernie's eyes. I felt his thoughts, zooming back and forth at amazing speed.

"Oh, no," Anya said. "You're going to drop the case, aren't you? I can feel it. Please don't. Please. I'll pay anything."

"We're not dropping the case," Bernie said. "And we can worry about the fee later."

Bernie: lock it in now!

But he didn't. Instead, he said, "Has Devin had much trouble from bullies?"

"Some little monster at school teased him for a while about being—about his weight," Anya said. "The teacher put a stop to it. That's how I found out—Devin hadn't breathed a word. The whole camp thing came out of that episode—Guy thought it would toughen him up."

"And what about bullying here?" Bernie said.

"None that I know of," Anya said. "The kids are supposed to write once a week, so I've just had the one card."

"Saying what?"

"You can see for yourself," Anya said. She dug a postcard from her purse, handed it to Bernie.

Bernie held it up to the fading light. "'Hi, Mom,'" he read. "'I'm at camp. Getting lots of exercise and not having seconds. The food's crappy anyway. I saw a real fox! I sleep in a tent with other kids. It's all right. Can't wait to get home. Love, Dev.'"

Bernie's face got real hard. Was that about the fox? I couldn't think of any other reason.

"Are you saying he's been bullied here at camp?" Anya said. Silence from Bernie. "Should I have known? How could I have?"

Bernie gave the postcard back. "C'mon, Chet. Let's get to work."

We met with Ranger Rob in his office in the big cabin. Ranger Rob sat on one side of his desk, us on the other.

"This is just a nightmare," Ranger Rob said. "What am I going to tell the campers? They loved Turk."

"They did?" Bernie said.

Ranger Rob looked up sharply. Hey! He was older than I'd thought. "What is that supposed to mean?"

"Turk's conduct up on the mountain was negligent at the very least," Bernie said. "And sneaking off in the middle of the night the way he did speaks of guilty knowledge."

"Guilty knowledge? What are you saying?"

"I suspect that Turk had inside information regarding Devin's disappearance," Bernie said, "may even have been an accomplice."

"Accomplice to what?" said Ranger Rob. "This is crazy."

"The nature of the crime—meaning the exact charges that will be filed when this is all over . . ." Bernie paused right there and looked Ranger Rob directly in the eye. Ranger Rob tried to meet his gaze but gave up pretty damn quick, maybe the quickest I'd seen. Loved when Bernie did that pausing and gazing thing, although what was going on could have been clearer to me. ". . . is what we're working on right now. Anything you can do to help will be appreciated by me, by law enforcement, and by the judge when this all comes to court."

Ranger Rob sat back in his chair. "You seem to be bullying me for some reason. I don't like being bullied."

"Funny you should mention that," Bernie said. "Some of the boys bullied Devin so badly that he slept outside the tent on the hike, up above thirteen thousand feet."

"I don't believe that."

"It's a fact," Bernie said. "There'll be more like it, and coming in fast, so your best move now is to stop fighting them."

Ranger Rob opened his mouth in a way that made me think he wasn't at all ready to stop fighting, but at that moment a big clunky phone rang on his desk.

"I thought you didn't have a sat phone," Bernie said.

"Do you question everything?" Ranger Rob said. "Park Service gave it to me this morning." He picked up the phone, said, "Big Bear," and listened. "All right," he said, and hung up. He turned to Bernie, the fight leaking out of him fast. "That was search and rescue, up on the mountain. No trace of the boy, and they're suspending operations for the night. Sheriff Laidlaw's coming back down in the chopper and . . . and he hopes that you stick around to help."

Bernie nodded.

"You can bunk in the guest cabin," said Ranger Rob.

"Thanks," said Bernie. "Right now I want to talk to Tommy, the boy from tent seven."

"What about?"

"Finding Devin."

"You think Tommy knows where Devin is?"

"There are leads that need following up," Bernie said. "That's what we do. And in missing kids' cases, time is always against us."

"Well, I suppose if I'm in the room—" Ranger Rob began.

"Nope," Bernie said.

"But I haven't even made the announcement about Turk yet."

"And you're not going to until we get done with Tommy."

Ranger Rob gave Bernie an angry look. "You'd better know what you're doing," he said.

Bernie said nothing. Of course we knew what we were doing. It went without saying, a favorite expression of Bernie's, and mine, too. Missing kids were our specialty. We'd worked a zillion cases—and if not a zillion, then at least many—and found every single kid. Every single kid, but once we were too late: can't leave that out. It was a case we thought about a lot, me and Bernie. First, I licked the little girl's face and then Bernie lifted her out of the broom closet and tried and tried to get her breathing again. Those parents when we brought the bad news: you don't forget things like that.

FOURTEEN

Night fell. Bernie and I sat in the dining hall, which was called the chuckwagon here at Big Bear Wilderness Camp. We have a wagon at home, and when Charlie was younger I'd pull him around on it. "Chet the Jet!" he'd be shouting. "Faster, faster, Chet the Jet!" Did we zoom around or what? This was back in the days when Iggy was still roaming outside. And guess what: Iggy didn't race along with us, oh, no. Instead he liked to jump on the wagon, crowd in with Charlie, and steal a free ride. That Iggy!

Nice and quiet in the dining hall, just the two of us. Bernie sat at the end of long old wooden table, eating a bowl of chili. I stood beside him on the floor—a floor made of wide boards worn down smooth, soft and comfortable—eating a bowl of kibble. All kinds of kibble out there on the market, but this one from Rover and Company was the best. The owner, Simon Berg, is a buddy of ours, sometimes sends over samples from the test kitchen. We were living the dream, me and Bernie.

He took out his cell phone, called Suzie for the zillionth time, and that didn't include the zillion times of not getting a signal. "Suzie? Suzie? If you're there, pick up. Are you there? Suzie?

Suzie?" He clicked off, looked at me. "How the hell did I forget she was coming up here? Took me by surprise. If I'd been prepared, I could have . . ." He didn't tell me what he could have done, but he didn't have to because I knew it would have been perfect. So maybe he didn't have to tell Suzie either, because she too would just know? A confusing thought, and not my usual kind at all. It slipped away, and I licked the last bit of kibble dust from the bottom of my bowl. Since licking was on my mind, I licked all around my mouth, and then the tip of my nose. Why not? It was something I could do, so I did. Once this perp named Walter "Honey" Potts bet Bernie a C-note that he could touch his nose with the tip of his tongue. Bernie took the bet—"No human can do that," he said. But maybe Honey Potts wasn't human— although he smelled, very powerfully, of human—because it turned out he could do it no problem. "Double or nothing?" he said. He was still laughing when we turned him over to Central Booking.

Hey! Bernie was watching me, head tilted at an angle. "Something on your mind, big guy?"

Me? Nothing at all. I got my tongue under control, sat down, shifted closer to Bernie, waited for whatever came next. How were we doing on the case? Not bad, right?

A kid came through the far door of the hall. I remembered him—a biggish dark-haired kid, a kid I liked, although I couldn't think of one I didn't, and then all of a sudden I could: Preston. But this wasn't Preston.

Bernie smiled and said, "Hi, Tommy."

Tommy came over, walking slow, the way humans—and especially kids—walked when they actually wanted to be going in the other direction.

"It's okay," Bernie said. "I don't bite."

Of course he didn't! What would be the point, with those little teeth of his, not little for a human, but still?

Tommy stood before us, shuffling from one foot to the other. At that moment, I drew my lips way, way back, exposing my teeth. I had not the least intention of biting anybody, but with the idea of biting somehow in the air, I just couldn't help it. Funny how the mind works.

Tommy stepped back. "His teeth are huge!"

I tried to get my lips back to where they belonged, but for some reason could not. It occurred to me to try licking my nose again, sort of on the way to reining in the lips, if that makes any sense.

"That's just because Chet's a big guy, period," Bernie said. The nose-licking method worked, and there I was: mouth closed, attitude professional. "He likes kids," Bernie said, "might even let you pat him, if you want."

What a joker Bernie is sometimes! Of course, Tommy could pat me. I turned my head to give him a nice, direct opening. He reached out, kind of cautious, and laid his hand on my head, went pat pat. Not a great patter, compared to Bernie, maybe, and nothing like Autumn or Tulip who worked at Livia's house of ill-repute and were off the charts when it came to patting, but still: no complaints.

"He has a nice coat, huh?" said Tommy.

"Chet likes spending time with the groomer," Bernie said. He could say that again—I waited for him saying it again to happen, but it did not. Janie's my groomer. She comes to us in her silver truck: what a great business plan. Janie's a strong woman with a broad face, big hands, and dirty fingernails: who wouldn't love her?

"Some dogs do well with allergic people," Bernie said.

"Yeah?" said Tommy.

"The Maltese, for one," Bernie said. "And Portuguese water dogs, if you want something bigger."

"Yeah," Tommy said. "Something bigger."

"Maybe your mom could spend an hour or so with a Porty, see how she does," Bernie said.

Tommy's eyes lit up: a nice sight, especially in a kid. "That's a good idea," he said, still patting me. He looked into my eyes, like he was trying to see something. I looked right back, trying nothing particular. "Chet helps you in your work?" he said.

"More the other way," said Bernie.

Tommy laughed. What was funny?

"What we're working on now," Bernie said, "is finding Devin and bringing him back safe."

Tommy stopped laughing. Then he sat down on the bench opposite us, his back to the table. Now we were all of us sitting together. Sitting conversations usually went better than the standing kind, the chasing after at full speed kind being the least promising; you learn these things in this business.

Bernie turned a bit, facing Tommy across the space between the benches. At that moment, I happened to spot what looked very much like the rounded end piece of a sausage lying under our table, in easy reach. I scarfed it up; yes sir, the rounded end piece of a sausage, nice and crunchy on the outside, juicy within. Nothing wrong with any part of a sausage, but end pieces were the cherry on the sundae, not that I'm a fan of either of those. This dining hall would be worth exploring if I had time, no doubt about that. Meanwhile, I'd maybe missed a bit of what was going down.

". . . play any sports, Tommy?" Bernie was saying.

"Little League," said Tommy.

"Got a favorite position?"

"Catcher."

Catcher? Tommy and I had something in common.

"Great position," Bernie said. "You like having the whole field in front of you, huh?"

Tommy looked surprised. "Yeah. I guess I do."

"That's kind of what Chet and I are trying to do right now, see the whole field," Bernie said. "Devin's out there somewhere."

"Um," said Tommy.

Bernie remained silent. That was a right we had, very important. One night over a bottle of bourbon, Bernie and Lieutenant Stine of the Valley PD had a big argument about it. How it turned out I don't know, because things got too exciting for me and I had to take five out on the patio.

"Like," said Tommy, after the silence had stretched on for what seemed a long time, "where?"

"We need help on that," Bernie said. "When someone disappears, we always talk to the people who saw him last."

"But you talked to us already," Tommy said. "In the tent."

"True," said Bernie. "But now Chet and I have been up to that campsite by the creek, had a look-see that raised more questions."

"You went up with Turk?"

"He showed us around—where the campfire was, the tent, all that."

Tommy nodded.

"Remember that sock of Devin's?"

Another nod from Tommy.

"Based on the scent off the sock, Chet was able to find the exact spot where Devin spent that last night." Bernie sat back, placed his hands on his knees, relaxed and patient. This was an interview—and Bernie's a great interviewer—but I didn't remember him ever sitting like that in an interview.

Tommy looked down at the floor. "He . . ." Tommy's voice got thick, the way human voices did when tears were about to enter the picture, but no tears came. He cleared his throat, looked up, even meeting Bernie's gaze for a moment or two, and said, "Devin didn't sleep in the tent. He slept on the ground outside."

"How did that happen?" Bernie said.

"It just seemed like a good idea," said Tommy.

"Yeah?" said Bernie. "Gets cold up there at night, even in summer. Devin didn't mind that?"

There was a silence, except for a faint scratching behind the nearest wall, the sort of scratching mice do, but no one except me seemed interested.

"I guess he kind of did," said Tommy at last.

"But?" said Bernie.

Tommy took a deep, deep breath and let it out with a groan. For a moment I was worried he was going to be sick, poor kid. "He just couldn't stand it anymore," Tommy said.

"Preston's bullying?" said Bernie.

Tommy took another deep breath. "Not just Preston," he said. "It was all of us."

"Okay," Bernie said. "And this idea—the good idea of Devin moving out of the tent—who came up with that?"

Tommy turned toward a window. Nighttime, now, the real dark nighttime you don't get in the city. "It was after supper, in the tent, and all this stuff about how the packs wouldn't have been so heavy if we didn't need so much food for Devin, and Devin sort of started crying for the first time, real loud and noisy, kind of scary even, and Turk opened the flap and said, 'What's all this shit?' and 'If you can't fuckin' get along, one of you's gonna have to sleep outside,' and . . ." Tommy went silent. Funnily enough, he was sitting like Bernie now, hands on his knees. He gazed down at his hands—nice, squarish hands, with a small scar on the back of one of them.

"So the idea was actually Turk's?" Bernie said.

"Sort of, I guess," Tommy said. "Did, um, you talk to Turk about this?"

Bernie has great eyebrows, if I haven't mentioned that already, eyebrows with a language all their own. Right now they were showing me that Bernie was surprised. "Good question," he said. "I did."

"And, uh . . ."

"You're wondering if he said the same thing? That it was his idea?"

"Yeah."

"He did not. Turk said it was Devin's idea."

Tommy shook his head.

Bernie rose, went to the window, gazed out at the blackness. Did he hear something out there? I listened real hard, heard nothing but the mice and a slight buzz from one of the ceiling lights.

"You don't believe me," Tommy said.

Bernie turned to him. "What makes you say that?"

Tommy shrugged.

"You think adults always take the word of adults over kids?" Bernie said.

Tommy shrugged again.

"The truth is," Bernie said, "in this business, we take the word of no one."

"Oh."

"But if what we hear matches up with what we already know, that's a different story."

"So you do believe me?"

"Yes."

"Are you going to tell Turk?"

"Tell him what?"

"That I, you know, ratted him out."

"No," said Bernie. "You don't have to worry about Turk."

The way Tommy was sitting on the bench changed, like something inside him had softened.

"Our only worry," Bernie said, "is Devin. So let's take it from when Turk poked his head in the tent."

"It was dark inside. Turk, uh, had the flashlight. He pointed it at Devin." Tommy went silent. He shook his head, a slight side-to-side movement.

"Something the matter?" Bernie said.

"He was crying."

"Right. You mentioned that."

"But the sight of it, all of a sudden like that. You know—his face."

"And then?" Bernie said.

"He kind of got his sleeping bag and stumbled out of the tent. Turk shone the light on us and said to shut our goddamn mouths."

"Which you did?"

"Yeah."

"Preston, too? He shut his mouth?"

"Maybe not that second."

"What was he saying?"

"Just more stuff."

"About Devin."

"Uh-huh."

"And then?"

"Things got quiet. We fell asleep."

"The kids in the tent?"

"Yeah."

"But not you."

"What do you mean?"

"You were noticing that the others—Preston, Luke, and Keith—had fallen asleep. So you were awake. How come?"

"I dunno."

"Are you a light sleeper?"

"What's that?"

"Someone who has trouble falling asleep, wakes up a lot during the night, that kind of thing."

"My mom says I sleep like a rock."

"So therefore . . . ?" Bernie said. That got my attention, which actually had been starting to slip, something that happens when humans get to going on and on, no offense. But I always perk up when Bernie starts with the so therefores, one of his top specialties.

"Guess I couldn't get to sleep," Tommy said.

"Were there noises outside?"

"That came later. Why I couldn't get to sleep was 'cause of how . . . how we, you know . . ."

"Treated Devin?" Bernie said.

Tommy nodded.

"You can take yourself off the hook about that, Tommy," Bernie said.

I glanced around. No hooks in the vicinity, a good thing: I'd had a nasty run-in with a fish hook in some perp's shed one time, ended up with stitches in my paw and a bandage that wouldn't stay on no matter how much I knew it was supposed to.

". . . much more interested," Bernie was saying, "in those noises outside."

"That was later," Tommy said. "I was almost asleep. Like first I thought I was dreaming these voices. But I opened my eyes and I could still hear them."

"Did you recognize the voices?"

"One was Turk."

"And the others?" Bernie said.

"There was only one other," said Tommy. "I'm pretty sure."

"Man or woman?"

"Man."

"What did he sound like?"

"You know, a man."

"Anyone you'd heard before?"

"No. I don't think."

"What were they talking about?"

Tommy scrunched up his face. Humans do that sometimes when they're thinking real hard. When we're thinking real hard— I mean, we in the nation within the nation—our faces stay the same. As for cats, I couldn't tell you.

"Coke," Tommy said.

"Coke?"

"Like the drink. Not drugs."

"What made you think that?"

"Because the man—this other man, not Turk, said, 'Things go better with Coke.'"

"And then?" Bernie said.

"Then the voices got farther away so I couldn't hear."

"How long did the talking go on for, all together?"

"Not too long."

"I'm assuming when you woke up, that the other man wasn't there."

"No."

"Did you hear him leave?"

Tommy shook his head.

"Did you say anything to Turk about all this in the morning?"

"I kind of forgot about it," Tommy said. "Turk was all upset, with Devin wandering off and having to search for him, and—" His eyebrows, dark and kind of prominent, sort of like Bernie's, rose suddenly. "Did the other man take Devin away or something?"

"Real good question, Tommy. I don't suppose Turk mentioned anything about him."

"No," said Tommy. "But you're going to ask him now, right?"

"That's the next logical move," Bernie said. "But—"

The door to the dining hall opened and in came Sheriff Laidlaw. He walked toward our table, a bit bowlegged in his cowboy boots, and said, "Got a moment?"

"Okay," said Bernie. He patted Tommy on the knee. "You've been a big help."

Tommy rose. "Are you going to find Devin?"

"We'll do everything we can," Bernie said. "Can't promise more than that."

Tommy nodded. He turned and left the dining hall, his arms hanging stiff and motionless.

The sheriff remained standing. "What was that all about?" he said.

"New information about Devin's disappearance," Bernie said. "We need to talk."

"That we do," said the sheriff. Then, over his shoulder, he called out, "Boys!"

Two uniformed deputies came through the door. One held a shotgun, pointed at the floor. The other was carrying Bernie's backpack—very easy to identify, on account of the duct tape patches. Where had I last seen the backpack? In Ranger Rob's office? I wasn't sure. All I knew was that Sheriff Laidlaw had changed a bit. His flat little eyes were no longer dull, now held a sparkle. Usually that makes a human more attractive, but not this time.

Bernie rose. Me, too. "What's going on?"

"Conducted a legal search of your pack," the sheriff said. "Here's the warrant, signed by Judge Stringer, funny old coot." The sheriff handed Bernie an envelope. "In the course of our legal search we came across a firearm."

"A licensed firearm," Bernie said.

"Good to hear," said the sheriff. "The thing is, your duly licensed firearm smelled to me—and the boys, correct, boys?—"

The two deputies nodded.

"—like it had recently been fired," the sheriff continued. "So based on that and other evidence we've been developing, and pending ballistics tests, I'm arresting you on suspicion of the murder of Turk Rendell."

Bernie laughed. "What's this? Some kind of backwoods humor?"

"Wish it was for your sake," said the sheriff. "One of you boys read Mr. Little here his duly licensed constitutional protections."

Both of the deputies were big and pear-shaped with real close-together eyes, one deputy's even more close-together than the other's. That was the deputy who took out a card and began reading.

FIFTEEN

"Gonna have to pat you down," Sheriff Laidlaw said to Bernie. I knew patting down, of course, which had nothing to do with patting. This hairy-faced dude—his mustache grew right into his sideburns—had it in mind to pat down Bernie? A soft growling started up in the dining hall at Big Bear Wilderness Camp.

The sheriff took a step back; afraid of me, no doubt about it.

"You're making a mistake," Bernie said. "Talk to Moondog."

"I intend to," said the sheriff. "But I also intend to pat you down."

"For Christ sake," Bernie said, his voice rising. "The ballistics aren't going to match, plus my weapon hasn't been discharged in months."

"No?" said the sheriff. "Sure didn't smell that way to me. How did it smell to you, Claudie?"

"Like it had been fired recent," said the deputy with the less-close-together eyes.

"Mack?" said the sheriff.

"Real real recent," said the other deputy.

They were talking about the .38 Special? I couldn't remember the last time we'd fired it, but if Bernie said months then it was months, whatever those happened to be. The growling grew louder.

"Control your animal," the sheriff said, backing away another step.

Animal? That was all of us in the room, amigo. I barked, loud and angry. The barrel of the shotgun rose, the muzzle swinging around to point in my direction.

"Chet," Bernie said, his voice soft and quiet. I went quiet myself.

The sheriff's eyes shifted, the way a thought inside the human head sometimes shifts the eyes. His gaze went to me, and then settled on Bernie. "Raise your hands," he said. "Spread your legs."

Bernie did what he was told, slow and careful. The look on his face, so hard, was one I'd seen only a few times before. The guys on the receiving end hadn't ended up well.

Sheriff Laidlaw stepped forward, patted Bernie down. "Somethin' in this pocket?"

Bernie turned out his pocket, handed the sheriff his cell phone.

The sheriff patted the other front pocket. "And this 'un?"

"There's noth—" Bernie began, then stopped. What was this? He looked a bit . . . hesitant. How was that possible?

"Turn it out."

Bernie turned out his other pocket. The big gold nugget fell on the floor, rolled up against the sheriff's boot.

There was a silence. The nugget glittered on the floor, made everything else seem dark. "Well, well, well," said the sheriff. "What have we here?"

"Um," said Mack.

"Kind of looks like a gold nugget," said Claudie.

"How about picking it up?" said the sheriff.

Claudie picked up the nugget and squinted at it, not a pleasant sight with his eyes being the way they were to begin with.

"Give," the sheriff said.

Claudie gave him the nugget. The sheriff hefted it in his hand. "Gold for sure." He turned to the deputies. "Either of you guys laid your baby blues on a bigger nugget?"

The baby blues thing confused me, and maybe the deputies, too; their eyes were muddy brown, for one thing. They shook their heads in a slow confused kind of way.

"Nugget like this remind you of anything?"

More head shaking.

"Think, for Christ sake," Sheriff Laidlaw said.

Claudie said, "Hittin' the lottery?"

The sheriff sighed. "Nugget like this, Claudie," he said, "takes me back to all them stories about what come out of that old mine back in the day."

"Oh, yeah," said the deputies.

"One of you boys care to inform Mr. Little here, hotshot private dick from down in more sophisticated parts, of the most important fact about that ol' mine of ours?"

"Like, uh, the abandoned part?" said Claudie.

"Or how it's kinda dangerous, what with the cave-ins and—" Mack began.

"What the hell's wrong with you morons?" the sheriff said. Those too-close-together eyes, for starters. Plus there was something rotten about their smells, like leftover fish was mixed in with their pear-shaped sweat. Hey! Was I cooking or what? I was just about to come up with more, when the sheriff said, "Start with the goddamn name of the mine," he said.

"The old Laidlaw mine?" said the deputies.

The sheriff smiled. He had a very small smile, just a slight uptick at the corners of his mouth, a nasty smile he turned on Bernie. "Been in my family for generations. But not the generations when they were diggin' out the gold. All we ever mined was dirt. Same for all the wildcatters we let poke around in there. Nothin' but dirt. So I'm kind of interested in where you got this little—what's the word? Bauble? Like that word, boys? Bauble?"

"Great word," said Claudie.

"'Cause he dropped it?" said Mack.

Bernie was silent for a moment or two, one of those silences where I could feel his thoughts, a feeling I loved. It was like the thoughts were in my own head, except I couldn't see inside them. But what was the holdup? The answer to the question about the nugget was me! I'd found it in the mine and brought it to Bernie. So therefore? So therefore was as far as I went: after that, Bernie took over.

"I found it," he said.

Bernie was saying he found the nugget? Not me? I could still just about taste the thing.

"Mind tellin' us where?" said Sheriff Laidlaw.

"Can't say exactly," Bernie said. "I spotted it on the hike up when we stopped by the stream for a drink. Not sure I could find the exact place."

"Bet you're not," the sheriff said. His smile faded away.

Bernie gazed at him, not smiling at all.

The sheriff tossed the nugget in the air, caught it on his palm. "What I'm going to do now," he said, "is take up that suggestion of yours, the one about checking out your so-called alibi with ol' Moondog. You boys make sure Mr. Little stays comfortable in my absence." He left the dining hall, pocketing the nugget on his way out.

We all sat down, the deputies on the table across from us, Mack holding the shotgun across his knees, me beside Bernie.

"What kinda dog is that, anyhow?" Mack said.

Bernie didn't reply. Some human silences are nice and comfortable, like when Bernie and Suzie are out on the patio, watching the sun go down. Others are not. This silence was one of those. The discomfort grew and grew until it filled the room and then Claudie said, "Reckon he's exercisin' his so-called right to remain silent."

If that was what Bernie was doing, he kept it up. I started getting real restless, but Bernie remained motionless, so I did, too. After a while, the door opened and Sheriff Laidlaw came in. He'd brought Moondog with him.

Moondog looked his normal self—tall and skinny with long stringy hair all over the place—but there was something strange about him, maybe the way he was looking in every direction except ours.

"Moondog here, one of our upstanding local citizens, has come forward of his own volition with some relevant testimony," the sheriff said. "Haven't you, Moondog?"

"If you say so," said Moondog.

"Appreciate your cooperation," the sheriff said. "Now why don't you repeat what you told me."

"The part about how I like three sugars in my coffee?"

"After that," said the sheriff. "When we were just about finished with the coffee and got to where you found the body."

"Yeah, um," said Moondog. He glanced up, the way humans sometimes do when they're trying to remember something. His lips moved and sound came out, but so soft I couldn't make out the words.

"Don't come over shy on us," the sheriff said. "Speak up."

Moondog cleared his throat. "I, uh, found the body and called him over."

"Him?" said the sheriff. "You're speaking of Mr. Little?"

"Uh-huh. He didn't look none too happy about it."

"About what?"

Moondog blinked. "About how I found the body. Isn't that what I'm sposta—" He went silent, although his lips, thin and cracked, kept moving.

"And then?" the sheriff said.

"And then he said . . ."

"Said what, Moondog? Let's move things along."

"That, um, ah, he hated goddamn meth dealers and wasn't sorry for what he'd done."

"Yeah?" said the sheriff.

Moondog nodded.

"Anything else?"

"Ain't that enough?" Moondog said.

"Do for now," the sheriff said.

Moondog walked out of the dining hall, eyes on the floor.

The sheriff turned to Bernie. "Got anything to say, hopefully in the nature of a confession?"

"You're embarrassing yourself," Bernie said. "That's all I have to say."

The sheriff's face went red, a redness that began in his neck and rose all the way up to his hairline. "Cuff the son of a bitch," he said.

The deputies stood up. Claudie unclipped a set of cuffs from his belt. Mack raised the shotgun. What was going on? They were planning to cuff Bernie? No way that was happening. The fur on my back rose, from my neck to the tip of my tail. Also the growling started up again. Plus was I baring my teeth? Yes, and I bared them some more. Both deputies stepped back. The shotgun swung around toward me. I wasn't afraid. I got my back paws under me, ready to spring. The deputy's finger curled around the trigger. Maybe he didn't know how quick I was.

"Chet," Bernie said, calm and gentle, like it was just the two of us, kicking back after a good day.

"Looks like you got a mad dog there, Mr. Little," the sheriff said. "We have ways of dealing with mad dogs here in the high country."

Bernie's face changed: he almost seemed like a different man, wild and dangerous. His voice didn't rise much, but it shook when he spoke. "If anything happens to Chet, I'll take you down, I promise."

That smile, small and nasty, appeared again on the sheriff's face. "Take me down meaning . . . ?"

"Kill you," Bernie said. "Is that clear enough?" He glanced at the deputies. "All of you."

"Sounds like you just threatened murder on three duly constituted officers of the law," the sheriff said. "You boys hear somethin' like that?"

The deputies nodded.

"Only a dumb country hick myself," the sheriff said, "but I wouldn't be surprised if you just opened yourself up for additional charges. DA's call, of course, but we've always seen eye to eye."

I like most kinds of human laughter, but not the snicker, which is what I heard from the deputies at that moment.

"Just funnin' with you, Mr. Little," the sheriff said. "DA's my kid brother, smartest Laidlaw that ever walked the earth."

"Meanest, too," said Claudie.

That led to guffawing, another bad kind of laughter. When the guffawing died down, the sheriff said, "Hands out in front of you, Mr. Little. Let's do this the easy way."

Bernie was silent for what seemed like a long time. Then he said, "First get my client, Anya Vereen, in here. I'm putting Chet in her custody."

"No problem with that last part," said the sheriff. "But, see, I'm the law, so what comes first is up to me. Hands out."

Bernie shook his head.

"You resistin' arrest?" the sheriff said.

The shotgun barrel moved again, the muzzle now pointed at Bernie's chest. Bernie didn't move, just sat very still on the bench. Was something real bad just about to happen? I hardly ever got that feeling, but I had it now.

"I do believe he'd dare you to squeeze that goddamn trigger, Mack," the sheriff said, "so you'll have to try something different."

"Different how?" said Mack.

"Think."

Mack thought, his face scrunching up unpleasantly. Then he swung the shotgun away from Bernie and aimed it straight at me.

"Somethin' like this?" Mack said.

"Read my mind," said Sheriff Laidlaw.

Bernie rose and held out his hands.

SIXTEEN

Sheriff Laidlaw snapped the cuffs on Bernie. Bernie didn't even glance at him. His eyes were on me the whole time and they were saying, "Be a good boy."

Being a good boy was the last thing I wanted at that moment. What I wanted was to spring on that horrible sheriff and sink my teeth deep into his neck. That probably sounds bad, but it was the truth.

"Ch—et?" Bernie has this long way of saying my name that gets my attention every time, or almost. I stayed where I was. The sheriff and his deputies walked Bernie to the door and out, slamming it shut behind them. Bernie kept his eyes on me the whole time.

The instant he was out of sight, I bolted right to the door, crashed into it hard. It didn't budge. I rose up and pawed at the knob. We'd been working on doorknobs, me and Bernie, and I'd figured out some, like the kind where humans pressed their thumbs down on a little metal thing, but this knob on the dining hall door—the round kind for turning—was still too much for me. I got both front paws on it, the way Bernie had said, and tried to push down with one and up with the other, or the other way around, or whatever he had said. Pushing and pulling, pulling and pushing, my claws slipping off the hard metal.

Bernie!

This sort of thing was so much easier with Bernie beside me. But he wasn't beside me. I heard a car start up outside in the night, heard it moving, the sound fading and fading and gone.

Bernie!

I pawed and pawed at that doorknob, maybe forgetting all about the push-pulling part. The dining hall filled with loud, angry barking. How much time passed before I realized it was me? I didn't know, but finally I shut up and my paws went still. Then they slid down the door, my claws scratching the wood lightly, and there I was, all paws on the floor. Did that mean I'd given up? I hoped not. We weren't quitters, me and Bernie.

I stood by the door. After a while, the lights went out, all by themselves. I was used to that: humans had things rigged to go on and off by themselves—take Bernie's alarm clock, except now it was broken on account of being thrown at the wall too many times. Darkness often bothered humans, but it never bothered me. Sometimes I even preferred darkness. You understand things different in a way that's hard to explain. Now, in the darkness, for example, I felt a very faint current of air in the dining hall, not coming through the crack under the door, but from the other way, back in the gloomy interior.

I turned and followed that current of air. It led me through the length of the dining hall, past all the rows of tables, to a pair of swinging doors at the back, slightly darker than the darkness. Swinging doors are the kind of doors I like. I pushed right through and entered a kitchen; knew it was a kitchen first thing, of course, the kitchen, besides being my favorite room in any house, always having a smell of its own.

The air current was coming from the far side, beyond some big fridges, gleaming faintly. This air current brought the night inside, kind of like the night was breathing into the kitchen. What a thought! Funny how the mind works, but no time to go into that at the moment. Probably never, in fact: I'd mulled over how the mind works more than once, and never managed to come up with anything. The point was I could feel the night, and looking up, I saw a black square high up on the wall: an open window. Too high? I didn't think about that until I was in midair. Leaping was just about my very best thing—will I ever forget that last day of K-9 school, flunking out with nothing but the leaping test remaining?—and I soared through that open window, scraping the top of my head, but hardly at all—I could barely feel it—and then soared some more before arcing down and landing lightly on nice mossy ground.

Out behind the dining hall the forest rose in a dark wall. I sniffed around, smelled all kinds of things, but not Bernie, and nothing was on my mind except him.

Bernie!

After some more sniffing, I remembered him being led by the sheriff and those pear-shaped deputies through the front door, and I took off, racing around to the front of the dining hall. Dim lights shone in a cabin or two, and beyond them, near the tents, a campfire burned low. I picked up Bernie's scent right away, the best human scent there was—so strangely like my own in some ways—and followed it down to the parking lot. There it dwindled away, losing itself in an invisible little cloud of exhaust fumes.

I stood in the parking lot, waiting for some idea to come to mind. When that didn't happen, I moved over to the Porsche and stood beside it. Definite scent of Bernie around the driver's-side door. I breathed it in for a while and then found myself trotting down toward the road, that long, long road that led past the stream, and the grove where we'd found that mushroom, and other things faint in my memory, and finally back home to our place on Mesquite Road. Yes: that was what I wanted, to be home. Home was oh so clear in my memory: I knew where every single bone was buried. I got a move on, ramped up to what Bernie called my go-to trot, a trot I can keep up just about forever. In no time we'd be back together, me and Bernie, doing what we did and feeling tip-top.

I'd barely gotten out of the parking lot when I spotted a big black car by the side of the road, headlights off but inside lights on, and two people sitting in the front. One, behind the wheel, was a man I didn't know; the other was Anya. They had the windows rolled down and I could hear them talking.

"You'll have to do better than that, Guy," Anya was saying. "Start by telling me the truth about why you picked this camp."

A guy named Guy? That rang a faint bell. I waited for it to ring louder, and while I was waiting, the guy named Guy—one of those very blond dudes, hair almost white, but with dark eyes that really stood out in all that paleness—said something like, "You giving the orders now, babe?"

And if not exactly that, then pretty close, but what came through clearest was the tone. One thing about human speech— and sometimes I think there's a bit too much of it, no offense, and besides that wasn't the one thing I was heading toward, which was about the fact that human speech has two parts happening at the same time. One is the words, often hard to understand—maybe even by humans, but that's just a thought I once had, back when Bernie and Leda were going through the divorce. That was the only time I saw Bernie cry, not when Charlie's stuff was getting packed up, but after, when it was just me and Bernie alone in the house. Never mind that; what I was getting to was that other part of human speech, the kind that's always a snap to understand: the tone. The tone's a dead giveaway, dead giveaway being one of Bernie expressions I really like. He has a bunch, which maybe I can go into later. But right now it was all about the tone of speech of the guy named Guy: nasty. I like just about every human I've ever rubbed up against—even the perps and gangbangers—except for the nasty-sounding types. This Guy guy was showing signs of being the nasty-sounding type.

"Why are you being like this?" Anya said.

"There's one I haven't heard for a while," said the Guy guy. "Takes me right back to our marriage." Aha! I had it now. Guy was the ex-hubby. Some kind of investment dude, and maybe Anya was afraid of him, which was why she'd come to us. For a moment, I thought I was real close to solving the whole case. But then: *Bernie!*

"Oh?" said Anya. "Your girlfriend—excuse me, girlfriends— understand your behavior? Don't tell me you've put a cap on the lying, the cheating, the temper."

"The inner bitch," said Guy. "Another fond memory."

Uh-oh. Bitch. I'd heard that one before, never really understood the mean tone that always seemed to go with it. I'd known a number of bitches—Lola down in Mexico came to mind, in fact was never quite totally gone from it—and I felt the opposite of mean, whatever that was, about all of them. I even wished there were more!

Anya shook her head. "We don't have time for this. Devin is missing."

Guy's voice rose, now nasty and loud at the same time. "Think I don't know that?"

"And what kept you? You were supposed to be here Saturday morning."

"None of your goddamn business," Guy said. He didn't like her, no doubt about that. But I had this memory, very faint, of that first time we met Anya in the parking lot at the airport hotel: hadn't she said something about Guy wanting to get back together with her, which was why she wanted Bernie to be her friend? Did he sound like a dude wanting to get back together? I sniffed the air, picked up not a trace of flowers. Dudes setting out to get back together with women always brought flowers. That was basic. We always got our flowers from Choi's Palace of Flowers, me and Bernie. The smells in there: they just about knocked me out every time. "She won't be able to resist these," Ms. Choi would always say, and Bernie would get a dozen more.

I moved a little closer. Anya was giving Guy a close look.

"What's with you?" he said.

"You don't seem very upset," she said.

"What the hell are you talking about?"

"Devin, what else?" Anya said. "I'm frantic. But not you. How come?"

"You're a crazy woman, you know that?"

She looked at him, even closer than before. "I'm getting this sick feeling you know something you're not telling me."

"Something like what?" Guy said, his voice going very soft but still nasty. That combo—soft and nasty—was the worst. I barked.

They both turned and saw me, standing in the road.

"Chet?" Anya called to me.

"Huh?" said Guy. "You know that mutt?"

Mutt? That settled it: Guy was definitely one of those humans who rubbed me the wrong way, almost an impossibility.

"Chet's a wonderful dog," Anya said.

"I thought you hated dogs," said Guy.

"Not Chet," she said, which settled any question that might have been in my mind about what side she was on, even though there wasn't one. She poked her head out the window.

"Chet? Where's Bernie?"

"Who's Bernie?" said Guy.

Anya paused. I could see her face clearly, mouth slightly open, some unpleasant thought darkening the expression in her eyes. That's a look you see sometimes in people: it means they know they just made a mistake. But if she had, I couldn't spot it. A wonderful dog: where was the mistake in that?

"Asked you a question," Guy said. "Who's Bernie?"

She turned to him. "Just someone I know."

"New boy toy?"

"No, as it happens. But to quote you, it's none of your god-damn business."

Then came a surprise, not a good one. Guy reached out, real quick, grabbed Anya by the back of the neck, and jerked her head in close to his.

"Who. Is. Bernie."

Anya's eyes, frightened now, were on Guy. They narrowed a bit and her chin came up, and I knew she was about to do something brave. "Bernie is a private eye—a brilliant private eye that I—I hired to look for Devin."

"Say that again?"

"You heard me."

There was a pause. Then Guy backhanded Anya across the face, with that surprising quickness of his, and real hard. She cried out, and maybe yelled something, and maybe he did, too, but none of that really entered my mind because I was on the move.

One bound, another, and on the next I was in midair, soaring right toward that open window on the driver's-side door, the wind rushing in my ears. Not a big space, and I only partly got through, barreling into Guy's upper body as he twisted around toward me.

"What the hell?" he said, and whipped one of those backhand blows in my direction. Real quick for a human, but I caught that backhanding hand in my mouth and bit down. He cried out, his voice suddenly high and scared and no longer nasty. Could it have hurt that bad? I didn't think so and gave my head a quick shake, back and forth, in the hope of sending the message about what was what. But maybe it didn't get through, because all that happened was more screaming, followed by flailing, and what was this? Brass knuckles appearing from under the seat? Then we were rolling around a bit, and he was fumbling with his free hand for the knucks—a weapon we hate, me and Bernie—and kneeing me in the face, and I was growling, and Anya was shouting, "Chet! Chet!" and then suddenly her door opened and we tumbled out, except for Guy, who somehow stayed inside.

I rolled over a few times, found my feet. By that time, the car had started up. It swung around in a wild circle, tires shrieking on the pavement, and sped off down the mountain road, headlights out, passenger door wide open. The smell of burned rubber rose in the night air. I turned toward Anya.

SEVENTEEN

The moon had risen over the treetops and I saw that Anya's nose was bleeding from both nostrils, the blood like two black streaks on her moon-whitened skin. She sat on the road, hugging her knees and crying softly. Poor Anya. I went over to her and licked off her tears and blood at the same time, a rich and heady mixture, I don't mind telling you.

She hugged me. "Oh, Chet," she said. "What's going on? Where's Bernie?"

I started panting, not sure why, and sat down beside her. She wiped her face on the back of her arm and pulled out her cell phone. Was that like panting? What a crazy thought: I forgot it immediately. Anya flipped open the phone, squinted at the screen, said, "No goddamn service." She stuck the phone back in her pocket. "What are we going to do?" Her eyes teared up. I gave her a little nudge with my head. Whatever we were going to do—and I had no ideas on that subject—we'd have to start by getting up.

Anya gave me a look. Her eyes cleared. "I told Bernie the truth," she said to me. "Maybe I just put the emphasis in the wrong places."

What did that mean? You tell me. All I knew was this: time to get up. I nudged Anya again, somewhat harder. She put her hand on my back and rose. At that moment, a flashlight shone on the path that led from the cabins down to the parking lot. The beam poked this way and that, then steadied, shining in our direction although not reaching us. We moved toward it. A man called, "Who's down there? What's going on?" I recognized the voice. It was Ranger Rob.

We came together at the entrance to the parking lot. Ranger Rob shone the light on Anya, then at me, then at the ground. His leathery face, illuminated from the bottom up, seemed older than before: people's faces aged quickly sometimes—I'd seen it more than once—and they never went the other way, even when things were going good.

"Ms., uh, Vereen?" he said, his voice not as strong as I remembered it, more like the voice of old Mr. Parsons next door back home in the Valley. "I thought I heard some commotion on the road, maybe an accident."

"Any word?" Anya said.

"Word?"

"About Devin, for God's sake." From the way Anya said that I could tell she was starting not to like Ranger Rob.

Ranger Rob shook his head, began talking again about a commotion.

"There was no commotion," Anya said. "We're looking for Bernie."

"Ah," said Ranger Rob.

"Ah?" said Anya. "What does that mean?"

"Just that there's been some, uh . . . shocking news on that score."

I felt Anya's hand on my shoulder, clutching my fur. "What are you talking about?"

Ranger Rob had a pickup. He drove us down the mountain road, Anya in the passenger seat, me in the cargo bed behind. It didn't take me long to discover that someone had been eating potato chips in the cargo bed, and pretty recently, judging from the crispness of the few I found. As often happens when a too-small snack puts in an appearance, I realized how hungry I was, but could I find one more measly chip, or anything else edible—and I'm not fussy—for that matter? I ended up licking the cold metal where the chips had lain, and then moved forward, gazing over the roof of the cab.

The wind blew in my face, a feeling I normally love, but my mind was somewhere else, namely on Bernie. I kept thinking he was back home on Mesquite Road, and I had to get there, too. Was that where we were going now? I peered into the night— hey, the same way our headlights were boring into the mountain darkness?—and caught a quick glimpse of a pair of orange eyes glittering by the roadside. Some big shadowy form faded away into the woods. I sniffed the air and picked up a whiff of that locker-room-laundry-hamper scent I'd first smelled on the trail. A puzzler, but I didn't puzzle over it for long: my mind swung back to Bernie.

We came to a fork in the road, our lights sweeping over a sign with writing on it. What did Bernie always say at a time like that? "In the words of Yogi Berra, when you come to a fork in the road, take it." Bernie always got a kick out of that, and so I did, too, although the meaning wasn't clear. Was Yogi Berra a perp? If so, his days on the outside were numbered, whatever that meant exactly.

Left and right were two directions. They came up over and over, but which was which? I never knew. Ranger Rob picked one of them and we kept going, first through a series switchbacks and then on a long winding stretch with some traffic and the glow of a town in the distance. Soon houses were going by, most of them dark, and we slowed down. The road broadened into the main drag of a small western town, the kind with a diner, a couple bars, a few stores, an office building or two. We'd had lots of adventures in small western towns like this, me and Bernie, so right away I felt pretty good about our chances. Chances for what was a question just starting to form in my mind when we parked in front of one of those office buildings. A blue light shone over the door.

Ranger Rob and Anya got out of the pickup. They both looked at me, standing in the back.

"What about Chet?" said Anya.

"The dog?" said Ranger Rob. "He'd better stay in the truck."

"Chet?" said Anya. "Stay!"

I hopped out. Did I stay for every Tom, Dick, and Harry? I knew plenty of Toms, Dicks, and Harrys, and stayed for none of them. I stayed for Bernie.

We went into the office building, not a very tall building, made of brick; I only mention that because bricks have a smell I like. There was a bit of confusion at the doorway and I ended up in the lead. The first person I saw was the deputy named Mack. He sat at a desk strewn with papers, eating from a big box of greasy fries; I knew they were greasy from the smears on his face. He looked up at us, selected a long limp fry, dipped it in a little paper cup of ketchup, and stuck it in his mouth.

We stopped in front of the desk. "Deputy?" said Ranger Rob.

"Yup," Mack said, and went on chewing, mouth open. I knew one thing right away: I wanted those fries.

"Is the sheriff around?" Ranger Rob said.

"Who wants to know?" said Mack.

Ranger Rob blinked. "I do," he said.

"Let's see some ID."

"ID? But you know me. Rob Townshend? Director of Big Bear Wilderness Camp?"

"Sheriff's orders," Mack said. "We got a dangerous prisoner locked up on the premises." He held out his hand, the ends of his fingers red with ketchup.

Ranger Rob gave Mack his ID. Mack gave it right back, didn't even glance at it. He made a little two-finger twitching motion at Anya. She handed over her ID. This time he looked carefully, and then looked just as carefully at her. "Picture don't do you . . . what's the word?"

There was a silence. Ranger Rob said, "Justice?"

"Yeah," said Mack. "That's it." Anya turned a stony-faced expression on him, gave Ranger Rob a dose of it, too. Mack reached for another fry, popped it in his mouth as he rose. "This-away," he said.

We followed him toward a door at the back of the room. Now I was in no hurry to be first, happy, in fact to lag far behind. Not to worry: I caught up real quick. Snagging a mouthful of Mack's fries took no time at all.

Mack knocked on the door. Voices speaking fast and low came from the other side. Mack knocked again. The talking stopped, and I heard Sheriff Laidlaw call, "Yeah?"

"Visitors," said Mack. "Civilians."

"The voting kind?" the sheriff said.

Mack eyed us. "Don' know. Want me to ask?"

The sheriff laughed. "Naw," he said. "Send 'em in."

Mack opened the door. We were in a small office that smelled of cigars. Sheriff Laidlaw sat at a desk, a shotgun rack on the wall behind him. On a couch along the side wall lay the cigar smoker, an old dude—string tie, cowboy boots, longish white hair—with his legs stretched out, feet resting on a pillow. Mack went out, closing the door behind him.

The old dude nodded to Ranger Rob. "Rob," he said.

"Judge," said Ranger Rob.

The old dude was a judge? There was only one judge I knew well—Judge Jaramillo, down in the Valley. I'd been Exhibit A, Exhibit B being a .44 Magnum I'd dug up out of some perp's flower bed. Judge Jaramillo had invited me up to sit beside him. Also he'd given me one of those nice pats that let me know he liked me and my kind. Plus, down under his big judging desk where no one could see, there'd been a quick handing over of a biscuit. So: nothing wrong with judges, in my opinion, and I was all set to like the old dude on the couch.

"Judge Stringer meet Ms. Vereen," Ranger Rob said. "Ms. Vereen's the mother of the missing boy."

The judge looked her up and down, real quick, but I caught it. Suzie had a thing about that, and I'd picked it up from her. Why she had a thing about it, and what the whole up-and-down thing meant was a mystery, but I loved Suzie, so it had to be important.

"My very best wishes to you, ma'am," the judge said. "You can be sure that the public servants of our beautiful county will not rest until little David is brought back safe and sound."

"Devin," said Anya.

"Devin?" said the judge. "Interesting name." He took a drag from his cigar, blew out a narrow stream of wonderful-smelling smoke.

Anya gazed at the judge, eyes narrowing. "Right now I'm not at all sure about your public servants," she said.

"Oh?" said the judge, tapping cigar ash into a coffee mug.

Anya turned to the sheriff. "Is it true you arrested Bernie Little?"

"'Fraid so."

"Why? What's going on?"

"Suspicion of murder," the sheriff said. "Specifically of the wilderness guide, Turk Rendell."

"That makes no sense," Anya said. "Why would Bernie do that? He didn't know Turk Rendell, hadn't ever been here in his life before Friday."

"If so," the sheriff said, "his attorney will have the opportunity to enter it into the record at the bail hearing."

"Speaking of which," said the judge, getting off the couch with a grunt, "since I'm presiding, I'd best not be participating further in this conversation." He nodded to Anya and Ranger Rob, stuck the cigar in his mouth, and went out through a side door, closing it behind him.

"When is this bail hearing?" Anya said.

"Tuesday, nine a.m.," said the sheriff. "In our small but historic courtroom upstairs."

"Who's Bernie's lawyer?"

"I believe he'll be represented by one of our fine public defenders."

"Are you telling us that Bernie hasn't called his own lawyer?" Anya said.

"Us?" said the sheriff. "That would be you and Rob, here?"

"Um," said Ranger Rob, looking down at the floor. I looked down, too, and spotted a popcorn kernel. Popcorn's not my favorite on account of the way it gets caught between my teeth, but I scarfed up this popcorn kernel anyway, realizing again how hungry I was. Square meal was one of my favorite human expressions. It had been way too long.

". . . information on that score," the sheriff was saying.

Anya's voice rose. "What's going on around here? My son is missing and instead of finding him you've arrested the only person who seems interested in bringing him home."

Sheriff Laidlaw sat back in his chair. "Gonna pretend I didn't hear that," he said. "Wouldn't want to think bad of anyone for how they acted in a moment of distress. Bail hearing's public, and you're welcome to attend. Meanwhile, Rob, I'm suggestin' you escort your friend back to wherever she's stayin'."

"I'm not leaving until I see Bernie," Anya said, folding her arms across her chest. I always watched for that in humans. Dust-ups often came next.

"'Fraid that's not possible under county regulations," Sheriff Laidlaw said.

"Fuck county regulations," said Anya.

Pink spots appeared on the sheriff's face, or at least on the nonhairy parts. Ranger Rob turned to Anya. She looked ready to say more, more and louder. Ranger Rob touched her elbow, very lightly. "Ms. Vereen?" he said.

She glared at him. He shuffled around and looked sheepish. That certainly described Ranger Rob's face at the moment, although I actually ran into an angry and unsheepish sheep once, resulting in a bit of trouble, perhaps a story for another time. Anya paused and took a deep breath. "All right," she said. She gave Sheriff Laidlaw the dagger look—another great expression of Bernie's—and turned to me. "Come on, Chet. Let's go."

"Not the dog," the sheriff said.

"Not the dog?" said Anya. "What does that mean?"

"Interest of being humane, believe it or not," said the sheriff. "No reason the dog can't share a cell with his master. Be a comfort, like."

Anya peered at Sheriff Laidlaw, head tilted to one side, like she was trying to see him from a new angle. We do the same thing in the nation within.

"That's a nice gesture, Sheriff," said Ranger Rob, who still had Anya's elbow. He began leading her toward the door.

I followed. Anya stopped and knelt beside me. "Stay, Chet," she said, laying her hand softly on my head. "There's a good boy." She and Ranger Rob headed again for the door. I followed.

Anya turned. "Chet? Stay. You're going to see Bernie."

I was? I didn't smell Bernie, not the least bit. Neither did I hear him. All I heard was a toilet flushing on the other side of the door the judge had gone through. While all that was on my mind—Bernie, toilet, Bernie, Bernie—Anya and Ranger Rob went out the main door. Hey! I bolted after them. The door closed in my face. Behind me, the sheriff laughed.

I turned my head, looked back at him, my paws still pointed to the door.

"Want to see Bernie?" the sheriff said.

Oh, yes, and very badly. But for some reason my tail wasn't wagging.

The side door opened and the judge came out, zipping up his pants. "Rid of them?" he said.

"Yup," said the sheriff. "But this dog here's got me a bit worried."

The judge glanced at me. "Think he's a biter?"

"It's not that," the sheriff said. "More like he's up to something."

"What the hell are you talking about?"

"Like he's plotting against us."

"Laidlaw?" said the judge. "Don't be such a goddamn moron. It's a dog."

"I know that, but—"

"Try to concentrate. Your job is to make sure everything goes smoothly Tuesday morning."

"You can count on me."

"Can I?" the judge said. "Is the prisoner going to look presentable, for example?"

The sheriff's eyes shifted. "No problem there," he said. "What kind of bail you got in mind?"

The judge smiled. He had just about the yellowest teeth I'd ever seen, almost brown. "High," he said. "Sky fucking high."

"What if—" the sheriff began.

The judge cut him off. "Don't want to hear your what-ifs," he said. "I'll do the thinking." He moved toward the door, saw I was in the way. "Here, boy," he said. I stayed where he was. The judge turned to the sheriff. "Got some kind of treat?"

"Treat?"

"Dog treat, for Christ sake."

"Why would I have a dog treat?" said the sheriff. "I'm a cat person—thought you knew that."

Cat person? I got the feeling, unusual for me, that things were growing worse and worse.

"Some snack then," the judge said. "A cookie, a doughnut."

"How about a Slim Jim?"

"Worth a try."

The sheriff opened his desk drawer and took out—yes!—a Slim Jim. He held it up. Who can resist a Slim Jim? I hurried over, barely aware of the judge moving behind me, leaving the office and closing the door. Oh, those wonderful Slim Jim smells.

I sat beside the desk, looking up at Sheriff Laidlaw, and waiting for him to come across with the Slim Jim. There were two ways of doing it, holding the Slim Jim close to my mouth where I could grab it, or simply dropping it at my feet. Both were fine with me but Sheriff Laidlaw did neither. Instead, he put the Slim Jim back in the drawer.

Whoa. Normally I liked surprises, but this was a bad one. I moved away from the sheriff, returned to the main door, and stood there doing nothing much. Soon the door would open and I'd be free. That was my only thought.

The sheriff reached for a folder and started leafing through papers. After a while he belched a couple times. That made me want to belch, too, but I had no belches inside me. The sheriff rose and went through the side door. I heard a toilet seat bang down. A moment or two later, a door at the back opened and Mack poked his head in. "Sheriff?" he said. He looked around and went away. But he didn't quite close the door behind him.

The next thing I knew I was through that doorway and in a long, not very well lit corridor with bare cement walls and no one in sight. I walked to the end, turned a corner, and right away smelled the smell I wanted to smell most in the world: Bernie!

I sped up. Cells appeared on one side of the corridor. I knew cells, of course, had helped walk perps into them on plenty of occasions. No perps here: all these cells were empty except . . . except for the last one. And—oh, no!—there was Bernie.

EIGHTEEN

What had they done to him? Bernie lay on his back on a hard metal bench, one arm over his face. That was a way he sometimes slept—just another nice thing about Bernie—but he wasn't sleeping. I knew that on account of the uncovered eye being open, although just barely. It was so swollen that just a tiny whitish sliver of wet gleam showed, the wet gleam of an eyeball. Around the eye was a big purple bruise, plus dried blood on his cheek and all over his torn shirt.

That poor eye wasn't looking my way. I stuck my head through the bars and tried to push through, but the space was too narrow for my shoulders. A whimpering started up. How terrible that was! I'd never heard Bernie whimper before, or anything close. *Oh, Bernie, please don't*—And then I realized the whimpering was coming from me. I put a stop to that pronto, changing to this low muffly bark I have for getting Bernie's attention but keeping quiet at the same time.

Bernie moved. He got a hand on the metal bench, pushed himself up to a sitting position, real slow. His other eye was even worse, but he saw me. He licked his lips—bloody and split—and said my name in a way I'd never heard before, all cracked and faint like a radio station voice when we're out in the desert and far away. Which was where I wanted to be at that moment, me and Bernie in the Porsche, free and easy.

"Chet." And then, louder and stronger, "Good to see you. Real good." He even gave me a little smile, his teeth so white in his bruised and bloody face. My tail started wagging. I was back with Bernie and that was the important thing.

He got off the bench, wincing hardly at all—but I caught it—and came to me. He gave me a nice pat between my ears. I pressed my head against his hand.

"You're a good man," he said.

My tail, still wagging, wagged more.

Bernie glanced down the corridor. "Did Anya bring you? Where is she?"

I kept wagging.

"Or was it Suzie?" His voice thickened. That happens some-times—I think when Bernie's having deep feelings. At that moment I was having deep feelings myself. "You didn't get here by yourself, did you?" He gave me a close look. I gave him a close look back. "No fair all these questions." Bernie knelt in front of me. "Listen, Chet, this is important," he said, and started talk-ing about something, maybe keys. But my mind was elsewhere, on account of Bernie's poor face, now within licking distance. I licked it, real, real gently.

Bernie laughed, just a tiny quiet laugh, but so nice to hear. "Okay, okay," he said, giving me another pat, "but right now I need those keys."

Keys? Right: he had been talking about keys. So maybe I hadn't missed anything at all. Chet the Jet, on top of the situation and don't you forget it.

"The keys, Chet. On the wall. Can you get them, big guy?"

Keys? Wall? The only keys I knew were the two on Bernie's key ring—a real cool key ring with a tiny white seashell I'd found on our trip to San Diego hanging off it—one for the Porsche and one for the house. We'd surfed, me and Bernie! What a life we had. My tail, which had stopped wagging, started up again.

"Hanging on the wall, Chet. Right behind you."

What was he talking about? I wasn't quite sure. All I wanted him to do was open the cell door and come out. Then we'd go get the .38 Special, wherever it was—Bernie would know—and come back here and do what needed to be done. Was that the plan? Sounded like a winner to me.

"Chet? Are you listening, buddy?"

Of course I was listening. Didn't I always listen to Bernie? I made myself listen even harder, and right away heard distant footsteps, on some level above.

Bernie gave me another quick smile. That meant he knew I was trying real hard, doing my best. "Look on the wall," he said and pointed behind me. I tried to listen even harder—footsteps, maybe a bit louder—but I was maxed out in that department.

"Chet! I'm pointing, big guy."

Pointing? We'd done a lot of work on pointing, me and Bernie, even more than we'd done on doorknobs.

"Follow my finger, Chet. You know how."

Yes, I did. And after that would come a treat, quite possibly a rawhide chew from Rover and Company. I gazed at Bernie's finger—his hands are the most beautiful I've ever seen, although a couple of the knuckles seemed a bit skinned and swollen, but that had to be a good thing, meaning we'd gotten in a few of our own, and . . . I lost my train of thought.

"Chet? My finger—follow it."

Right. I knew this, knew it backward. Well, not that. There were lots of strange human expressions, knowing something backward being one of the strangest.

"Chet."

I followed Bernie's finger, turned my head toward where it was pointing. And there, hanging from a hook fairly high on the cement wall of the corridor, was a long black key on a black ring.

"Good, good boy," said Bernie. "Go get it."

Fairly high on the wall, but really no challenge for a leaper like me. In a flash I was in midair—hey! actually too high, would you believe that?—and snagging that black ring on the way—

But oops. Not quite. Snapped my teeth around the ring, but somehow lost my grip, the key still up there, now swinging back and forth. I jumped again and the same thing happened: no problem getting to the key. The problem was . . . I wasn't sure about what the problem was.

"That's okay, Chet," Bernie said, behind me. "You'll get it."

If Bernie said I'd get it, that was that. I jumped and jumped, the same thing happening, that cold hard ring—now all slobbery—slipping through my teeth. I jumped and jumped and—hey!—missed with my teeth completely, instead hitting the ring with the tip of my nose and knocking it off the hook and high in the air. Key and ring landed on the hard floor with a clank and a jingle, very nice to hear.

"Good boy."

I scooped up the key ring, trotted over to the cell, and dropped it inside. Mission accomplished. Next mission? I waited to find out.

Bernie grabbed the key ring, reached through the bars, twisted his hand around, stuck the key in the keyhole in a small metal square on the cell door, turned it, and: *click!*

And then he was out! I jumped right up into his arms. Had I ever been this happy? Yes, and it was always the best possible feeling.

"Easy, big guy," Bernie said.

I got all paws down on the floor, stood still, a professional through and through. Bernie put his finger across his lips: our signal for quiet. "Quiet as a mouse," Bernie sometimes said; not sure why, since mice, scratching away behind the walls of many houses I'd visited, weren't especially quiet.

We started down the corridor, not making a sound, except for Bernie, although he was being very quiet for him. But I heard those other footsteps, moving somewhere in the building.

We went past all the cells, turned the corner, and came to the door that led to the sheriff's office. Bernie paused for a moment, gazed at the door, and kept going. We rounded another corner at the end. Just a few steps away stood another door, a door with a high little window in it, and through that window I saw the moon. We were home free! Bernie reached for the doorknob, and then a strange thing happened. Just before he could touch it, the knob started turning on its own.

Bernie stepped back, hugged the wall. I hugged the wall with him. I got the idea, even kind of remembered us doing it once before: the old hiding-behind-the-opened-door trick. I loved tricks! Next the door would open, and in would stroll whoever was strolling in, with us meanwhile hidden behind the door so the newcomer would just keep strolling, maybe whistling to himself the way humans sometimes did when they thought they were all alone, and then out the door we'd scoot, me and Bernie, into the night and gone.

But that wasn't what happened; none of it. First, I heard those footsteps again, now clack-clacking not above us but on our level. Then—it sounded like Claudie—came shouting: "What the hell?" An instant later, alarms went off and a red light over the door began flashing. The door itself made a loud firm click. Bernie grabbed the handle and tried to turn it, but it wouldn't turn.

On the other side, the judge said, "What's going on?"

Bernie pivoted, facing back down the corridor. At about the same time, Mack and Claudie came running around the corner. Claudie—he had a bandage wrapped around his head, nice to see—was reaching for the gun on his hip and Mack was waving a nightstick. We were trapped, a feeling I hated. But Bernie and I could handle these dudes, no problem, as long as I took Claudie down before he brought that gun into play.

I charged forward, full speed.

"No, Chet!"

That was Bernie, saying something behind me, something I didn't quite catch. I bounded toward those two deputies, bad guys for sure despite the stars twinkling on their chests. Growling started up—wild, savage, dangerous; that was me, bucko, better believe it. Mack and Claudie skidded to a stop, their eyes widening in fear, no doubt about it and no surprise: that growling was coming close to scaring me, kind of crazy. Claudie pulled the gun from his holster, but before he could raise it, I hurled myself on him, front paws right in his face, and teeth bared as much as I could bare them. *You're going down, bad dude, and staying down.* I remember having that thought. I also remember catching a glimpse, off to the side, of Mack's nightstick—it had one of those lead-weighted ends—swinging my way in a hurry.

NINETEEN

Some very bad dreams blew into my mind, kind of like a storm. Lots of shouting went on in these dreams, plus fighting and hitting and maybe even a gunshot or two, and there was nothing I could do about any of it, which was the way of dreams. Once Bernie and Suzie got into a big discussion about dreams and what they mean. The candles looked so nice on Suzie's table that night, their light flickering on the wineglasses. Bernie slipped me the fatty part from his steak, a juicy—

Bernie!

Did I smell him? No. I opened my eyes. That set off a pain in my head. I ignored it, tried to get my bearings. Where was I? In a big shadowy sort of place, weak light coming from a hayloft high above. I knew haylofts. We'd once found a perp trying to hide out in one, Bernie poking around with a pitchfork, the fun we had. But the point: haylofts meant barns, so I was in a barn. And no Bernie. No humans, no other life of any kind.

I was on a wooden floor, worn smooth, a nice feeling under my chest, but most of me wasn't feeling nice. I rose, kind of slow for me, the pain shooting around a bit in my head. I ignored it.

Also, I was pretty thirsty. The scent of water was in the air. I followed it.

But not far. All of a sudden I got jerked to a stop, one of my front paws in midair. I looked back. Oh, no! A chain? Yes, a chain, the kind with strong thick metal links. I looked back, saw that one end was attached to a big hook hanging from the ceiling. The other end was attached to my collar; I could feel the cold metal links on the back of my neck. I knew all about links like that from one or two bad adventures in the past—adventures that had all ended up good, meaning the bad guys got theirs—so I already knew you could gnaw and gnaw at them, gnaw your very hardest, and still get nowhere. Instead I twisted my head, twisted and twisted it, at the same time trying to slip right out of my collar. I'd twisted out of my collar more than once, on account of Bernie always leaving it kind of loose. But for some reason it didn't feel loose now: in fact, it felt tight—uncomfortably tight, even if I wasn't twisting and pulling against it.

I went on twisting and pulling, digging my back claws into that soft wooden floor, straining with all my strength, and I'm a hundred-plus-pounder. No use: my collar was on me, but good. I stopped all that twisting, pulling, straining, and began gnawing at the metal links.

I gnawed and gnawed. Most times gnawing feels good on your teeth, plus it's always interesting finding out how things come apart. But this gnawing did not feel good, and nothing came apart or even gave the least sign that it would. I kept gnawing.

After a while, I went back to twisting and pulling. Then gnawing. Then twisting and pulling. After that I tried charging across the floor at my very fastest. Not too clear how long that went on. All those charges ended with me getting jerked to a halt so sudden my legs would fly out from under me. I kept doing it. By that time I was seeing red, even if Bernie says I can't see red.

Bernie!

We don't give up, me and Bernie, part of what makes the Little Detective Agency what it is. I charged, picked myself up, and was gathering my strength—still plenty left, amigo—when the barn door opened, letting in a cold, silvery shaft of light. In that shaft of light stood a man.

"Well, well, well," he said, looking at me.

I looked at him. A real skinny guy. Was this someone I knew? Hard to tell, with the light behind him and the still air in the barn not bringing me any scents from that direction. But the voice seemed a bit familiar, and then he turned slightly, revealing sunken cheeks and a thick black mustache. There's something about mustaches that makes it hard for me to look away, so I didn't. And right about then it hit me: Georgie Malhouf.

Georgie! Georgie was a friend! He'd invited Bernie to speak at the Great Western Private Eye convention—where Bernie had done so well!—and then cut a nice check. But . . . but maybe Bernie hadn't accepted it. What was that all about? I tried to remember.

Georgie came forward. He stopped, just out of my range on the chain, and studied me with those small brown eyes of his. "A little worse for wear, maybe, but not bad at all," he said. "A tough son of a bitch, aren't you?" He laughed. "Literally."

What was Georgie talking about? I wasn't sure, was no longer sure about anything when it came to Georgie.

"You thirsty?" he said. "I'll bet you're thirsty."

That was a bet Georgie would win. My tongue came out a bit, sort of on its own. Georgie walked over to a rusty faucet sticking out of the barn wall, took a ladle off a hook, filled it with water, came back.

"Water," he said, moving into my range, the ladle extended in front of him.

Ah, the smell of water. I started to have a strange thought, something to do with if there was only one smell left in the whole world, please could it be . . . but I let it go and sat down.

Georgie smiled. He had one of those smiles where teeth showed—yellow, in Georgie's case that dark smokers' yellow—but the eyes didn't join in. There were also a few humans who could smile with only their eyes—Suzie was one of those. None of that mattered at the moment; all that mattered was the water in that ladle.

Georgie held it out for me.

I drank.

Lovely. I lapped up that water, lapped and lapped.

"Drink your fill," Georgie said. "Plenty more where that came from."

I drank my fill. We were getting along great, me and Georgie. I drained that whole ladle, began feeling more like myself; maybe not tip-top, but at least the ache in my head was almost gone.

I looked at Georgie. He looked at me. What was this? He had a biscuit hidden away in his pocket? How had I missed that till now? I really hadn't been myself, not close. Georgie reached into his pocket—he wore his pants very high, the belt almost up to the level of his hollow little chest—and took out the biscuit, not big, but I've never been fussy about things like that.

Georgie held up the biscuit. "See this?" he said. What kind of question was that? "If you're good, you'll get it," he said. "But only if you're good. If you're bad, you won't. And there'll be other consequences. Got that?"

Consequences? A new one on me. But I had no problem with the takeaway: any moment now, I'd chewing on that nice biscuit.

Georgie rose on his tiptoes—hey! he wore tassel loafers. Something about tassel loafers always got that gnawing thing going in me. Not now, of course. Georgie, on his tiptoes, reached up and unhooked the chain. Holding the end, he said, "Now we walk out of here and get in the car." He waved the biscuit in my face. "Once we're settled in the car, nice and cooperative, this is yours."

One thing about Georgie that I was starting to notice: he talked kind of fast. The last flow of words zipping by, for example: what was all that? I wasn't clear. But I was very clear on the biscuit right in front of my face. Who wouldn't have been? I could even make out the tiny logo stamped into it, the happy face of a member of the nation within. In short, I snagged that biscuit right out of Georgie's hand.

And, being hungry—when was my last real meal?—I made quick work of the biscuit, gobbling it down in two snaps. Maybe not a Rover and Company–caliber biscuit when it came to taste, but not bad at—

WHACK! The end of that chain: I was so busy with the biscuit I hadn't seen it coming. The end of the chain got me pretty good, right on the side of the face. Georgie had done that to me? Why? I had no idea. But I didn't take that from anybody. I lunged at Georgie. Then came a surprise. He was ready for me, ready with a sort of black cloth bag. Lunging the way I was, I stuck my head right into it. I couldn't see a thing. A drawstring tightened around my neck. I went a little crazy, tossed my head around, trying to get the horrible thing off. It wouldn't come off. Georgie yanked on the chain. I yanked back, way harder, pulling him across the floor.

"Butch," he yelled out. "Butch!"

I heard running footsteps, kept pulling Georgie across the floor. I had no plan, except to drag Georgie until he finally gave up and let me go. The running footsteps came closer.

"Take it, Butch!" Georgie said. "He ripped off my goddamn fingernails."

Then someone much stronger than Georgie was on the other end of the chain, someone much harder to pull. In fact, he was pulling me. I dug my claws into the floor. This Butch dude grunted and kept dragging me—across the floor, outside— I could feel the sun—over some stubbly grass, and then all of a sudden I got picked up, lifted clear in the air, and thrown into a small hard space. I scrambled up. A door slammed down with that heavy car door thump.

I bashed around, clawing blindly at my surroundings. Even clawing blindly, you start to figure things out from the different feel of what's getting clawed. I figured out that I was in the back of a station wagon, with a cage-type grille separating me from the rest of the car. I'd seen many members of the nation within the nation riding in setups like this, and somehow that calmed me. I bashed around a little bit longer and then lay down.

The front doors of the car opened and people got in. Two moving bodies, that was easy to hear, and then I picked up their scents: Georgie—there was sickness in his smell—and this new strong dude, Butch, all about needing a shower plus lots of deodorant. From the passenger seat, Georgie said, "Let's get out of this hellhole."

"Hell, yeah," said Butch. "Never wanted to—" I heard another car driving up. "Who's that?" said Butch.

"Quick," Georgie said. "Get that hood off the goddamn dog."

"But—"

"Move!"

Then came a lot of confused banging around, maybe someone climbing over the seats, followed by grunting and clunking, and suddenly that black bag went whooshing off my head and I could see. The first thing I saw was the neckless, shaved-headed dude, Georgie's driver. This had to be Butch. I surged toward him just as he snapped the grille back in place.

"Christ almighty," Butch said. "He's a beast."

"Shut up," said Georgie. "And let me handle this."

Handle what? I looked out. A taxi was parked beside us—always easy to spot, from that little boxy thing on the roof—and getting out of it was Anya. Anya! She came striding over, her face angry. I had no problem with that—I was angry, too.

Georgie got out of the car. "Hey, there," he said. "What can I do you for?"

Anya pointed at me. "What are you doing with Chet?" she said.

"The Chetster, as we like to call him?" Georgie said. "Taking care of the big fellow, that's what."

The Chetster? No one had ever called me that in my life. I was Chet, pure and simple. Fact one, as Bernie liked to say. Fact two: I was real happy to see Anya. Other than those, I had no facts.

"We like him and he likes us," Georgie said. "See how happy he is?"

Was that my tail, stirring up a lively breeze? I dialed that down, but not as fast as I wanted, my tail resisting for some reason.

"Uh," Anya said, "that's good. But I'll be taking over now."

"Oh?" said Georgie.

"Chet belongs to Bernie Little," Anya said. "Bernie's . . . indisposed at the moment. I'm a friend of his, so I'll be looking after Chet in the interim."

"Have you talked to Bernie about this?" Georgie said.

"Not yet," said Anya. "But I know it's what he'd want."

"Not so sure of that, all due respect," said Georgie. "See, I'm friends with him, too. We go way, way back, me and ol' Bern." *Bern?* Bernie hated that. "In fact—Butch? Mind passing me that envelope from the glove box?—Bern has already made his wishes clear in case the kind of unfortunate situation now happening ever happened, if you follow."

"I don't," Anya said.

Georgie held out the envelope. Anya's gaze shifted for a quick moment to Georgie's bloody fingertips—a nice sight in my opinion—before she took the envelope and unfolded the sheet of paper inside.

"Duly signed, dated, and witnessed," Georgie said, stuffing his hand in his pocket.

Anya read, "'In the event I am temporarily or permanently incapacitated, I entrust without reservation the care of Chet to my longtime friend and colleague, George Malhouf. Signed, Bernie Little.'"

"You follow now?" Georgie said.

TWENTY

"B oss?" Butch said. We were on the move, driving down a long sloping canyon with mountains on both sides, tall green trees growing on their lower slopes but all rocky and steep above that. "Got a question."

Georgie took a deep drag at his cigarette, spun the butt out the window. The incoming air, rich and full, more like the air I was used to, felt good in my chest. "What kinda question?" he said.

"About what you're doing," said Butch. "For my own development, like."

"Development?"

"In case I'm ever in your shoes," Butch said. "Running a company."

Georgie choked on the cigarette smoke. I'd seen the same thing happen with Bernie from time to time. After, Bernie would always say, "That's it, cold turkey." So I was expecting Georgie to say that, too, and looking forward to what would happen next, specifically: would a turkey—it wouldn't even have to be cold—

finally put in an appearance? But instead, Georgie said, "Let's hear it," and didn't mention turkeys at all.

Outside a field of yellow flowers went by, a creek running through them, a winding blue line in all that yellow, kind of familiar. I had one of those memory tastes—does that ever happen to you?—almost as strong as a real taste, in this case of the delicious mushroom Bernie had found. Where was he? I didn't know. I lay down in the back of Georgie's station wagon, out of ideas.

"Thanks, Boss," Butch was saying. "What I'm wondering is if you made all this happen from the get-go or whether it's more of an on-the-fly situation."

"Made all what happen?" said Georgie. I wondered about that, too. Flies are something I'm very aware of, and I knew there were none in the car.

"This whole thing with Bernie Little," Butch said.

Bernie? I listened my hardest. High above a big black bird was making slow circles in the sky, up and up. The sight made me uneasy, hard to say why. I rose.

Georgie was lighting another cigarette. "Bernie Little," he said, blowing smoke through his nose, always an interesting sight. "Been on my mind for a long time."

"Yeah?" Butch said, sounding surprised.

"Why wouldn't he be, for Christ sake?" said Georgie. "He's competition. Competition's gotta be watched at all times. Stamp it out if you can—what do you think made this country great?"

"You're right, Boss."

"'Course I'm right."

"But how's Bernie Little competition? We're big."

"Ever heard of reputation? Word-of-mouth reputation—can't buy that for love or money. And Bernie's is good and getting better. I'm talking in certain circles downtown. Stine, for example. And Torres. Plus the DA loves him."

"Yeah? How come?"

"On account of the past few years, since he hooked up with—" Georgie, not looking back, jerked his thumb in my direction. "—he's been taking on some tough cases and bringing home the bacon."

Bringing home the bacon: how often had I heard that, followed by no bacon coming forth? Couldn't tell you how many times, but if Georgie thought I was going to fall for the gag yet again, he was mistaken. We have our—something or other, can't quite remember the expression—me and Bernie.

"I thought they hated him downtown," Butch said.

"The old guard hates him. The reformers love him. Suppose the reformers win out? This election coming up? Heard of it? We gotta be prepared. Which is how come I tried to bring Bernie into the fold. Not taking into consideration that a pigheaded bastard like him's too good to work for me."

Whoa. What had Georgie just said? Something very nasty. I wasn't going to forget that, not ever.

". . . follow-up," Georgie was saying, "meaning at least separate him from his number-one operative."

"You're talking about the . . . ?"

"I am," said Georgie. "But if you're asking whether I knew all this backwoods shit was going down, the answer's no. What I knew was that some shit like this shit was going down eventually with Bernie—in his DNA, plain and simple. The lucky part was happening to know Laidlaw, way back when. But here's something to remember, Butch. Luck is the residue of design."

"Wow," said Butch. "That's fuckin' brilliant."

Georgie made a little nod.

"Wow," Butch said one more time. Then, after a pause, "What's residue, again?"

Georgie turned slowly to Butch. "Remind me what I'm paying you," he said.

"Thirty-nine K," Butch said. "Plus bonus."

"Unfamiliar with that last word," said Georgie. "How do you spell it?"

I don't remember lying down, but I must have, because soon I was back in dreamland. Riding in cars can do that to you. When I opened my eyes, I found myself on my side in the back of Georgie's station wagon and the sun in a different part of the sky. Once Bernie had explained all about that to Charlie. All I knew was that the explanation had involved a soccer ball and a tennis ball, which turned out to be a little too much fun for me. As for the sun, things moved, right? So why shouldn't the—

Whoa. What was that? Flashing by and towering above, just beyond my window: the giant wooden cowboy who stood outside the Dry Gulch Steakhouse and Saloon, one of our favorites, mine and Bernie's. They had a patio out back where my guys were welcome. The scraps on that patio—don't get me started. But that wasn't the point. I scrambled up. Yes, the wooden cowboy, just off the freeway, and beyond it the Dry Gulch parking lot, and—and was that Suzie's yellow Beetle? I was back in the Valley! That was the point. From right where we were at that moment I could find my way home to our place on Mesquite Road no problem. I rose, got one paw on the glass, ready to—

And then, out of nowhere, I heard Bernie's voice—the best human voice in the world—so clear he might have been right next to me. If only he was! He was telling me something he'd told me many times, something that had never made any sense to me, in fact was still pretty startling: *There's more than one way to skin a cat.* Something with a cat in it was important for me to know? That was as far as I'd ever gotten on this. But now for the first time, I took another step. What was skinning a cat, anyway? I didn't know, but it sounded vaguely . . . positive. So: something vaguely positive could be accomplished in more than one way? Was that it? Wow. Was I cooking or what? I took my paw off the glass and sat down, calm, obedient, no trouble to anybody.

The wooden cowboy shrank and shrank and finally disappeared from view. Suzie's Beetle in the parking lot! All at once I couldn't get her out of my mind. Dry Gulch made a real nice smelling drink with mint leaves that Suzie loved. She was probably drinking it right now. If only—but Bernie always said not to waste time with if-onlies, so I stopped the whole Suzie train of thought cold, just about.

We were headed downtown. I could see the towers rising into that strange yellow downtown air. Then came the exit for the college. I thought I glimpsed a Frisbee soaring low in the distant sky—just a bright orange dot. Traffic was as light as it ever got except for at nighttime, and Butch had a heavy foot on the gas. Downtown zipped by and the warehouse part of South Pedroia appeared. And then, all of a sudden: a siren.

"Christ," said Butch.

Georgie grabbed the rearview mirror, twisted it so he could see, and said, "Comes out of your pay, unless you talk him out of it."

Butch pulled over. Getting pulled over was something I knew well. Bernie never argued, always said the same thing: "Couldn't have been over ninety." And the cop would say, "How come?" and Bernie would say, "'Cause this babe tops out at eighty-nine," and then the cop would give him a second look and say, "Hey! Bernie!" We knew just about every cop in the Valley, never got a ticket.

A cop appeared at the window, face kind of obscured by his motorcycle helmet. "License and registration," he said.

Now was the moment for saying "couldn't be over ninety," but Butch did not. Instead he went with, "Seventy-one on this speedometer, officer—gonna write me up for bein' six over?" Which I knew was a loser.

"License and registration," the cop repeated. He took them, returned to his motorcycle, soon came back with a ticket. "Clocked you at eighty-five," he said. "Have a nice day."

A vein throbbed in the back of the Butch's neckless neck. The sight made me bark, not loud, don't know why. The cop crouched down a bit, peered into the car.

"Hey!" he said. "Is that Chet?"

I peered back. If it wasn't Fritzie Bortz! A terrible motorcycle driver with lots of crashes on his record; we'd visited him in the hospital not that long ago, he and Bernie downing a bottle of bourbon, but not the real big size. It was great to see Fritzie. My tail started wagging.

"Chet?" said Georgie.

"The dog," Fritzie said. "Looks so much like this dog I know—" He peered in closer. "Gotta be him."

My tail wagged more.

"Well," said Georgie, "it's not. This here's, uh, Wilkie, and I've had him since he was a puppy."

"Yeah?" said Fritzie. "Sure looks like Chet. The spitting image."

Wilkie? I was getting called Wilkie? And something about

spitting, a not-very-pleasant human habit, although pretty much men only? I barked.

"Ha ha," said Georgie. "Wilkie knows we're talking about him."

"Knows his name, like," Butch said. Georgie shot him a quick glaring look. "Which is Wilkie," Butch added. "Ha ha."

"Sure looks like Chet," Fritzie said again.

"Lots of dogs look alike," Georgie said. "On account of they're bred to."

Fritzie's eyes got thoughtful. I didn't know what he was thinking. I was thinking: check my tags. But instead Fritzie nodded, straightened, tapped the roof, and moved away.

Butch pulled back onto the freeway. "Wendell Wilkie was a ballplayer, right?" he said after a while.

"B-o-n-u-s?" Georgie said. "Forget it."

We took the last South Pedroia exit, the one before the interchange where you could decide on the spur of the moment to take off all the way to San Diego. We'd surfed, me and Bernie! I thought about that over and over, and then we were parking in front of a low white building with a sign on the roof.

"Read the sign," Georgie said.

"Our sign, you mean?" said Butch.

"What other goddamn sign is there?"

Butch gazed at the sign. "'Malhouf International Investigations.'"

"Ever wonder what the 'International' part was all about?"

"Nope."

"Now you're going to find out."

They got out of the car.

"What about the dog?" Butch said.

Georgie gazed at me. "On second thought," he said, "you stay here with him."

"Okay."

"And while you're at it, take off his tags."

"How am I sposta do that?"

"You'll figure it out," Georgie said.

"What if he tries to run away?"

"Didn't you hook up the chain like I said?"

Uh-oh. News to me, and not good.

Georgie entered the building. Butch walked around to the back of the station wagon, stood watching me through the window. "Gonna be good?" he said.

Of course not. The instant that door opened up—if that was in the cards, as Bernie liked to say, although he'd stopped that after the Mama Reenya Tarot card case, a case I hadn't understood from the get-go, except for what a great patter Mama Reenya had turned out to be, right up there with Autumn—I planned to be as bad as bad gets. But then, just as Butch was reaching for the door, I remembered about the chain. And coming right on top of that memory, so fast, was Bernie's—what would you call it? advice? Yes! That was it. Thank you, Bernie! Even if it had to do with cats, the point was: *more than one way, big guy.*

I lay down, chin right on the floor, eyes gazing up at nothing in the least-threatening way imaginable, like I was just one big softie. You hear that about a certain kind of big guy: *oh, he's just one big softie.* Not this big guy, amigo. When that door opened, I was going to rip—

Whoa.

More than one way. I'd come close to forgetting the whole thing.

Butch looked through the back window. "You gonna make this difficult?"

I yawned, no idea why, a real big one, mouth open wide as wide could be.

"You are, ain't you?"

What was wrong with Butch? Scared of a yawn? But then I remembered, maybe a little late, that yawns show teeth. I shut my mouth and went right back to being Mr. Softie.

"That's better," Butch said. He licked his lips, how humans do when they're nervous. We in the nation within get nervous, too, but show it in different ways, although I couldn't think of a single one at that moment, maybe because I didn't feel nervous myself, not the least bit. That was Bernie for you every time: just hearing his voice made everything all right.

"Now," Butch was saying, "what I'm gonna do is raise this here door, slip off those tags, and let you out, nice and easy, no crazy shit. Got that?"

I gazed up at nothing, my eyes as blank as I could make them.

"On three," said Butch. "One, two, three." He raised the rear door, then jumped quickly back. I didn't move a muscle. "Okay, then, so far so good. Now I'm gonna reach in here like so." He reached in like so, if that meant real slow and cautious. His hand—stubby, with fat fingers, nothing like Bernie's, moved past my mouth. I could have . . . done just about anything, but somehow I knew for sure that that was the wrong play. He unclipped my tags and said, "Whew. Now I'll just lean over here a bit, grab onto the chain, move back—and there we go!" Butch, standing outside the open door, wiped sweat off his upper lip. "Come on out."

I just lay there. Being Mr. Softie was growing on me.

"Huh?" Butch said. "Hop out. You're free."

Free? Butch was forgetting the chain, one end of which he had in his hand. But maybe I'd made my point. I rose, in no hurry, had a nice stretch, butt way up, head way down and then stepped out of the car, landing lightly in the parking lot. Maybe something about that landing alarmed Butch. He was eyeing me like mayhem might be on my mind. And of course it was—always, actually, something to probably not get into at any time. *But not now, big guy.* I sat down, gazing up at him like an obedience-training star. Which I never quite was—have I mentioned about my days in K-9 school?

"Hey," said Butch, "gettin' with the program, huh?"

Sure thing. And then came another thought, not my usual kind: *Sure thing, if the program is skinning a cat.* A lovely feeling went through me from nose to tail, the feeling of being in command.

Butch jiggled the chain. "Need to piss or anything like that?"

Not really, although marking this and that was never a bad idea. I had a sudden crazy urge to mark Butch. What a good mood I was in!

"Well, then," Butch began, just as a black limo pulled into the lot. At about the same time, Georgie came out of the building and hurried over to meet the limo. He opened one of the rear doors and a short round man with glossy black hair stepped out. They shook hands, talked for a moment or two, and walked over to me and Butch.

"This is Butch," said Georgie, "one of our junior operatives." Whatever that meant, it seemed to come as a surprise to Butch, judging from the look on his face. "Butch, say hi to Mr. Han, president and CEO of the biggest private investigation company in Shanghai."

"Wuhu," said Mr. Han.

"Excuse me?" Georgie said.

"Wuhu," Mr. Han said. "No Shanghai."

"Six of one," Georgie said. "And this here, Mr. Han, is, uh, Wilkie. Wilkie," he went on, looking at me for some reason, "meet your new owner, Mr. Han."

"Master," said Mr. Han, "and only if animal is passing test."

"Understood," Georgie said. "Let's get started."

TWENTY-ONE

"What I was thinking, Dezhang—okay to call you Dezhang, or you want I should stick with Mr. Han?" Georgie said. In the station wagon again, Georgie now at the wheel, Mr. Han beside him, Butch in the backseat, me in the very back.

Mr. Han made a little nod, kind of a bow.

"Dezhang it is," Georgie said. "Pronouncing that right?"

Another little nod.

"Cool," Georgie said. "Takes some getting used to, first name coming last."

"Excuse, please?" said Mr. Han.

"We do the opposite—first name first. Maybe when you guys take over, I'll be Malhouf Georgie." Georgie laughed, glanced at Mr. Han, maybe to see if he was joining in. Mr. Han was not.

"Hey," said Butch, "you think in China they order rolls egg?"

There was a silence. Then Georgie said, "Your résumé in shape for sending out?"

Butch shrank down in his seat.

"What I was proposing, Dezhang," Georgie went on, "was we use a real case for this test."

"Real case?" said Mr. Han.

"That's on the books right now," Georgie said. "Show you what Wilkie here can do in game conditions. You're stealing this dog, Dezhang, believe me."

What was this? Was Georgie talking about me? What was all this Wilkie business all of a sudden?

"Twenty grand no steal," said Mr. Han.

That seemed to bring on another silence. Georgie cleared his throat, something humans do when they want to make a fresh start. "This particular case involves the restaurant business, just about the flakiest business out there."

"Test first," said Mr. Han. "Then eat."

Georgie shot him a quick glance. "Gotcha," he said.

We drove through some bad South Pedroia streets, all familiar to me. For example, down that street—a mean one, as Bernie would say—was where a perp name of Darren Quigley had lived not so long ago. I had no problem with Darren—hadn't I scarfed up a Cheeto or two in his living room?—but he'd come to a bad end anyway, south of the border down Mexico way.

Georgie turned onto a street full of potholes, the high smoke-stack that never stops spewing rotten-egg-smelling smoke—the tallest thing in South Pedroia—towering overhead. Mr. Han pointed to it. "Who is owning?" he said.

"Good question," Georgie said. "You wanna get the environmentalists on their case?"

Mr. Han stared at Georgie for a moment. Then he started laughing, the red-faced, doubled-over, tears-streaming laughter that's almost scary. Georgie joined in. They laughed and laughed, high-fiving each other.

"I don't get it," Butch said.

Georgie stopped in front of a small cement-block house at the end of the street, dirt yard with rusted appliances in front, a garage bigger than the house in back.

"Man of the house drives a truck for the biggest restaurant supplier in the south Valley, longtime client," Georgie said. "Constant inventory shortfalls, especially in big-ticket items, steaks, chops, ribs—big concern. Malhouf International has narrowed down the suspects to three, truck driver being numero uno. He's on the road at the moment and the missus is a flight attendant, working the—Atlanta route today, was it, Butch?"

"Miami," said Butch.

"Miami," Georgie said. "We dot the i's at Malhouf International."

Whoa. Mr. Singh's mother had a red dot between her eyes, the only person I'd ever seen doing the eye dot thing. Was she mixed up in this restaurant scam? This case—at least it wasn't one of ours—was getting complicated.

". . . point being," Georgie was saying, "that now would be an opportune time for sniffing around."

We got out of the car, approached the front door of the little house, Butch holding my chain. The house was silent, except for the hum of a fridge inside. Georgie crouched down, examined the lock, then took out a key ring loaded with keys and selected one. We were going into the house? Why was that? The steaks were in the garage in the back. What could be more obvious? A soft breeze blew from that direction, and it smelled like the Police Athletic League picnic just before the grilling starts.

Georgie stuck the key in the lock and turned it. "Presto," he said, and pushed the door open. "Do your thing, Wilkie."

Here's a bit of strangeness: every time Georgie said Wilkie, my mind went straight to him hitting me across the face with the chain.

We went inside: me and Butch, then Mr. Han, and Georgie last. Shotgun house: I'd been in a zillion, maybe more. A tidy kitchen, everything put away except for two mugs sitting on the counter. Did anyone else notice the steam rising from them? No sign of it. Bernie would have, first thing. By now, he'd have had his hand on the butt of the .38 Special. But would we have been in the house in the first place? No way: we'd have been in the garage, packing up all those steaks. My mouth started watering, just at the thought.

We left the kitchen, moved down the hall. Behind me, Georgie sniffed the air. "Picking up anything, Wilkie?" he said, his voice low.

In fact, I was, coming from behind the very first door we reached. Human beings—and this is true as well in the nation within—give off unmissable odors during certain encounters in their lives. I paused by the door.

"In here?" Georgie said. He turned to Mr. Han. "Dollars to doughnuts goddamn room's full of freezers."

"What is doughnuts?" said Mr. Han.

That was a shocker. I wasn't close to being over it, when Georgie opened the door and—

What was that word Bernie liked? Pandemonium? When all hell breaks loose? We always loved that, me and Bernie; we were a lot alike in some ways, don't forget.

When events speed up, it's hard to keep them straight. The first thing I saw was a naked woman lying on a bed, perhaps not lying, more scrambling around for the sheets and trying to pull them up over her. Was she screaming at the same time? I thought so, but my mind was more occupied by the fact that the old hiding-behind-the-open-door trick was about to get played on us.

What else?

Mr. Han was saying, "Excuse, excuse."

Butch was saying, "What the hell? She's supposed to be thirty-five thousand feet over Texas right now."

And Georgie was saying, "You're fired."

At this point, a real big dude, almost Butch's size, sprang out from behind the door. Real big, and like the woman, not wearing clothes. He was screaming, too, but not in the scared way; his screams were all about rage.

"Whoa," said Georgie. "All a mistake. And aren't you supposed to be in your truck today?"

"Um, Boss?" Butch said. "This ain't hubby."

"Well, then," Georgie said, "since no one here comes off as lily-white, why don't we forget the whole—"

And last, the most important fact of all: the big screaming dude suddenly had a meat cleaver in his hand, or maybe had had it the whole time. Again, hard to keep everything straight in situations like this, plus I was on my own. But even on my own, meaning no Bernie, I knew a few things right away. First, the screaming dude was in on the whole meat scam. Second, Mr. Han had already booked, was nowhere to be seen. No time for the other things, because the screaming dude was swinging that cleaver.

Georgie dove one way, Butch the other. The cleaver missed Butch's head by not much and sank deep into the doorjamb. One interesting detail about that: Butch hadn't let go of the chain, so it had gotten straightened right out, stretched flat against the doorjamb. And that cleaver had sliced through it clean. By the time I realized that, Georgie and Butch were crawling frantically every which way and the screaming dude was trying to twist the cleaver out of the wall.

I booked, just like Mr. Han, down the hall and out the front door, which he'd conveniently left open. Did I happen to take a quick nip out of Georgie's leg somewhere along the way? I have no recollection of that.

Outside, Mr. Han was already in Georgie's car, snapping down the locks and pulling out his cell phone. He looked at me. I looked at him, a nice enough gentleman but with a lot to learn, beginning with doughnuts. Screaming rose from the house, everyone inside joining in now. I ran into a neighbor's yard—the chain so short it didn't drag on the ground, not bothering me at all—saw a fence at the end, not high enough to pose a challenge, kind of disappointing, and leaped over. Chet the Jet in action, the free wind in my face!

I landed in a small parking lot next to one of those self-storage places, and not only that, but—amazing!—our self-storage place, at least the end unit was, where we kept the Hawaiian pants. There were stacks and stacks of them inside, Hawaiian pants with bird patterns, fish patterns, flower patterns, palm tree patterns, martini glass patterns—you name it. Bernie still didn't understand why Hawaiian pants hadn't taken off and made us rich, and if Bernie didn't understand it, neither did I. I trotted right up to that end unit, stood outside, and sniffed. What was I hoping for? Bernie's scent? I didn't pick it up, not a trace. Meanwhile: sirens, and getting louder. I glanced around, spotted a narrow alley, and headed that way, breathing my kind of air again—hot and dry, smelling of all sorts of Valley things: flowers and mesquite, grease and smoke, and always—you didn't even have to be near a grate—the smell of sewage on the move.

SPENCER QUINN

The alley led to another alley, lined with boarded-up build-ings on both sides, lots of graffiti on the walls, and suddenly: a rat, practically in front of my face. Those nasty eyes, that nasty smell: of course, I took off after the rat, chasing him around the corner and almost snapping him up, before he darted into a tiny gap at the base of a brick wall.

I kept going, soon found myself on a street with strip malls, gas stations, fast-food joints, stretching on and on. *Blight, big guy:* that's what Bernie would have said. He hated blight, whatever exactly that might be, but in my opinion there was good in every-thing. For example, when I strolled around to the back of one of those fast-food joints, there stood a trash barrel, and when I knocked it over, out came lots of interesting stuff, including a perfectly good burger or two, which I made short work of, on account of how long it had been since my last square meal.

Ah. I sat on the broken pavement and licked my muzzle. The back door of the fast-food joint opened and a guy appeared, squeezing out a mop. His gaze went to me, then the trash barrel, and back to me; he yelled something and shook the mop.

I rose and trotted off, soon settling into my go-to trot, the trot I can keep up pretty much forever. The sun was sinking down in the sky, and I had it at my back: that was important. My mind went kind of blank. I was aware of the downtown towers coming closer, and a little later I reached the dried-up riverbed that ran all the way across town to the airport. Not too long after that I was moving alongside one of the fenced-off runways. A plane rolled down the tarmac, picking up speed. A kid near the back looked out the window, saw me, and waved. That was nice. Then I thought of Devin. Where were we with that? My mood changed. The plane lifted off, made a sweeping turn, and got small in a hurry. By that time, I was partway down the steep slope beyond the runways, the slope that led into the canyon.

And not just any canyon: this was our canyon. My mood changed back to normal, kind of my go-to mood. I was still far from home, but Bernie and I had once hiked all the way from Mesquite Road to the airport. What a picnic we'd had, watching the planes come and go! I sped up, couldn't help it.

The sun was just going down as I made my way along the high ridge that ended at the big flat rock across the gully from Mesquite Road. Standing on the big flat rock—a soft, red rock that felt nice and warm under my paws—I could gaze down and spot—yes!—our place. Home always looked strange from up here, so small and mostly just orange-tiled roof. But there was our patio, with the flower pots and the swan fountain that Leda put in. The water flowing from the swan's beak glinted in the soft, early evening light; I could just make out the splashing on the stones. A lovely sound: my ears were already home.

Kind of a strange thought, and I was just starting to forget it, when from out of nowhere a very small member of the nation within came running over the crest of the ridge. Real small but fast for a little guy. He scooted toward the rock, saw me, and tried to put on the brakes, but lost his footing and tumbled in the dust. He scrambled up, gave himself a shake—just as I would have done, dust rising in little clouds—looked up at me, and started barking.

Hey! He turned out to be just a puppy. Still, no one barks at me and gets away with it, so I barked back. He barked. I barked louder. The little guy barked louder, too; a funny-looking little guy: for one thing, his ears didn't match, one being mostly white, the other mostly black. My mind almost caught on that fact, as though wanting to stop there for a bit, but then I got busy barking still louder. And damned if he didn't get louder, too, high-pitched and very irritating. I gave him a quick *bark bark bark,* each one louder than the last. And he came right back at me! And then— what was this? From down below: *yip yip yip,* the most irritating bark in creation. Iggy?

I checked the house next door to ours, a pretty good distance away, but not so far that I couldn't make out Iggy, standing on the upstairs balcony, front paws on the railing. Somewhere behind him and out of sight, I heard old Mr. Parsons saying, "Iggy, what the hell?"

Meanwhile, this little bugger planted on his solid little bugger legs wouldn't stop! *Bark bark bark!* Not quite as high-pitched as Iggy, but there was a throatiness to it, like he was—could it be possible?—trying to intimidate me. I barked. He barked. Iggy went *yip yip yip.* I whipped around and barked at Iggy, real fierce. The little length of chain still on me came loose and fell to the ground. Whoa. I'd barked it off? No time for getting anywhere with that, because now old Mr. Parsons appeared on the balcony, stumping along on his walker. He stood beside Iggy and peered out in my direction, shielding his eyes with one hand.

"Edna?" he called. Voices carried in the desert air; Bernie had made that point many times, especially when we were in stealth mode, one of our favorites. "Are you awake? Something here you should see." I heard Mrs. Parsons's voice somewhere back in the house, but couldn't make out the words. Then Mr. Parsons said, "Chet seems to have gotten loose." Mrs. Parsons spoke again, and Mr. Parsons said, "Right, no news there. But he's got this little puppy tagging along. And Edna? The puppy's Chet in miniature, to a T."

TWENTY-TWO

The puppy barked again. I'd had enough. I jumped down from the red rock, gave him a bump with the end of my nose, just hard enough to get his attention. He flew into the air, landed with a thump, and rolled down the slope, all the way to the bottom of the gully. *Got your attention now, little friend?* I was just thinking that thought when the puppy bounced up, glared at me, and went right back to barking! Hard to believe. At the same time, that kind of behavior reminded me of someone; couldn't quite think who. I just stared at him. Meanwhile, Iggy was back to *yip-yip-yipping*. I glanced over at him. Was he trying to scramble over the balcony railing? Didn't he realize it was a long way down? What did Bernie say at times like this? Something about problems in stereo, stereo meaning . . . I wasn't quite sure. I barked at Iggy, barked at the puppy, barked at myself, not sure why. It was time for . . . for Bernie to do something. Maybe he was back in the house, safe and sound, in the middle of one of his naps. I barked at him, the loudest yet: *BARK BARK BARK.*

A sudden silence fell, almost like the whole world had stopped, that somehow I had stopped it. And in that silence, I listened my very hardest for Bernie's call: "Chet? Where are you?" or "What's all the racket, big guy?" or something along those lines. But nothing like that happened. Then, from way across the canyon where all the new houses were sucking up what was left of the aquifer—as Bernie had mentioned to the developer at a meet-and-greet cookout, the conversation going downhill fast after that—came a bit of a surprise: the sound of one of those human inventions we could do without in the nation within, namely, a dog whistle. Is that nice, to make a sound like getting pricked with a sharp stick deep inside the ears, with the added touch that you yourself, the blower, can't hear it? They really can't! Humans, I mean. In the nation within, we hear it all too well. The puppy, for example, ears stiff and pointed, was already climbing the slope as fast as he could, his paws—how big they were considering his size!—churning up clods of dirt. This was the being-called game; I knew it from K-9 school. The only way to stop the horrible noise was to run as fast as possible to whoever was responsible for making it. Not much of a game, compared to fetch, for example. The little fella zoomed back up the ridge and over the crest, disappearing from view. I went the other way, climbing the trail that led to the back gate of our house.

We have a high adobe wall at the back of the house, with a high wooden gate in the middle. High, yes, but not quite high enough to keep me from leaping over, a fact no one knows but me. I've only leaped it in emergencies, once on an interesting night when . . . hey, when I heard some she-barking across the canyon. All at once, I got the feeling that a brand-new thought, a real big one, was about to enter my mind. But it didn't. I jumped over the gate.

I landed—front paws touching down just ahead of the rear ones, feeling hardly any jolt at all—on the patio, and headed right to the swan fountain. Ah, the lovely taste of our very own water.

The next thing I knew, I was wading around in the circular stone basin to my heart's content. After lots of that, I hopped out, shook off, and went to the back door. Our back door is wooden at the bottom and glass on top. I rose up, paws on the glass, and gazed in at our kitchen and the entrance to the hall leading farther into the house. Nothing moved, except—except a mouse nibbling on a slice of toast that had been left on the counter.

That was maddening. I barked and barked. The mouse paused for a moment and went back to eating our toast. I barked some more, the mouse now ignoring me completely. *Bernie! Wake up! Let me in!*

But no Bernie. He wasn't napping? Then where was he? All of a sudden—oh, no—I remembered the last time I'd seen him. Bad sights came popping into my mind. I didn't want to see those sights again but couldn't stop them. My front paws slid down the glass. I stood by the door, doing nothing.

After some time, I noticed a flip-flop of Bernie's lying under the patio table. I went over and sniffed it for a while, started feeling better; Bernie's feet had a lovely smell—not something you could say of all humans—quite a bit more peppery than the smell of the rest of him, with a nice added suggestion of the scent that comes off those tiny bits of a pencil eraser that you find after lots of erasing has happened. When I'd done with sniffing, I picked up the flip-flop, getting a good taste of it, and felt better still.

Carrying the flip-flop, I moved around the side of the house, meaning the side next to Iggy's; old man Heydrich, no pal of me and my kind, lived on the other side. I passed the coiled-up hose, the trash barrel, and Charlie's old bike, now too small for him. The fun we'd had when he was learning how to ride the thing, so wobbly! I'd raced round and round him, helping out as best I could. Sometimes, especially after a drink or two, Bernie says he'd like to make something else out of that bike and hang it on the wall; no idea what that's all about.

There's a small gate at the side of the house, closing off the narrow space from the front yard. Not a high gate at all: I hopped over without really thinking about it, trotted into the front yard and started digging. Had I forgotten about that bushy-tailed squirrel burying something under my favorite tree, the shady one in the middle? That wouldn't be me.

I dug the thing up—turned out to be some kind of nut, which I reburied, but deeper. A job worth doing, Bernie says, is worth doing well. Bernie: always the smartest human in the room. After that, I went to the front door. Closed. I pawed at it for a while, not getting anywhere. I pawed some more.

Sometime later, I walked over to the shady tree and marked it, saving some squirts for the other two trees—and keeping a reserve just in case—and sat down, the flip-flop still in my mouth. At that point, I saw Mr. Parsons at his front window. He had a cell phone to his ear and his eyes on me.

The phone rang inside our place. And then I heard Bernie! "Little Detective Agency," he said. Yes! That was us! "Please leave a message after the tone." Oh. I'd forgotten about the message machine, also remembered what I'd been trying to forget, namely how Bernie had looked the last time I'd seen him. Now I couldn't get it out of my head.

Meanwhile, Mr. Parson's lips were moving although the sound of his voice came from our place. How weird was that?

"Bernie? Dan Parsons here. Uh, next door. Sorry to bother you, but Chet seems to be out on his own. Not complaining—we like Chet, Mrs. Parsons and myself—but he seems to be acting a bit strangely, like he's . . . hard to say, really. Anyway, not to alarm you. If you're away or something and I can help, give me a call."

I sat in our front yard. Darkness moved across the sky, kind of like night was slowly leaking in. What a thought! I forgot about it and just sat, facing Mesquite Road. There was nothing to do but wait for Bernie to drive up. And the moment he did, I'd go bounding over and jump right into the Porsche and climb all over him. Was it going to be soon? I listened for the Porsche. It has a very distinctive sound that I can hear from far away, a kind of growl a bit like my own.

I growled; lay down; rose and marked the trees again; sat; growled. Stars appeared. Bernie had explained all about them to Charlie. All I remembered was the muffin part. *Imagine poppy seeds in a muffin,* he'd said. I could do that easily: I was familiar with exactly that kind of muffin, a specialty at Donut Heaven. I realized that I was getting hungry. When had I last eaten? There'd been a quick burger or two, snatched on the fly, but that seemed like a very long time ago. I got up and marked the trees again.

"Chet?"

I turned to Iggy's place. Mr. Parsons stood in the doorway, the porch light shining on his worn old face. Somewhere behind him, Iggy was going crazy.

"You all right, Chet?" Mr. Parsons said.

No complaints.

He gazed at me. I gazed at him. "Hungry?" he said. "Want to come inside?"

What was he saying? That he was going to let me into our place? How was that possible? Bernie was the only one with the key. I could see it in my mind, hanging off the seashell key ring, the Porsche ring beside it. Keeping track of the keys was all about security, and security was part of my job.

"Come on, Chet," Mr. Parsons said. "Got a treat for you."

Iggy went crazier. I was wondering: *Treat? What kind?*

"A nice treat."

I liked nice treats, no doubt about that. Come to think of it, I'd never known a not-nice treat. I rose, crossed Iggy's yard—like ours, not a grass lawn, but full of desert plants, unlike old man Heydrich's, whose sprinkler system went on twice a day, a sight that bothered Bernie no end—and stood in front of Iggy's porch.

"Come on in," Mr. Parsons said.

I stood there. Iggy went silent. Somewhere in the house, Mrs. Parsons said, "Daniel? What's going on?"

"Trying to get Chet to come in."

"Offer him a treat."

"I did."

"Tell him he can play with Iggy."

"He wouldn't understand that, Edna, he's—"

And some more along those lines, which I missed on account of already being past him and inside the house.

First time in Iggy's house! Of course, I've been in lots of houses not my own, and knew the drill: best behavior and nothing but. Remember, Bernie always said, you're a—something or other, couldn't come up with it at the moment, and also too busy sniffing my way around this nice rug in the front hall. A nice rug, but wow, had Iggy messed up on it or what? All cleaned, in human terms, meaning no messes to see—or probably even smell, in their case—but there were traces left, believe me. That rug—soft and nubbly, with a pretty cactus and sagebrush pattern—reeked!

I sniffed my way down the hall, hearing the front door close behind me, and Mr. Parsons saying, "All clear, Edna." Old humans have a different smell from young ones. This house had that smell, sort of like newspapers when they get old and yellow;

young humans smell milky. Also there was kibble, and not far from where—

A door opened and out came my pal, Iggy! And was he flying or what, that strange stubby tail straight up and stiff, his tongue, so weirdly long, flapping all over the place. He barreled right into me, bounced straight back, somehow crashing into a tall sort of display table—we'd once had a similar one—with a flower vase on top. The vase wobbled one way, another, and then came down with a smash, plus a splash, on account of all the water in the vase. Iggy bounced up, now with a long-stemmed flower in his mouth. I wanted one, too, forgetting for the moment that I still had Bernie's flip-flop in my mouth, and then I forgot about everything, and we were motoring, me and Iggy.

Through the door Iggy had just come through and into the kitchen. Was that Mrs. Parsons in the wheelchair and with the oxygen-breathing thing in her nose? Maybe, but we were picking up speed, me and Iggy, side by side, ears flattened by our own wind, nipping at each other every chance we got, and in situations like that it's hard to notice every single detail. Next we were bombing upstairs—what was that in my mouth? kibble chunks? I made quick work of them—and racing along a corridor and through a bedroom, the air suddenly full of down feathers, and pivoting as one, back down the stairs, through the kitchen—hey! the flip-flop, now on Mrs. Parsons' lap? I snatched it back up and we rounded a corner and careened into a bathroom, our claws scratching deep in the hardwood floor. My pal Iggy, best friend from way back! Was it good to be with him or what? We stuck our heads in the toilet and had lapped up just about every drop when the door slammed behind us.

Uh-oh. We turned. Yes, the door, definitely closed; and more bad news: that round knob, impossible for me. I heard Mrs. Parsons, somewhere down the hall. "God in heaven."

And then much closer, just on the other side of the door, Mr. Parsons, breathing heavily: "All over, Edna. I got 'em trapped."

"Where?" Mrs. Parsons's voice, kind of wavery to begin with, was more so.

"Powder room."

"Oh, Daniel. My soap collection's in there."

"They're not interested in soap."

Soap collection? Were they talking about all those itty-bitty brightly colored round things that had gotten into the toilet somehow? The toilet which now seemed to be filling up with water again, the water rising and rising? I looked at Iggy. He looked at me. What was this? He had the flip-flop? I snatched it back.

"What's all that crashing around in there?" said Mrs. Parsons; I heard the squeak of her wheelchair wheels, coming closer.

"Not sure," said Mr. Parsons. "Why don't you lie down in the den? You're not supposed to get upset."

"Daniel?"

"Yes?"

"Make sense."

"Sorry."

Iggy made a play for the flip-flop. I put a stop to that.

"Maybe if I open the door just a crack—" Mr. Parsons began.

"Don't be a fool. Try Bernie again."

Bernie? Something about Bernie? I went still. Iggy snatched the flip-flop right out of my mouth. Meanwhile, my paws were getting wet, a bit of a mystery.

I heard little beeps of a phone being dialed. Then, after a pause, "Still not picking up," Mr. Parsons said. "I think he's out of town."

"What about calling the ex-wife?"

"That harridan?"

"You never used to be so judgmental, Daniel."

"You couldn't be wronger."

There was a pause. Then Mrs. Parsons laughed, a nice, musical sort of laugh that didn't sound like an old person's laugh at all. "You're something," she said.

"Likewise," said Mr. Parsons. I didn't understand these people at all.

"How about the girlfriend?" Mrs. Parsons said. "Suzie something. She's nice."

TWENTY-THREE

Not long after that, I was walking out of Iggy's place in the company of Suzie. I was so happy to see her, although Suzie herself didn't look all that happy. Suzie had great eyes, dark and shining like our countertops, but now they'd lost the shining part.

"Were you a good guest, Chet?" she said.

Guest! That was the word I'd been trying to remember. We passed the plumber coming the other way.

Suzie's Beetle was parked on the street, and I was all set for a ride, but instead we crossed back over to our place and went to the front door. I didn't know why: I'd given up on Bernie being inside. Suzie knocked and called, "Bernie? Bernie? Are you in there?"

Our house was silent.

"But of course he's not," Suzie said. "Otherwise the car would be . . ." Sometimes when humans went silent like that, you could almost hear their voices carrying on inside their heads. She glanced at the driveway. There was nothing to see but the oil stain from the leak Bernie could never quite patch.

Suzie slid her phone from her pocket, dialed, checked the screen. "His phone's switched off, or . . ." She reached into her bag, took out a key. Suzie had a key to our place? And I didn't know? I felt my tail drooping: security was part of my job. Suzie unlocked the door and opened it. We went inside.

Home. *Home is the hunter:* something Bernie often said when we came home, even though we'd never gone hunting, not even once, and I wanted to, pretty bad. Other times he said: *No place like home.* Amazing, the things Bernie knew. But what kind of place was home with no Bernie?

Suzie switched on the lights. Everything looked the same as always, maybe not quite so messy, but don't trust me on that: Bernie and I aren't fussy about mess, unlike Leda, say, or Neatnik Nolan, this perp we'd cuffed who refused to get into the car until we'd cleaned out all the fast-food wrappers. My tail rose back up, just at the memory of him.

Suzie sniffed the air. She had a beautiful nose for a human, finely shaped, her two tiny nostrils exactly the same, which you hardly ever saw in humans—but that was the point: tiny. Her nose was tiny. Could she actually sniff out anything? Hard to believe. But maybe—and here came a new idea, very slippery, about to slip clear away from me—maybe Suzie was thinking that there was something sniffable in the air, if only she could sniff it. What a thought! Had to love Suzie, although in this case there didn't happen to be anything sniffable, other than that damned mouse.

I charged into the kitchen.

"Chet, Chet! What's going on?"

And there was the little bugger, caught red-handed, whatever that meant. You don't need hands for catching perps, a fact I knew better than practically anything: cases at the Little Detective Agency almost always ended with me grabbing a perp by the pant leg, as I couldn't have failed to mention. And this mouse—

frozen for a moment on the countertop, not much toast left—was a perp, pants or no pants.

I tore across the kitchen, flew up to the counter, leading with my front paws. The mouse unfroze but quick, darted around the toaster, and—what was this? Disappeared into a tiny hole where the wall joined the countertop, a hole I'd never seen before? I pawed uselessly at that hole.

"Are you really that hungry?"

I turned—there was Suzie, looking almost angry with me, an impossibility—and lowered myself down to the floor. This had nothing to do with hunger, was all about that pilferer trying to—

I realized, too late, that I had the toast—what was left of it— in my mouth. I tried to wag my tail and drop the toast at the same time, but had trouble with the toast part.

Suzie knelt in front of me, looked into my eyes. Poor Suzie: she was so worried. "Where's Bernie?" she said. "Can't still be up at that stupid camp—you're here and you didn't go three hundred miles on your own." Her eyes shifted. "Is he shacked up with that woman?"

Suzie rose and started walking through the house. I followed her. We went from room to room, entering the office last. The office is next door to Charlie's bedroom, where Charlie sleeps on some weekends, not enough. A basket of kid's blocks lies in one corner of the office—the room was meant for a little sister or brother that never came along; sometimes I played with the blocks myself. The rest of the office is mostly Bernie's books—on shelves, in stacks here and there, sometimes scattered on the floor; plus the desk; the two client chairs; the wall safe, hidden behind the picture of Niagara Falls; and the whiteboard on the wall, where Bernie figures things out. Suzie went to the desk, picked up a framed photo and gave it a close look. I knew this photo because

Bernie often gazes at it, too: Bernie and Suzie laughing, their eyes on each other.

Suzie put the picture back on the desk. "Bodyguarding duty," she said. There was a little pause, and I had the strange idea that she would lay it facedown, but she didn't.

She turned to the whiteboard. Normally when we were working a case, there'd be lots of writing on the whiteboard, plus arrows, boxes, and even some drawings, often big ocean waves; Bernie would spend time on those waves, getting them just right. But there was none of that now, the whiteboard almost totally white.

"Anya," Suzie said, pointing to a bit of writing. "No last name. She would be the babe, no doubt. Then there's this arrow to someone named Devin. And a second arrow to a nameless guy. 'Check out guy,' is all it says. What guy would that be?" She made a tut-tut sound. Love the tut-tut sound—loved, in fact, a lot of those human nontalking sounds. I hoped Suzie would do some more, but she didn't.

Instead she sat down at the desk, picked up the phone and started calling our pals: Rick Torres, Lieutenant Stine, Cedric Booker, Otis DeWayne, Simon Berg, Mr. Singh, Nixon Panero our mechanic, Prof down at the college, and lots more, and calling places, like Max's Memphis Ribs, Dry Gulch, Donut Heaven, asking everybody if Bernie was there or if they'd seen him. I could see the answers on her face.

Suzie hung up the phone. "Can I picture him shacked up somewhere with this Anya person?" she said. She got a faraway look in her eye. "My mom would say he's a man and men do what men do." Suzie's mom? This was new. I liked new things, but was Suzie's mom part of the case? It was getting complicated. "On the other hand, Mom's a four-time loser when it comes to marriage, so maybe she's not . . ." Suzie turned to me. "But one thing I can't imagine is him letting you run off and doing nothing about it."

What was all this? I didn't know. All I knew for sure was how much I liked Suzie. I shifted closer to the desk. She patted me, and right between the ears, an excellent choice. "You know what attracted me to him in the first place? How he was with you." Or something along those lines: I was pretty much concentrating on the feeling between my ears.

Suzie rose and paced around a bit. That was a sign of her brain shifting into high gear; Bernie did the same. "What's the logical next step?" she said.

She had me there.

"Begin with the last place I saw him, maybe? What was the name of that stupid camp?" She took some device from her purse—humans had so many!—smaller than a laptop but bigger than a phone, and started working away. Soon she was back on the phone. "Voicemail? I don't want goddamn . . ." She hung up. "We could drive up there, I suppose."

I headed toward the door.

"Or," she went on, "I wonder if . . ." Suzie went back to her screen. I lay down, stretched out. Time passed.

"Here we go," Suzie said. "Under the registration tab, a list of campers. No parents, but . . . but here's a Devin. One and only. Last name Vereen. All they've got for an address is North Valley. How about we try a search for Anya Vereen, see what we can . . ."

And more like that. I closed my eyes. So good to be home, back to lying on the rug while work went on close by. The only problem: Bernie wasn't the one doing it. My eyes opened and stayed that way, refusing to close, not letting me sleep, not letting me not think about Bernie.

"Okay, Chet." I raised my head. Suzie was getting up, packing her bag. "Let's roll." Suzie could move very fast when she wanted. She almost beat me to the car.

We drove to the North Valley, Suzie behind the wheel of the Beetle, me riding shotgun. Riding shotgun in the Beetle wasn't like riding shotgun in the Porsche—the Porsche having no top made it just about perfect—but I had no complaints, especially after Suzie slid my window right down.

"Was that what you were barking about?" she said. "It's hot as hell out there." She cranked up the AC, so we had a cold breeze coming from one direction and a warmish one—this was the time of year when the Valley stays hot long after the sun goes down, the heat beating up instead of beating down—from another. Just a little thing, maybe, cold and heat at the same time, but there was lots of fun in little things.

We got off the freeway, entered Anya's development. Yes, one of those developments Bernie hated with mostly cul-de-sacs and houses that looked the same, but they don't all smell the same, which was how I knew we were in the right place. Somewhere in this particular development lived a believer in compost heaps, and there's no way to hide that from the likes of me.

Suzie pulled into Anya's driveway. A light shone somewhere at the back of the house. We hopped out, or rather Suzie walked around and opened the door for me, the window space being a little on the tight side for hopping through, although you couldn't say I actually got stuck, not to the extent where I couldn't have managed without Suzie's help. We went to the front door—I gave myself a quick shake on the go—and Suzie pressed the buzzer.

Bzzz. Then the house, already quiet, seemed to grow quieter, hard to explain. Suzie made a fist—how small hers was, compared to Bernie's—and knocked on the door: a surprisingly loud knock for a fist like that. Suzie cocked her head and listened. Maybe for footsteps from the back of the house? Was that a human-type thought? I myself was listening to breathing, very soft, from just behind the door. Also I was catching a faint scent of dynamite, kind of strange.

"Hello?" Suzie called. "Anyone home? Anya Ver—"

The door whipped open, so quick and hard it made a breeze. On other side stood a man, real big, his face shadowy, the gun in his hand less so.

"Who the hell are you?" he said.

"Suzie Sanchez," Suzie said. "Reporter for the *Valley Tribune*. Put that gun away."

He lowered the gun. I noticed that his non-gun hand was bandaged, a nice sight. I already knew who he was, of course: one taste of your blood and I'd never forget you either.

"Reporter?" he said, leaning forward a bit; the streetlight shone on that light blond hair of his, almost white. "What do you want?"

"I'm looking for Anya Vereen," Suzie said. "Isn't this her house?"

"I paid for the goddamn—" He cut himself off, clamping his mouth shut. That was when he noticed me. "What the fuck?" He took a quick step back: the guy named Guy, beginning to get the picture. The gun rose again, this time pointed in my direction.

"Put down that gun or I'm calling the police," Suzie said.

"It's licensed," Guy said, his eyes still on me. The hair on my back was up from nose to tail.

"We'll let the cops sort that out," Suzie said. The smell of fear? I picked up none from Suzie, not a whiff.

Guy tucked the gun in his belt.

"What's your name?" Suzie said.

"None of your business."

"The reason I ask is that Chet here seems to know you."

Damn right I did. And I was looking forward to getting to know him even better.

"Huh? You talking about the dog? Never seen him in my life."

"Then how come he's growling?" Suzie said.

News to me, but she was right, no question. I toned it down.

"How about because he's a bad dog?" Guy said.

Suzie shook her head. "This isn't normal," she said. "Normally he likes people. So why doesn't he like you?"

"How would I know? It's an animal, for Christ sake."

Suzie gave him a hard look. Her gaze moved over to his bandaged hand. He stuck it in his pocket.

"Is Anya here?" Suzie said.

"I got no more to say."

Suzie raised her voice: "Anya! Anya!"

No response, unless you counted a cat meowing—which is what humans call that horrible sound—from a few houses away. I got the feeling that things weren't going well.

"Satisfied?" Guy said.

"Nowhere near," Suzie said. "Where's Bernie Little?"

"Never heard of him."

"You're lying—I can see it on your face."

Guy's hand tightened on the gun. "Enough lip," he said, "unless you want it fattened for you."

Now I did smell a little fear coming off Suzie. Mostly anger, yes, but a little fear, too; had to be honest. Having the gun pointed at her didn't do it, but just that palaver about fat lips or whatever it was did? A mystery.

A little afraid, yes, but did Suzie back up? Not a step. "If something's happened to Bernie, I'll make you regret it for the rest of your life."

"I'd be shaking in fear if I knew what you're talking about," Guy said. "But since I don't, it's adios. Happy trails."

He started closing the door. This was the moment for the foot-in-the-door trick, but Suzie didn't seem to know it. The lock clicked. A bolt thunked into place. Footsteps moved away.

Suzie raised her fist to knock again, then paused and lowered it. "Come on," she said.

That was it? We weren't busting down that damn door, charging inside, grabbing Guy by the pant leg?

"Chet?"

Suzie, part way to the car, had stopped and turned toward me. We exchanged looks.

"Ch—et?"

She said that just like Bernie did. I left the doorstep and went over to her. We got in the Beetle and backed out of the driveway.

Suzie drove up the street, turned onto the next one, then the next one, lost the headlights, and—hey! we were doing the round-the-block trick, one of our best moves, mine and Bernie's! Suzie was catching on.

TWENTY-FOUR

We parked in a real good spot, on a curve where we could just see Anya's house, between a car in front of us and a tree across the street. Lights off, windows open: this was how it was done. Popping noises came from the motor and soon went silent. We sat up straight and watched Anya's house, looking as it had before, just that one light showing at the back.

"He paid for the house, that's pretty clear," Suzie said after a while. "And none too happy about it, meaning ex-hubby." She drummed her fingers on the steering wheel. Finger drumming was something I couldn't stop watching, for some reason. "Coming to the door with a gun like he did—who's he afraid of?"

Me, for one.

Suzie glanced at me. "Besides you, I mean."

Hey! She was right there with me, practically inside my head. Suzie: she got better and better.

"Could it be her?" Suzie said. "Anya? Oh, God, don't tell me he's set up to ambush her. Maybe calling the cops is the right . . ." She went silent. A moment or two later she reached over, rested her hand on my the back of my neck. "Wow, Chet—where'd you get all those muscles?"

I had no idea, but nice of Suzie to mention it. I pressed against her hand.

"What did Anya hire you two to do?" Suzie said. "That's the piece I need." Were we back to the very beginning of the case? I remembered Anya approaching us in the parking lot, a curvy little woman with . . . with trouble in her blue eyes. Had I seen the trouble then, or was I just seeing it now? Funny how the mind works, sometimes on your side and sometimes maybe not. Hey! Kind of a scary thought, like having an enemy within. I switched over immediately to thinking about nothing.

Suzie sighed. "I jumped to conclusions, Chet," she said. "I'm a fool."

Jumping? Weren't we on a stakeout? Jumping had never come up in any stakeout I'd been on. I kept my eye on Suzie, just in case she was about to make some rookie mistake. But at the same time—my eyes being a little better placed for this kind of thing— I was still aware of what was going on in Anya's house, namely that the light at the back had suddenly gone out.

Suzie leaned forward a bit: she hadn't missed it. We watched the house. A few moments later, the garage door opened and a dark car rolled out, turned onto the street, and came toward us. Guy was at the wheel, talking fast on a cell phone, even waving his hand around; he didn't come close to looking our way. The black car passed under a street lamp.

"Black Mercedes," Suzie said. "Vanity plate PAYME. This shouldn't be too hard."

Good news: soon I'd be back with Bernie. Or did Suzie mean something else? I gave her a close look, learned nothing except that I liked her face. Which I already knew, right? But no harm in reknowing.

The black Mercedes came to the end of the block, went through the stop sign. Suzie turned the key. "Bet you've done this a thousand times," she said. "If you've got any pointers, give me a shout."

Had to love Suzie, and of course pointing was part of my repertoire. She had nothing to worry about.

We followed the black Mercedes through the development— Suzie keeping the lights off, just as Bernie and I would have done—and then up onto the freeway, where she turned them on. She was doing great, although we wouldn't have eased in so close, me and Bernie, and also we hardly ever got in the same lane as the suspect. But it didn't matter: Guy was still on the phone, didn't once check the rearview mirror.

We came to spaghetti junction, this nightmare, as Bernie always called it, where a bunch of freeways met. Round and round some ramps we went, and then, zoom, we were headed toward the moon, low in the night sky and kind of reddish, the way the moon often was in the Valley. Suzie pulled out her own cell phone. For a crazy moment, I thought she was calling Guy.

"Hello?" she said. "Rick Torres, please."

Rick Torres, our buddy in Missing Persons! Was Donut Heaven in the near future? It didn't feel like that kind of future, hard to explain how, so I tried not to get my hopes up, something I'm maybe not that good at.

"Suzie Sanchez," Suzie said. "I need a quick favor—ID on state tag PAYME, black Mercedes."

Rick's voice came through the phone, all shrunken. "This is for Bernie?"

"No. Well, maybe, in a sense. I'm not sure where he is, Rick, but I've got Chet with me. He was home alone, locked out of the house. I'm actually a bit concerned."

"There's hundreds of possibilities."

"I know but—"

"But the main thing is Bernie can take care of himself. So no need for worry."

"Rick? Are you coming across or not?"

There was a pause. "Does Chet seem upset?" Rick said.

Suzie glanced my way. I was sitting up straight in the shotgun seat, not letting that black Mercedes out of my sight.

"Not that I can tell," Suzie said. "He's very alert right now. Very, very alert."

Rick laughed. "Car's registered to a Guy Wenders. Address is Wenders Associates, 14221 Old Apache Road."

"Thanks, Rick."

"Don't do anything dumb." *Click.*

"A guy named Guy," Suzie said. Yes, exactly, and that was just part of the problem. "Bernie could have made that diagram a little—" she began, and then got busy again with the phone. "Carla?" she said.

I knew Carla, a friend of Suzie's at the *Tribune,* and one of those humans who was fond of me and my kind, even made sure to always carry a little something in her purse. I hadn't seen Carla in way too long.

"Working on anything important right now?" Suzie said.

Up ahead, Guy was changing lanes. What was this? We were starting to pass him? Following from in front was one of our specialties, but no way Suzie knew how. I barked, just once, the low, rumbly kind.

"Oops," said Suzie. She took her foot off that gas. We settled back to where we were supposed to be.

". . . sewer extension hearing," Carla was saying, "plus the strippers at the Lion's Den just went on strike—Mike wants to slide over there and take some pictures."

"I'll bet he does," Suzie said. "I need anything you can dig up on Wenders Associates in the Northwest Valley."

"Call you back." *Click.*

Digging was about to happen? I liked Carla more and more.

Not long after that, Guy slowed down and took the next ramp. We took it, too, following way too close, in my opinion, but Guy was still on the phone, his shoulders hunched in an intense kind of way. He led us past a golf course, spray from the sprinklers sparkling in the moonlight, and through a gate and down a long cobblestone lane with palm trees and flowers beds on both sides. Hey! I knew where we were.

"Rancho Grande," Suzie said. "Remember, Chet?"

Of course I remembered. Rancho Grande, oldest hotel in the Valley. We'd come here for a drink in the gardens out back, me, Bernie, Suzie, and not so long ago. The bill turned out to be a bit of a surprise for Bernie, and then came another surprise, some credit card problem, but everything turned out great, and the homemade potato chips, so crispy, were the best I'd ever tasted.

Rancho Grande wasn't one of those tall hotels you see downtown; instead it spread out wide in both directions in kind of U-shaped wings, U-shape being something I've learned from U-turns, of which I'd seen plenty, often at high speeds. Humans have invented a lot of things, but the car was the best, nothing else even close. Guy followed one of Rancho Grande's wings to the end, parked, glanced around—we'd come to a full stop, lights out, just as though Bernie'd been behind the wheel—and walked away on a gravel path that led to the other side of the hotel, a path I'd been on myself at one point on that visit with Bernie and Suzie, a brief interruption concerning a rabbit who'd hopped onto the grounds without warning, maybe startling me out of my best behavior.

Suzie parked, leaving plenty of distance between the Beetle and the Mercedes. We were getting out of the car when Suzie's phone buzzed.

"Hey, Carla." Suzie listened for a moment or two and then said, "Investor? What does that mean?"

On the other end, I heard Carla say, "Not sure. But he's got a record."

"What for?"

"DA initially charged him with money laundering, but it got pled down."

"Yeah?" said Suzie. "Any details?"

If there were, I missed them, but it didn't matter: money laundering was a complete mystery. We'd worked some money-laundering cases, me and Bernie, and I'd been pretty hopeful the first few times—I knew laundry very well, of course—but no laundry ever turned up, and I'd sniffed for it diligently.

Suzie clicked off. "Let's see what's what," she said.

That was more like it. We crossed the parking lot, passed the Mercedes, and moved onto the gravel path. I picked up Guy's scent, even the bloody bandage part. Some thought about that bandage and laundry started taking shape in my mind and then collapsed, kind of like a bridge in a war movie Bernie and I liked, name escaping me at the moment.

We came to the back part of Rancho Grande, a huge expanse of lawn and flowers and more palm trees—with a tall fountain in the center, a fountain I knew I had to stay out of no matter what—and far in the distance the tennis courts, lit for night play. Tiny players made tiny jerky movements, but it was too far away to see the ball, the most interesting thing about tennis by far. I took a step or two that way, then remembered myself.

Suzie was scanning the back of the hotel—fire pit, patio, bar, restaurant, piano player. "Don't see him," she said. "Where'd he go?"

Actually, toward the tennis courts. I led Suzie down a path that went by sitting areas here and there, people having drinks at a few of them, but most unoccupied. Not far from the fountain, Guy had left the path and veered onto the lawn, which sloped down to a garden of tall cactuses—an unlit garden, but that didn't keep me from seeing two men seated at a small round table. I smelled cigar smoke and went still.

"What, Chet?" Suzie said, squinting into the darkness in not quite the right direction; but at least speaking in a low voice. At that moment a cloud passed over the moon and the night got even darker. "Can't see a thing," Suzie said.

I led her in a long circle that brought us to the cactus garden from the other end. We came up between two big close-together cactuses—a tall flat spiky one, surfboard-shaped; the other barrel-shaped and even taller. I got down low, flat on my belly—Suzie getting the idea right away and doing the same—and peered through the narrow gap.

Two shadowy men, sitting silent at the table. Then came the orange glow of a cigar tip heating up, and in that glow I saw: Guy Wenders, a glass in his hand and a worried look on his face; and the cigar smoker, also with a glass in his hand but not looking at all worried: Judge Stringer. A funny old coot, Sheriff Laidlaw had called him. I didn't see it.

Judge Stringer sipped from his glass, ice cubes clinking. "Fine hotel," he said. "An institution. You realize that every president since TR has stayed here, with the single exception of the present occupant? What do you think that means, Guy?"

"How the hell would I know?" Guy said. The cigar glow faded and their faces went dark. I was aware of Suzie feeling around in her bag. Was she carrying? That would have been a big surprise.

"Not a student of history?" the judge said. Guy didn't reply. "In that we differ," the judge said. "I find the study of history infinitely rewarding. Here are just two things I've learned. First: history only moves in one direction. Second: once it gets started, it has no brakes."

"For Christ sake," Guy said. "Give it to me in plain English."

The cigar glowed again. Guy looked more worried than before; the judge looked like he was enjoying himself. "What happened to your hand?" he said.

Guy stuck his bandaged hand under the table, out of sight.

"Hope it's one of those you-should-see-the-other-guy situations," the judge said. Hey! Was he talking about seeing me? No way was I letting myself get seen now. This kind of close-up surveillance didn't work if you got seen: that was basic.

Guy said nothing. He picked up his drink and took a big swallow. I could hear it going down his throat.

"You're a tough customer," the judge said. "Still remember how you played football, boom boom boom. You could hear those hits in the parking lot."

"That was a long time ago," Guy said.

"But it made an impression, that's the point," the judge said. "Best damn football player ever come out of the county, full ride with the Buffaloes—made us all proud." The judge smoked some more, blew out a thick stream of smoke that glowed orange and then vanished, but my mind was on buffaloes. If they were in the picture, the case was getting away from us and fast.

"I just need a little more time," Guy said.

"Not happy to hear that," the judge said. "I'm more in the mood for good news."

"I can give you ten grand," Guy said.

"I hear that right? T-e-n?" The judge tapped his cigar. A fiery little cylinder fell to the ground, and in the momentary light I saw he had a gun in his lap, under the table. "I hope you don't think that's the number that'll make me happy."

"I've got it on me," Guy said.

"Cash?"

"Cash."

The judge sighed. "Kind of defeats the purpose, doesn't it?"

"You want it or not?" Guy said.

"Really want to be taking that tone with me?" the judge said. "Under the circumstances?"

Guy was silent.

"There's an age-old lesson here," the judge said. "A nice set of folks works up a nice little business and then one of 'em gets greedy and screws it all up for everybody."

"I was never going to actually keep all—"

"Don't want to hear it," said the judge, his voice rising over Guy's. "Let's have what you got."

"Meaning this is over?" Guy said.

"Over?" said the judge. "Over is when we're made whole."

"You will be," Guy said. "For Christ sake, why wouldn't I do that, Judge? But it's all getting out of control."

"My worry, not yours," the judge said. "And I'll accept your partial payment."

The moon came out again and things brightened up, but in

a strange way, making it almost like I was looking at a photograph. A very clear photograph, clear enough to show the sweat on Guy's face, even though the Rancho Grande grounds had to be the coolest place in the Valley; the wad of cash he was holding out; the judge, cigar, down to a stub, in his mouth, reaching with one hand for the money; and the gun, under the table in his other hand. Suzie must have seen the gun: I heard a quick little intake of breath.

The judge paused, then looked over in our direction. His hearing was good—especially for a human—but not his night vision. He turned away, took the money, and pocketed it.

"Aren't you going to count it?" Guy said.

"I trust you," the judge said. "Trust you now, if you see what I mean. And as long as you've absorbed this lesson, I'll be trusting you into the long and prosperous future."

Guy gave him a hard look, but maybe the judge didn't see it, on account of the moon getting covered up again.

"How about we drink to that, Guy? The future."

They clinked glasses. Guy downed what was left of his and rose. "I'll be in touch," he said.

"I know," said the judge.

Guy moved away, stepped around a saguaro, not a big one, and headed toward the hotel. The judge sat quietly for a little while. Then I heard a sound coming from him, kind of rustling or riffling. He took one last puff on his cigar and in that last glow I saw he was counting the money.

TWENTY-FIVE

The judge dropped the cigar butt onto the crushed-stone floor of the cactus garden and ground it under his heel. Then he rose with a little grunt, his knees creaking as human knees sometimes did, especially old ones, and walked away in the direction of the tennis courts. Or not quite: off to the side of the courts lay a small parking lot, and the judge had turned that way.

"Who do we follow?" Suzie said. "Guy? This supposed judge, assuming Judge isn't his name? None of the above?"

I knew a tricky question when I heard one, waited for Suzie to come up with an answer.

"Did you see that gun, Chet? He was ready to blow Guy away, unless . . . unless he didn't get the ten K? Or was it something else? Guy has a gun, too, as we well know. Did he have it on him? Was he ready to do some shooting of his own?"

More tricky questions, not a good sign in my experience. Once we worked a case so tricky that Bernie lost his temper and ended up locking all these dudes into a small room until it got sorted out. The smells in that room when it was over: one of my favorite memories.

"Or," said Suzie, "should we back up a bit, maybe hunt down . . ." She went silent, but I was already on board. Was hunting ever the wrong move?

Back in the Beetle, back in Anya's neighborhood, back on her street, parked in our old spot across from her house. Was this part of hunting?

"Why do I think Guy won't be here?" Suzie said.

Maybe because no lights were showing in the house? I couldn't come up with another reason. And it turned out to be one of those nice times when I didn't even have to, because almost right away a small sedan went past us and turned into Anya's driveway. The driver's door opened and Anya got out.

"Anya, maybe?" Suzie said. Her eyes narrowed. "The little curvy type, huh?"

Couldn't get much past Suzie. She herself was not the little curvy type. She wasn't without curves, not at all, but she was taller than Anya, more the coltish type. The coltish type: that was what Leda had said to Bernie, after meeting Suzie for the first time. "The coltish type, Bernie? I'm surprised." The whole thing was confusing to me, since I was pretty sure that colts were a kind of horse. Bernie had looked a bit confused himself; we're a lot alike in some ways, me and Bernie, don't forget that.

Anya walked toward the front door of her house. Suzie got out of the car. I got out, too, on her side and possibly a little ahead of her, and we started across the street.

"Excuse me," Suzie called.

Anya wheeled around, startled.

"Anya Vereen?" Suzie said.

Anya put her hand to her chest. "Who are you?" she said. She did something with her keys and the light over the front door flashed on. A bad mistake: you never lit yourself up in a night-time situation. That was basic. On the other hand, as humans say—and once at a bar Bernie made the point that if humans had only one hand they'd think a lot differently, but no one seemed interested, except me, of course—we hadn't come to take Anya down. Or had we?

"How do you know my name?" Anya said.

We were in her driveway now. "It's one of those long stories," said Suzie.

"What the hell are you—" Anya began, and then she noticed me. "Is that Chet?"

Who else? Of course it was me. I trotted over to Anya, gave her a nice greeting.

"Easy, easy," she said. She looked up at Suzie, now beside us. "How did you get him?"

Suzie waved that question away, one of my favorite human gestures. "Where's Bernie?" she said.

"Um," said Anya, looking down at the ground. "He's, ah, still . . . up there. But who—"

"Doing what?" said Suzie. "I understood you hired him for bodyguard duty."

Anya nodded.

"Bodyguarding you, specifically?" Suzie said. She pointed her finger at Anya; the human finger pointing like that makes me think of a gun every time.

Anya nodded again.

"And here you are, back in the Valley, and he's not."

"It got more complicated," Anya said. "Are you, like, his girl-friend or something?"

"Why do you ask?" Suzie said, her voice sharpening, and her posture sharpening, too, if that made any sense.

"Didn't mean to pry," Anya said. "But if he is your boyfriend, you're a lucky girl."

Suzie gave Anya a long look, and then nodded herself, a very small, quick nod, there and gone. "How about we move this discussion inside?" she said.

Sometimes humans want to say no—you can see it on their faces—but they don't, no idea why. This was one of those.

Inside Anya's house, I picked up Devin's scent right away, but it was old and weak. A lot of talk got going around the kitchen table, not always easy to follow. And maybe not easy for the humans either, at least not for Anya, because she was saying, ". . . and they've suspended the search, I'm not sure why—I'm so confused." Tears rose up in her eyes but didn't spill over.

Suzie wasn't at all teary. "But Bernie must have explained the situation," she said. "What did he say?"

"About what?" Anya said.

"Why they suspended the search, what he thinks is going on, the whole story," Suzie said. "And didn't he know Chet was missing? What's going on with that?"

"We, uh, didn't discuss any of those things," Anya said.

"What about Chet?"

Anya bit her lip; I always watched for that one. "The paper seemed, you know, legitimate."

"Anya? What the hell are you talking about?"

Anya started crying. She put her face in her hands and ramped up to the sobbing stage. That often upsets me, but it didn't this time, on account of my noticing how hard Suzie's face was. She and I were together on this, and that was what I had to keep in mind; and besides, at that moment, there wasn't room for more.

Suzie let Anya cry for a moment or two. When she spoke, she didn't say "there, there," or any of that, and her voice was as hard as her face. "What goddamn paper?" she said.

"The one that Georgie person showed me," Anya sobbed behind her hands.

"Georgie Malhouf?"

Anya nodded, got the sobbing under control but still kept her hands over her face. "And he called him the Chetster."

The Chetster? I never wanted to hear that again.

"What about this paper?" Suzie said.

"I hope I didn't do anything wrong," said Anya.

Suzie's voice rose. "What about the paper?"

"Oh, God. It said that if anything happened to Bernie—"

Suzie reached across the table, grabbed Anya's hands, and tore them away from her face. And now Suzie's voice filled the room. "Has something happened to Bernie?"

Anya's features got all twisted up. "I'm not supposed to say—" and then the sobbing took over again.

Suzie rose and slapped Anya across the face, pretty hard. That shocked me, but in a good way, I admit it. It shocked Anya, too. The waterworks dried up just like that. She gazed open-mouthed at Suzie.

"He found this body in a mine way up there," Anya said. "A dead body."

"I get it. Go on."

"It was the trip guide—from when Devin got lost. And they arrested him."

"They arrested Bernie?"

Suzie was leaning over Anya now, so close their faces were almost touching.

"For murder," Anya said. She was afraid of Suzie: I could see it and smell it. "But I'm not supposed to say," Anya went on quickly. "So please—"

"You're saying, Anya, and that's that. Who told you not to talk?"

"The judge. At first, I thought he was horrible—the way he looked at me—but I think he's really on Bernie's side. Simpatico— that was the word he used. He met me before I left and said if we just let the excitement die down, he'd be inclined to set a low bail and we can work from there. He said 'we,' so—"

"Judge?" said Suzie. "What's his name?"

"I'm not sure."

"Describe him."

"Sort of old. Dresses western—cowboy boots, string tie, that look. Oh, yeah—and he smokes these smelly cigars all the time."

Suzie took out a device, the palm-sized kind. She held it up, pressed a button. And then we heard:

"Not a student of history? In that we differ. I find the study of history infinitely rewarding. Here are just two things I've learned. First: history only moves in one direction. Second: once it gets started, it has no brakes."

Suzie hit the button again and the device went silent.

"That's him," said Anya.

"Sound simpatico to you?"

"I don't know, maybe not. But where did you get that record- ing? I don't understand."

"I made it," Suzie said. "An hour ago at the most." She pressed the button. And now:

"For Christ sake. Give it to me in plain English."

Suzie clicked it off. Meanwhile, I was watching Anya's face lose all its color. Her skin turned an unhuman shade of whitest white; even her blue eyes suddenly seemed white. "That's—" For a moment she couldn't get her breath, as though she'd been running a long race. "That's Guy. My ex." She raised her hands palms out, shook her head from side to side. I'd seen that one more than once in my career: it meant being out of ideas.

"He had a meeting with your judge friend tonight, on the grounds of Rancho Grande," Suzie said. "The meeting seemed to be mostly about money. Your ex handed over ten thousand dollars, but the judge wanted more, much more."

"I'm not following this at all," Anya said. "Guy doesn't have ten grand—he's a year behind on child support."

"The judge counted it," Suzie said. "I trust him on that."

"But—but what's going on? How come you were even there in the first place?"

"We—meaning Chet and I—followed Guy from here to Rancho Grande."

Anya's voice shrank down to something very small. "Guy was here at the house?"

"In, actually," Suzie said.

"Inside?"

Suzie nodded.

"But how? I changed the locks, and, and . . ." Anya rose very slowly and walked down a hall off the kitchen. We followed her. She led us to the back door. It was partway open, hanging from one hinge, and a big chunk of the doorjamb was missing.

"Oh, my God," Anya said. She gazed at the broken door and then all at once whirled around, so abruptly I couldn't help barking. Anya pushed past us and ran back down the hall, darting into a room.

We went after her. The room turned out to be a bedroom: pink sheets on the bed; TV with a stack of DVDs beside it; a little table with one of those mirrors with lights for putting on makeup. A typical sort of woman's bedroom. Not so typical was the wall safe, but you do see them sometimes, although not like this one. The door was open and hanging in a lopsided way that reminded me of the back door of the house. Anya stood before it, mouth and eyes wide open. I picked up that dynamite smell—we'd spent a whole morning on it at K-9 school—much more obvious now.

"Goddamn it," Anya said. She smacked that hanging safe door real hard. It banged against the wall and fell clanging to the floor.

"The ten grand?" Suzie said.

"Twelve," Anya said, her voice harsh, like metal things were in her throat. "The bastard skimmed two. He's the skimming champion of the fucking western world." She staggered a bit, like she was about to fall, then sat heavily on the bed. "What am I going to do?"

"How about leveling with me, for starters?" Suzie said.

"What do you mean?" said Anya. "Are you accusing me of something?"

"Not yet."

"Not yet? I thought you were on my side."

"What side is that?"

"They've suspended the search for my son. Do you know how that feels?"

Suzie gazed at Anya. "I'm on Bernie's side," she said. "Got it?"

Anya tried to meet Suzie's gaze, gave up almost right away.

"Let's start with the cash," Suzie said. "Why did you have so much lying around?"

"It wasn't lying around."

"Or earning interest," Suzie said. "What do you do for a living?"

"I'm an accountant by training," Anya said.

"Where do you work?"

"I don't see why I have to answer all these questions," Anya said. "I feel like you're attacking me."

"Here's some advice I learned from Bernie," Suzie said. "In a situation where everyone's going to cave eventually, you want to be first."

Hey! Suzie had a good memory. I'd forgotten that one completely.

"Are you a detective, too?" Anya said.

"Something much worse," said Suzie.

"I believe it," Anya said. "You're not nearly as nice as he is."

"That's the truest thing you've said so far," Suzie said. "Try to keep it up. Where do you work?"

"Why is it important?"

"I need facts."

"And I need to hold on to my crummy job."

"I'm not looking to get you in trouble."

Anya took a deep breath. "E-Z Tax," she said. "It's one of those strip mall tax places. We have the worst software in the business."

"Why aren't you someplace better?"

Anya shrugged.

"Did it have anything to do with Guy's money-laundering bust?"

Anya made a little gasping sound. "How do you know about that?"

"Isn't it a matter of public record?" Suzie said.

"But I wasn't involved, and the DA believed me."

"Cedric Booker?"

"Christ," said Anya. "You know him?"

"Yes," Suzie said. "But if you stick to the truth, I'll have no reason to bring him in on this."

And then came some more back-and-forth, but my mind was stuck on Cedric Booker, the tallest human I'd ever seen. Could have gone to the NBA, Bernie said, but he never learned to play with his back to the basket. That back-to-the-basket thing was a puzzle to me. I puzzled over it again, and when I'd had enough of that, Anya was saying,

". . . Guy's plea bargain, which was when I left him, but everything was all commingled, so the IRS cleans out any bank accounts, which is why—"

"—you keep cash in the safe."

Anya nodded. "Anything else?" she said.

Suzie thought for a moment or two. "Just the Buffaloes," she said.

"The Buffaloes?"

"Didn't Guy play college football?"

"I didn't know him then," Anya said. "Something happened and he lost his scholarship. No surprise in hindsight." She gazed at the open safe. "There was a boy who wanted to marry me in those days. I didn't think he was exciting enough." Anya shook her head. "I heard he ended up in Hong Kong, making millions."

Suzie handed Anya her card. "If you need to get in touch with me."

Anya checked the card. "You're a reporter?"

"Not at the moment," Suzie said. "Come on, Chet."

"Where are you going?" Anya said.

Suzie started to say something, quickly cut herself off. "Get that door fixed tomorrow," she said. "And sleep somewhere else tonight."

TWENTY-SIX

We rode through the night, Suzie behind the wheel, me in the shotgun seat. Suzie drove differently than Bernie—not as fast, both hands on the wheel—and the Beetle didn't have that—how would you describe it? growl?—yes, that deep growl of the Porsche, that said *Clear the track, amigo, here we come.*

"Chet? What are you growling about?"

Uh-oh. That was me? I got a grip. Were we on the job? It kind of had that feel, except for one big thing. No Bernie. No Bernie, no Bernie went round and round in my mind.

"I don't trust her at all," Suzie said after a while.

Who was she talking about? I waited to find out.

"But it's a side issue. Got to keep our eye on the ball."

That made total sense to me. Suzie was a fine thinker, although probably not in Bernie's class. The only ball around was a tennis ball under my seat. I could smell it, also smell that I'd played with it before, the only problem being that the Beetle was on the small side, with not much room for me to twist around and get my paws—

"Chet? What are you doing?"

Jammed way in there, so frustrating. I got back up on the seat, alert and professional. Outside we were leaving the freeway, turning onto two-lane blacktop, rising up into some hills; the air got fresher and cooler. A sign flashed by.

"State line," Suzie said.

I remembered that from before, also remembered this air, kind of nice except there not being quite enough in every breath. We were going to Bernie. I barked, found I was angry, and barked again.

Suzie glanced over at me. "Exactly," she said. She got on the phone. "Carla? I need a favor. Home address for a Judge Stringer, probably in the same county as a summer camp, Big Bear Wilderness, I think it's called." She waited, and while she waited started up with that finger-drumming again, this time on the steering wheel. I was liking Suzie more and more. She listened, said, "Got it, thanks. I owe you." She clicked off.

I sat straight up, watching the traffic coming and going, not much in either direction. I couldn't wait to get there, wherever we were headed, and not being able to wait is always hard for me, which was probably why I gnawed at my shoulder a bit. I tried sticking my tongue way, way out and that helped a little, but not for long.

After a while we entered a canyon with steep rocky slopes rising high above, the moonlight glittering on flat surfaces here and there, turning them the color of bone. This was the road to the camp. We were close. Knowing that made the can't-wait feeling even stronger. I started panting.

Suzie glanced over. "Need a pit stop?"

No, no, Suzie, just floor it! I stopped panting, tried licking my face.

Suzie peered into the night. No traffic at all now, and we'd lost the moon behind the mountaintops. "We're looking for . . ." she began, and then: "There it is." We came to a fork. "Why does Bernie always get such a kick out of that Yogi Berra thing?" Suzie said, and I remembered this fork from the last time, with Ranger Rob at the wheel. Much better to be with Suzie. She took the turn and we zigzagged down to the town, almost completely dark, at the bottom of a valley.

"Big Bear, county seat," Suzie said. "All the good burghers asleep in their beds."

Burgers: yes to that—who would ever say no?—but Bernie came first.

We drove down the main drag, the diner, bars, stores, all shut up for the night.

"Goddamn one-horse town," Suzie said, looking around.

That was news, and not good. I saw no horse, but I trusted Suzie. Horses had been nothing but trouble in my career, prima donnas, each and every one.

We went past the brick office building with the blue light hanging in front. I got angry again—I seemed to have so much anger in me these days, not like me at all, and I didn't feel good about it—and did some more barking.

"Easy, Chet," Suzie said. "Everything's okay."

Nice to hear, but how was that possible?

We came to the end of the main drag and Suzie squinted at the sign by the crossing street. "Oro Road," she said. "Here we go."

Oro Road took us out of town and along a mountain ridge with views of the town and more mountains in the distance. We could see the moon again, very bright. It illuminated two gate posts up ahead with a wagon wheel over the top. Suzie slowed down, eyes on a pattern of red reflectors on one of the posts.

"Nine," she said. "My lucky number."

Bernie had a lucky number, too, but I couldn't remember what it was. I stopped at two when it came to numbers, and that was plenty.

Suzie drove between the gate posts. "Lights on or off?" she said. Made no difference to me. Suzie left them on.

We followed a pebbly lane that curved around a huge rock and ended in front of a house made of logs, but very fancy, with tall windows, balconies, and two stone chimneys.

"My, my," Suzie said, parking behind a big and shiny SUV. "Judging turns out to be lucrative."

We got out of the Beetle and walked to the front door, a thick-looking wooden door with a horseshoe knocker. I already knew horses were somehow in the case, so the horseshoe knocker made sense, but why horses wore shoes was something I'd never understood.

The house was quiet. Suzie took a deep breath, raised the knocker, and brought it down hard. Outdoor lights flashed on all over the place. Never get lit up in the darkness, but what could we do? I looked at Suzie. She raised the knocker again and banged it against the door even harder. We could work together, me and Suzie.

I heard footsteps somewhere back in the house. They got louder: a woman—I could smell her—and not young. From behind the door, she said, "Who is it?" in a high, shaky voice.

"Sorry to bother you at this hour," Suzie said. "We're looking for Judge Stringer. It's urgent."

"But who is this?" the woman said, her voice getting even higher and shakier.

We knock on many doors at the Little Detective Agency and it's always a tricky moment when they want to know who's there.

One favorite of Bernie's is that they've won a prize; and then it turns out to be breaking rocks in the hot sun!

Suzie's eyes shifted. "We're friends of Guy Wenders's."

"Guy Wenders? But he moved away years ago."

"Nevertheless," Suzie said.

There was a long silence.

"My husband is asleep," the woman said.

"He'd want you to wake him," said Suzie.

Another silence, but not as long. Then the woman went padding away—*pad pad pad*—bare feet on a tile floor.

Suzie looked at me. I looked at her. "Don't let me screw this up," she said at the very moment that voices started murmuring somewhere in the house, costing me the chance to hear what it was about, so maybe a screwing-up just from talking about screwing up—wow! What a lot of thinking. And what it did it matter? Suzie was a gem.

Pad pad pad. Approaching footsteps, but a man's this time, and he was wearing slippers.

"Who are you?" he called.

"Open up, Judge," said Suzie.

"I asked you a question."

Suzie was silent. So was the judge. All this silence weighed on me in a way that's hard to explain. I just knew I had to get rid of it. I barked. Once was enough; I felt better right away.

A bit more silence, but it wasn't the same. There's a silence when nothing's going on, and then there's a silence when someone's having thoughts, very different, almost not a silence at all. This was that kind. The door opened.

Judge Stringer peered out. He wore a purple robe over pajamas, and slippers with rawhide laces, a distraction I knew I had to ignore, and his white hair, of which he had lots, was sticking up all over the place. His gaze went to me and widened immediately.

"What the hell?" he said. The judge's breath wafted my way in an invisible little stream: whiskey, tomato sauce, and cigar smoke, very, very stale, all the appeal of cigar smell lost. He turned to Suzie. "Who are you? Where do you get off, waking my house at this ungodly hour?"

From somewhere out of sight came the woman's voice.

"What's going on, Clarence? Is something wrong?"

"Everything's fine, Shirley," the judge said, not turning, his eyes glued on us. "Go to bed."

"Everything's not fine, Clarence," Suzie said.

He lowered his voice, down close to a hissing sound; I don't like that in a human—or in a snake, for that matter, but a snake can't help it. "What do you want?"

"To make things a little less ungodly," Suzie said. "Where's a good place to talk?"

Before the judge could answer, Shirley spoke again, "Did I hear a dog, Clarence? I don't want a dog in the house."

Grabbing an old lady by the pant leg? That wasn't going to happen, but my mind was now at rest on the question of who the bad guys were.

"Tell her Chet's an old friend," Suzie said.

Little pink spots appeared on the judge's face. "I don't understand a word you're saying."

Suzie shook her head. "You know him—that was obvious. And Chet sure as hell knows you."

Shirley called out once more: "Clarence?" She was getting on my nerves.

"If you like, we can have this conversation right here," Suzie said. "On the assumption that you and your wife share all aspects of your lives."

All those pink spots on Judge Stringer's face joined together and he turned red. Then he made a quick little motion for us to come in.

"Clarence?"

The judge called over his shoulder. "Go to bed, goddamn it."

Somewhere back in the house a door slammed. We followed the judge down a long hall lined with big paintings of cowboys and Indians, and into an office with wood-paneled walls, a big dark wooden desk, brass-studded leather chairs, and a rack full of guns. I stood by that. The judge sat behind the desk. Suzie perched on a corner of the desk. The judge didn't like that—you could tell by the curl of his lips.

"We can talk in here," the judge said. "So talk."

Suzie took out her device. "Do you have one of these?" she said. Her voice sounded good, nice and even, but she was scared. I could smell it. The judge was scared, too. So the smell of fear spread through the room. I myself couldn't think of anything to be scared of at the moment.

"They come in handy," Suzie said. The judge's eyes were locked on the device. Suzie pressed the button.

Then came Guy's voice, very clear. *"I just need a little more time."*

"Loud enough?" said Suzie. "Or do you want me to turn it up?"

The judge didn't answer. He was gripping the desk top with both hands, as though the whole room was suddenly picking up speed. His own voice was now coming out of the machine; it actually sounded a little better that way.

"Not happy to hear that. I'm more in the mood for good news."

"I can give you ten grand."

"I hear that right? T-e-n? I hope you don't think that's the number that'll make me happy."

"I've got it on me."

"Cash?"

"Cash."

"Kind of defeats the purpose, doesn't it?"

"You want it or not?"

"Really want to be taking that tone with me? Under the circumstances? There's an age-old lesson here. A nice set of folks works up a nice little business and then one of 'em gets greedy and screws it all up for everybody."

"I was never going to actually keep all—"

"Don't want to hear it. Let's have what you got."

"Meaning this is over?"

"Over? Over is when we're made whole."

"You will be. For Christ sake, why wouldn't I do that, Judge? But it's all getting out of control."

"My worry, not yours. And I'll accept your partial payment."

"Aren't you going to count it?"

"I trust you. Trust you now, if you see what I mean. And as long as you've absorbed this lesson, I'll be trusting you into the long and prosperous future. How about we drink to that, Guy? The future."

Clink.

The redness had faded from Judge Stringer's face now, but it was shiny with sweat, even though the AC was keeping the big log house nice and cool. When he spoke, his voice was hoarse, like he'd been shouting for a long time. "Who are you? What do you want?"

"Who I am isn't important," Suzie said, "except for the fact that I'm the kind of person who would make sure that arrangements had already been made for the wide dissemination of this recording in the event I didn't return home safely."

What was all that? You tell me. But the judge seemed to get it: his face got sweatier and a little tic appeared in one of his eyelids. This wasn't the kind of tick you can take drops for, but no time to get into that now.

"As for what I want," Suzie said. "You have a bail hearing in a few hours. All you have to do to make this go away forever"—she held up the device—"is your job."

"My job?" said the judge.

"Making sure that justice happens," Suzie said. "Didn't that come up in law school?"

TWENTY-SEVEN

We drove back down Oro Road. The moment we lost sight of the judge's big log house, Suzie reached over with one arm, pulled me close, and said, "Yes!" And then, "Whew," and "Wowee!" I broke free—getting held real tight can be nice, but in very short bursts—and licked the side of her face, or maybe the back of her head, on account of the way the Beetle was swerving a bit.

We turned onto the main drag. "Never been so scared in my whole life," Suzie said. Then she sniffed under one of her arms. Was that fascinating or what? Suzie was full of surprises, all good. She glanced to the side. "There's a hotel, but somehow I don't think . . ." We kept going. As we passed the office building with the blue light hanging over the door, another light went on inside. "I slept in a car once, back in high school," Suzie said. "Supposed boyfriend. What the hell was I doing?"

Couldn't help her with that, high school being a bit of a puzzle to me. We'd worked a case once, me and Bernie—something about prom limo scams, never clear in my mind—and I'd bumped up against high school kids. They weren't happy. How come? College kids were another story.

We drove out of town, headed up the road to the camp, soon came to a lookout with a couple of benches. "How's this?" said Suzie. She swung in, parked, switched off the engine. Then she switched it back on, turned the car around, and reparked, this time facing the road.

We got out, walked to the edge, and checked out the view, dark mountains rising against a dark sky.

"Thirsty?" Suzie said.

I was. She had a bottle of water in the car but no bowl. I sipped from her cupped hand. A car started up somewhere in the distance, and another.

"Better grab some shut-eye," Suzie said. She curled up on the backseat; I took the front. I was conscious of Suzie being restless and wide-awake, and then I wasn't.

"Eight fifty-five," said Suzie, checking her watch as we parked on the main drag. A nice morning, sunny and bright. She opened the door under the blue light and we went inside.

The first person we saw was Mack, leaning against a desk, belly hanging over his belt and nightstick hanging from it. The hair on my back rose up. Mack paused in midbite—he was eating a cupcake with sprinkles on top—and gave us a hard stare.

"Morning, Officer," Suzie said. "We're looking for the courtroom."

Mack pointed toward an elevator with the remains of his cupcake. We crossed the lobby and got to the elevator just as the door slid open. Claudie, an open box of cupcakes in his hand, started to step out, stopped when he saw me. We moved around him.

He got out, turning his head to watch us. Things seemed tense to me, but Suzie was cheerful. "Have a nice day," she said to Claudie as the door closed. Then came a thump. Had Claudie kicked the door? I wasn't sure. I didn't like elevators at any time. Suzie smiled at me and pressed a button. The elevator, small and old with lots of brass work and mirrored walls that had gone all milky so you couldn't really see yourself, shuddered and started going up.

"You're not a popular guy here, Chet," Suzie said. "Why is that?"

A complicated story, and some of the details were already unclear to me, kind of like those milky mirrors, but one thing I knew for sure: Bernie had been in this elevator, and not long ago.

The elevator shuddered again and stopped. The door opened and I saw we actually hadn't quite reached the floor, were about a half step short. "If I ever write this up," Suzie said, "that's where I'll start—this place isn't on the level."

What did that mean? No idea. We got off the elevator, found ourselves at the back of a courtroom. I'd been in courtrooms before, even been Exhibit A for my buddy Judge Jaramillo, down in the Valley, but never one this small. It had only two benches on either side of a narrow aisle, then two long desks, and in front of that and raised up on a dais another desk, at which Judge Stringer was sitting. He wore a black robe and looked real tired. At each of the two desks sat a group of two people, their backs to us. One of those people was Bernie. He was wearing an orange jumpsuit! This was the worst moment of my life.

Suzie put her hand on my neck, actually sort of around my collar. We took a seat—the only spectators—Suzie on the end of the bench, me in the aisle. It was kind of a nice Old West–type room—all the furniture polished dark wood with lots of curlicues, pictures of long-ago soldiers on the wall behind the judge. Bernie loved the Old West. That was my only thought and it made me feel a bit better. The judge checked his watch and rapped the gavel.

"Court is now in session," he said. "File number C-6319, bail hearing, the State versus Little."

A woman in a business suit at one of the tables—not the one where Bernie was sitting—rose and said, "Your Honor?"

Judge Stringer nodded.

"There's been a—" the woman began, then came to a halt. She glanced at the man beside her. He glanced at her and I saw who he was: Sheriff Laidlaw. The sheriff looked as tired as the judge, maybe more. He gave the woman an impatient kind of nod.

"The state wishes," said the woman, "to direct Your Honor's attention to a slight change in the supporting documentation concerning this hearing."

The judge nodded again. This was not a judge I was fond of, like Judge Jaramillo, but you had to give him some credit for being able to follow all this.

"Specifically, Your Honor," the woman went on, "the medical examiner, Dr. Laidlaw, has just this morning submitted a revised autopsy report, which, with permission, the state wishes to submit for the consideration of the court."

Judge Stringer motioned for her to come forward. She handed him some papers and returned to her seat. The judge put on glasses and spent some time with the papers. I watched Bernie's orange back. He was sitting up straight and motionless. I did the same.

The judge stopped reading, took off his glasses, arranged the papers in a neat little stack. Then, eyes straight ahead, looking at nobody, he said, "Case dismissed."

Meaning what, exactly? I felt Suzie's hand gripping my back in an excited sort of way, so it had to mean something. No one moved for a moment, and then the man next to Bernie rose—a young man, I saw as he turned slightly sideways, with not much happening in the way of a chin—and said, "Your Honor? You're dismissing the whole case against my client? Or does this ruling apply only to the terms of the bail, or—"

"Case dismissed," Judge Stringer repeated, this time banging down the gavel.

"But—" began the young man.

"Are you intending to file an opposing motion to the dismissal of the case against your client?" the judge said.

"No, sir, of course not, it's just that—"

"Then zip it, Counselor."

The young man shut his mouth and sat down heavily, as though his legs had gotten weak.

"This hearing is adjourned," the judge said. He turned to Bernie. "You—" he said. His voice shook a little, but he got it under control. "You are free to go. In the matter of the demise of Turk Rendell, the ME has returned a finding of death by suicide."

Suzie shot to her feet, face shining. Death by suicide: one of those human expressions that could fool you. It turned out to be a great thing.

Bernie rose. The judge left quickly through a small door behind the dais. The woman in the suit came down the aisle—a puzzled look on her face—and got in the elevator. That left the sheriff and Bernie alone up front. The sheriff approached Bernie. Bernie turned to him, raising his arms, and I saw he was cuffed. The sheriff took out a key and Bernie turned a little more, and that was when he saw us.

He looked a little better, both eyes nice and open, at least.

The expression on his face didn't change, but his eyes did, and in a beautiful way, hard to describe. He was happy to see me! And probably happy to see Suzie, too, no getting around that. She had her hand on my collar again, for some reason.

The sheriff unlocked Bernie's cuffs, then bent down—what was this? they'd shackled his legs?—and got those leg cuffs off him. A nice sight, the sheriff down at Bernie's feet, but Bernie wasn't taking it in; his eyes never left us.

The sheriff stood up, spoke to Bernie for a few moments in a low voice. All I heard for sure was: ". . . set foot in these parts ever again." Bernie gazed at the sheriff and didn't say a word. The sheriff handed him a plastic garbage bag and an envelope, mounted the dais, and went out the back door.

Then there was just us in the courtroom: me, Bernie, Suzie. We came together in the aisle—I got to Bernie first, Suzie somehow losing her grip on my collar—and we all hugged. Oh, the smell of Bernie, and the touch of his hand! Suzie ran her own hand over Bernie's poor face, very lightly.

"Good to see you," she said, her voice sort of low and thick.

Bernie kissed the top of her head. I rose up, and put my front paws on his shoulder, maybe getting between them. My tail had—what's that expression?—taken on a life of its own, although it sort of did have a life of its own anyway, so therefore . . . I didn't know, but Bernie handled the so therefores, and now he was back! How that eased my mind, I can't tell you.

Bernie opened the envelope, took out the keys to the Porsche, the ones with the seashell I found in San Diego on the ring. There was also a note. Bernie scanned it. "The car's in the county lot," he said. "Let's get out of here."

Good idea, but in that orange jumpsuit? The next thing I

knew, I was kind of clawing at the orange jumpsuit, the idea of ripping it to shreds suddenly very powerful in my mind, leaving no room for anything else.

"Hey, big guy," Bernie said. Then he laughed, just a little quiet laugh, but nice to hear. He opened up the plastic bag and there were his real clothes. Bernie changed on the spot. The big purple bruises on his chest and stomach: I didn't like those at all. Bernie left the orange jumpsuit on the judge's desk.

We walked to the Beetle.

"Want to drive?" Suzie said.

"Yeah," said Bernie. She gave him the keys. We got in the car—me maybe losing my concentration for a moment, because I ended up in the backseat—and headed out of town. Suzie started telling a long, complicated story. After a while I realized it was all about me, and Georgie Malhouf, and Anya, and Guy, and Rancho Grande and lots of other things. Bernie listened without making a sound. I didn't make a sound, either, but I stopped listening early on. Did Suzie get out her device at one point and play it for Bernie? Quite possibly.

Meanwhile, we followed the road toward the camp for a while, before turning onto a gravel track. It took us around the back side of a steep hill, and came to an end in a big dirt parking lot, no one around. On one side, by a gas pump, stood some big trucks, a front-end loader, a couple backhoes. On the other side was the Porsche, looking the way it always did, brown with yellow doors, very old, no top, bullet hole in the rear plate, Maxwell's Memphis Ribs bumper sticker; in short, it looked great. Bernie pulled in beside it, turned to Suzie, and finally spoke.

"Devin?" he said.

"They've suspended the search," said Suzie. "The whole thing stinks, doesn't it?"

Bernie nodded. Interesting, because I was detecting no strong smells whatsoever.

"How about we start with a quick visit to the camp?" he said.

"What about your promise to leave the county and never come back?" said Suzie.

"I didn't say when." Bernie smiled, but not a real one, more just showing teeth. I showed mine, too, even though no one was looking my way, stuck in the backseat. "You don't have to come," he said. "I already owe you more than—"

"Zip it, Counselor," said Suzie.

Bernie smiled again, this time a real one. He opened the door, put a foot outside, and then paused. I—starting to squeeze between the seats on the off-chance of getting out first—paused, too.

Bernie was gazing at the Porsche. "I've had kind of a crazy thought," he said. "Maybe a little paranoid."

Lost me there, but that new scent I was picking up from outside? Very faint, but it worried me a bit, and—

Bernie closed the door, stayed in the car. I sniffed the air. That new scent had faded almost to nothing, not enough for me to work with. I hated when that happened.

"What?" said Suzie.

He pointed at the Porsche with his chin. "An old model like that—no one's going to think it has a remote starter."

"I don't get it," Suzie said.

"But Nixon"—our car guy, Nixon Panero, also a former perp we'd put away, a story maybe for another time—"installed one for free last month. Probably wants something, but he'll let some time pass before asking—that's his way. Point is"—Bernie held up the Porsche keys—"we do have a remote starter."

"So?" said Suzie.

Bernie turned the Beetle around, drove back across the parking lot to the other side. We got out.

"Stand over here," Bernie said. We moved behind a backhoe.

"What's going on?" Suzie said.

"I'm just being a wuss," Bernie said.

Bernie a wuss? That was a good one.

He pointed the key ring in the direction of the Porsche and pressed some kind of button. Then came a flash from under the Porsche's hood, a *BOOM*, a fireball, and smithereens.

TWENTY-EIGHT

After that came the most silent silence I've ever known. Then Suzie said, "Got your gun?"

"Couldn't be located, according to the sheriff," Bernie said.

Suzie gazed at where the Porsche had been. "He turns out to be a belt-and-suspenders guy," she said.

Bernie laughed. Belt and suspenders? I didn't worry about the meaning of that, not for a moment. For one thing, I was too busy worrying about the Porsche. I loved that Porsche—and I'd loved the Porsche before it, the one that had gone shooting off a cliff. What was life without a cool ride?

Bernie stopped laughing, touched Suzie's shoulder. "This isn't a good place for you right now," he said.

"Meaning?"

"How about heading home?"

Suzie shrugged herself out from under his hand. "You can if you want. I'm not walking away from a story like this."

Bernie gave her a long look—not hard, not at all, just long. "There's a lot about journalism I don't understand," he said.

"But your job makes perfect sense," said Suzie.

Of course it did: Suzie didn't miss a beat, whatever that happened to be; different from a beat-down—I was pretty sure of that. What made more sense than rounding up perps? We had the best job in the world, me and Bernie. No worries at all on that score. But I was worried about something. What was it, again? Oh, yeah, the Porsche. Just as I remembered that, it was time to get in the Beetle, and in the . . . well, not struggle, really, more like a friendly contest, to see who would sit where—and amazingly I again found myself in the backseat!—I forgot whatever it was once more.

Ranger Rob was in his office, typing on his laptop, door open. We went in, just as he pressed a button and a printer in the corner started whirring. He looked up and saw us.

Sometimes with humans you get to see the face behind the face. Take Bernie, for example: when we're alone that's the only face I ever see. Back to Ranger Rob: his normal face, the one I'd seen before, was the kind of good-buddy, weather-beaten face you saw a lot, roaming around the West the way Bernie and I did. Now, for just an instant, like a camera had flashed at him in a dark room, out came the face behind the face of Ranger Rob. Whew! Way too complicated, and good buddy returned fast, but underneath was an unhappy dude—surprised, scared, even a little panicky. Humans were at their very worst when they got panicky. Take the time when that pet-store-robbing perp, name escaping me at the moment, thought the best way to get the python off his leg was to point his gun down there and pull the trigger. I got ready for anything.

"Well, hello," said Ranger Rob. He rose, a little abruptly, his chair rolling away from him. "Well, hello, there. Take a seat.

Caught me all on my lonesome. Annual Rodeo Day—bussed everyone over to Durango. But still, this is, uh, a nice surprise."

"Is it?" Bernie said.

"Of course, I heard the good news—your exoneration, and all, and believe me I never even dreamed for a second that you, uh . . . but I just didn't think I'd be seeing you so soon, is all. Have the pleasure, I meant to . . ."

Bernie and Suzie sat on chairs opposite the desk. I stood between them. From a standing position to leaping across that desk would take no time at all.

"My friend, Suzie Sanchez," Bernie said.

"Pleased to meet you, miss, ah, ma'am," said Ranger Rob.

"I'm also a reporter for the *Valley Tribune*," Suzie said.

"Oh," said Ranger Rob.

You heard "oh" like that in this business from time to time, almost always a sign that things were going well. Ranger Rob pulled up his chair and sat down carefully, like maybe he'd stopped trusting it. His gaze went to Bernie's face then quickly away. The worst bruise, the one around the eye, was starting to turn yellow.

"Some, ah, ice for that?" said Ranger Rob.

"I'm fine, thanks," Bernie said. "You must have just found out about the hearing."

"News travels fast up here."

"Have you had time to think about the medical examiner's finding?"

"What aspect of it, exactly?"

"The suicide aspect."

Ranger Rob rubbed his hands together. They were on the small side for a guy his size. "Frankly, I was taken aback. But as for what goes on inside a man, can we ever really know?"

Bernie glanced at me, not sure why. Then he turned to Ranger Rob. "Sometimes we can," he said. Ranger Rob's eyes shifted. "But leaving aside philosophical questions for the moment," Bernie went on, "I think the ME—what's his name again?"

"Doc Laidlaw," said Ranger Rob.

"Blood relation of the sheriff?"

"Great-uncle, I believe."

Bernie smiled, just a small quick one. I loved to see him enjoying himself. "Doc Laidlaw," he continued, "would have been better advised to have ruled it death by accident."

Ranger Rob shook his head, kind of like he was getting buzzed by insects, which he wasn't because I'd have heard them, even the smallest. "Lost me," he said.

"What's certain," Bernie said, "is that Turk died of a gunshot wound. I saw it myself. What I didn't see was a gun. That's rare in gun-suicide cases, for obvious reasons." I tried to think of one and couldn't, but I didn't spend much time on it. "Whereas it's possible to imagine Turk in the mine, gun in hand, maybe because he hears a sound of some kind, and all of a sudden the roof falls in, the gun goes off at the worst possible angle, and then it gets buried under tons of rock, lost forever." Bernie glanced at Suzie. "Can you imagine that?" he said.

"Only if I close my eyes real tight," said Suzie.

"I think I see what you're saying," Ranger Rob said.

"I'll spell it out," said Bernie. "Your employee, Turk Rendell, was murdered. I'm asking whether you have any idea who did it."

"No," said Ranger Rob.

"Just no?" Bernie said.

"That's my honest answer. I don't know."

"Care to speculate?"

"In what way?"

"Start with the two essential facts—Devin's disappearance and Turk's murder. How are they related?"

"I just—I . . . this is all . . . all out of my experience."

"What is your experience, Ranger Rob?" Bernie said, his voice kind of gentle.

"I don't understand your question," Ranger Rob said.

Suzie piped up, her voice not gentle at all. "Bernie's trying to find out what sort of man you are," she said; and then, in her normal voice: "Is that right, Bernie?"

Bernie made a funny little shrug, a she's-right-what-can-I-do? sort of thing.

Hey! Was this good-cop bad-cop? With Bernie as good and Suzie as bad? At first I thought, wow, are we cooking or what? But then came another, not thought, really, more a glimpse of a strange future where Suzie was grabbing perps by the pant leg. That was my job! I found myself inching sideways and forward a bit, maybe getting into the space between Suzie and what we called the interviewee in this business, lingo Suzie probably wasn't familiar with.

"So," said Suzie, kind of leaning around me, "information on your background might be useful."

"I don't see—" Ranger Rob began.

"Starting with how you got this damn job," Suzie said.

Ranger Rob sat back in his chair. "I'm qualified. I've had a long career in the camping industry. You can check it out."

Suzie pulled out her cell phone.

Ranger Rob looked at her in surprise, not the good kind. "Coverage is a bit spotty, I'm—" he began.

"Clear signal, thanks," Suzie said. And then: "Carla? One

more thing—can you run a quick search on Ranger Rob Town-shend, director of Big Bear Wilderness Camp? Work, marital, criminal, the usual. Thanks." *Click.* "Where were we?"

Ranger Rob's face had gotten kind of greenish. That can sometimes lead to puking in a human. I shifted back a bit. "I'm going to have to ask you to leave," he said.

"Noted," Bernie said. "Let's move on to the ownership of the camp."

"Why?" said Ranger Rob. "It's a typical five-oh-one c three nonprofit."

"But where did the money come from—land, buildings, equipment?" Bernie said. He rose, went to a window, looked out. "There must have been substantial start-up costs."

"Before my time," Ranger Rob said. "The board handled all that."

"But you're the director."

"Correct."

"Who's the chairman of the board?" Bernie said.

I knew that one: Frank Sinatra; we'd gone through a period of listening to him nonstop, me and Bernie.

But that wasn't Ranger Rob's answer. "Judge Stringer," he said.

Bernie nodded, that slight nod he did when he already knew. He wandered over toward the printer in the corner. Ranger Rob swiveled around, kept a close eye on Bernie. Human anxiety has a smell, not as sour or strong as fear, but in that line. It drifted over to me from across the desk.

"One last thing," Bernie said. "Why was the search for Devin called off?"

"That had nothing to do with me," said Ranger Rob. "The sheriff and the head of rescue made the decision, because of the bears."

"Bears?" said Bernie, speaking exactly what was on my mind.

"A number of bears have been spotted up by Stiller's Creek in the last few days. It was felt that most likely there'd be no, ah, remains. A sad, sad situation and—would you please not do that?"

Bernie had removed a sheet of paper from the printer and was reading it. "Sending out your résumé, Ranger Rob?"

"Just testing the waters, more or less."

"I would in your place."

At that moment, Suzie's phone beeped with that special beep for a text, whatever that happened to be. She glanced at the screen. "Good old Carla," she said. She walked over to the desk and held the phone so Ranger Rob could see.

He licked his lips. Tongue so white, face so green: I got a little pukey myself. "I suggest you talk to Turk's mother in Jackrabbit Junction," he said. "But you didn't hear it from me."

"That will depend on how this plays out," Bernie said. "Where's Jackrabbit Junction?"

"Actually not far from Stiller's Creek," Ranger Rob said. "But you have to come in from the back side, so it's seventy miles by road. You need four-wheel drive for the last ten or so."

"Can you hike in from the creek?" Bernie said.

"It's doable," said Ranger Rob.

"Christ," Bernie said. He banged his fist into his open hand, real loud, almost like gunshot. Ranger Rob jumped. So did Suzie. Not me.

"We'll need a few things from you," Bernie said. He placed the sheet of paper in the paper tray, but it got away from him and fluttered to the floor.

"You mad at me?" Suzie said.

"Nope," said Bernie.

"You haven't said a word in two hours."

We were on the trail that led up to Stiller's Creek, and the spot where Turk and the boys had camped, and the mine; me first, then Bernie, then Suzie. They carried packs given to us by Ranger Rob. Ranger Rob had also parked the Beetle in a shed behind one of the cabins, locked the door, and said something about some embezzlement that wasn't really embezzlement, totally beyond me, to which Bernie only replied, "You haven't seen us."

And Ranger Rob had said, "I haven't seen you."

But he'd been seeing us at that very moment! I hadn't gotten that at all, but I did know that humans sometimes didn't think their best when they were feeling pukey.

We rounded a corner and saw those rocky mountaintops streaked with white—snow, I knew that now—for the first time. Suzie huffed and puffed and said, "How come?"

"How come what?" Bernie said.

"Is that nice, making me do a lot of explaining when I'm struggling for breath? How come you're not talking, for Christ sake?"

"I'm struggling for breath, too," Bernie said.

"You're not."

It was true. Bernie had huffed and puffed pretty much non-stop our first time up this way, and now his breathing was real quiet. That was Bernie.

"So," Suzie said, "explain."

Bernie stopped and waited for Suzie to catch up. She was bent a little from the weight of the pack, her face shiny pink. We'd reached the place where the white-bark trees petered out and the Christmas trees began. I found myself sniffing around the last of the white-bark trees, a big one with strips of the bark hanging off. And what was this? That locker-room-laundry-hamper scent again? Yes, and lots of it.

Meanwhile, Bernie was handing Suzie a water bottle. "I'm mad at me, not you," he said.

"But why?" said Suzie.

Yeah, why? When had Bernie ever done anything wrong?

"I blew the whole goddamn case," he said. "Had it and dropped it."

Huh? None of that made any sense. For one thing, Bernie had great hands—he'd played ball for Army, don't forget that. I trotted over and gave him a little bump.

"What do you mean?" Suzie was saying.

Bernie recovered his balance and said, "I'll show you in a while. Keep going, or do you want a breather?"

"Never say that again," said Suzie.

We wound our way up and up through the Christmas trees, the trail shrinking down to a narrow crest, steep drops on either side, the snow-streaked mountaintops much closer now. I got this crazy impulse to leap into that deep blue sky, so beautiful. Not a good idea, of course. Way up high a big black bird was doing what I wanted to do. I'd never been fond of birds.

After a while the ground leveled out and gurgling water sounded through the trees. Moments later, I was on that broad flat rock in midstream, lapping up lovely cold water to my heart's content.

"Stiller's Creek," Bernie said.

"Chet seems to like it," said Suzie.

"He's a connoisseur of water."

Meaning what? You tell me.

Then we were all on the other side. "Campsite was up there," Bernie said, pointing up the slope. "The mine's this way."

We headed upstream, Stiller's Creek getting smaller and smaller, the trees disappearing, the footing turning to broken rocks, not so easy for Bernie and Suzie. I had to double back so many times I lost count, although I actually stopped trying when I got to two. Bernie and Suzie were both huffing and puffing by the time we reached the mine. Suzie gazed at the opening for a moment—those old timbers and darkness beyond—and then strapped on her headlamp and started inside.

"What are you doing?" Bernie said.

"I want a picture."

"Why?"

She glanced back. "This is a story, Bernie."

Bernie gave me a look. I gave him a look back. Not sure what that was about, but whatever it was, we were on the same side.

Bernie strapped on his headlamp. We went in. He gave her a little tour. "Here's where some old-timer carved his name. There's what's left of the side tunnel where Chet found the nugget. Here's the main tunnel, the one Moondog was working." That kind of thing. And not long after that, we were standing over the rubble pile where we'd found Turk's body. Suzie took out her camera. No body here now, of course, so—whoa.

I barked and barked.

"Chet?" Bernie said. "What's up, big guy?"

"Do you think he's upset, remembering what was in there or something?" Suzie said.

Bernie shook his head, although I couldn't be sure of that, because by that time I was clawing at the rubble for all I was worth, which I now knew was twenty grand, by the way, not too shabby.

"What's going on?" Suzie said, her voice echoing deep in the mine.

Bernie didn't answer. He was down on his knees, digging alongside me to the best of his ability, which was pretty good for a human. Dust swirled in the light of the headlamps, and the air got thick and hard to breathe. We uncovered the chest first, worked our way up to the face. It was Guy.

TWENTY-NINE

Guy, and shot in the head, just like Turk.

"I don't understand," Suzie said. Bernie turned to her, lit her up in his headlamp. She had her hands on her face; her eyes were wide; her shadow on the wall wasn't steady.

"This is what arrogant men do," Bernie said. "The kind who think they're smarter than everyone else."

Good luck with that. Bernie was always the smartest human in the room, end of story.

"What arrogant men are you talking about?" Suzie said.

Bernie knelt again and started covering Guy back up, reburying him under the rubble. I did what I could to help, but uncovering is more my thing.

"Judge Stringer, for one," Bernie said.

"He killed Guy?"

"Or had it done."

"Why?" Suzie said.

Bernie glanced over his shoulder at her, laid a last rock over Guy. "Let's get out of here," he said.

* * *

So nice to be back outside in the sunshine, maybe the nicest the outdoors had ever felt in my whole life. I was together with Bernie again, and of course Suzie was a gem; and maybe soon she'd be heading back to the Valley, leaving us to crack this case the way we always did, except for once when we got there too late, opened up that broom closet and—I didn't want to think about that night. So I didn't, but at the same time I no longer felt quite as tip-top.

Suzie hunched her shoulders and shivered. "I'm developing this sickening theory," she said.

My ears—which didn't match, something I'd learned from people commenting about them right in front of my face—pricked up. How often had I heard Bernie say that it helped to have a theory of a case? Take the Dalton divorce, where Bernie made a chart on the whiteboard all about Mrs. Dalton's improving golf scores and realized she was having an affair with the pro, case closed.

"Go on," Bernie said, his voice quiet.

"Maybe the judge thought that Guy had made the incriminating recording himself," Suzie said. "And was using us as a weapon against him."

"That sounds about right," Bernie said.

"Oh, my God," Suzie said. "Don't you see what that means?"

"Means Stringer's on the losing side," Bernie said, "whether he knows it or not."

Suzie backed away a little, blinking. "You're a hard man, Bernie, aren't you? Don't you understand? I got Guy killed. I'm—I'm responsible for the death of a human being."

"No, you're not," Bernie said. He reached out and took her chin in his hand, not roughly but not gently either. "Not even one percent." Percent! I loved when Bernie brought that up—it meant his brain was working at its very best. He let go of Suzie's chin, leaving faint finger impressions on her skin; they faded right away. "Stringer and whoever helped him are responsible," Bernie went on, "and Guy started all by himself on the road to getting killed."

"How do you know?" Suzie said.

"He's—he was—a type, Suzie. A type we've dealt with many times."

Bernie couldn't have been more right about that, and given time, I'm sure I could have come up with an example or two. But Suzie had her face set in a way that made me think she wasn't buying it, like she was . . . could it be possible? She was digging in her heels? Wow! Suzie and I had something in common.

"What you learn in this business," Bernie went on, "is that the most you can usually expect is to clean up at the margins. Big changes are hardly ever possible, dealing with the kind of people we deal with. But every so often, you get a chance to pull off something big. This is one of those times."

"What are you talking about?" Suzie said.

"Devin," said Bernie, shrugging his pack up a bit, the way he did when it was time to hit the trail.

Suzie rubbed her chin, then nodded. She did that pack-shrugging thing, just like Bernie. "All set," she said.

Bernie smiled. Then he picked up a stick and began drawing in the dirt.

"Ch—et?"

Uh-oh. Bernie drawing in the dirt with a stick always got me going. I trotted over to a nearby rock and lifted my leg. Over the splashing sounds—turned out I'd been holding on for a while—I heard Bernie saying things like, ". . . here on the back side of the mine . . ." and ". . . where this ridge should lead to . . ." and ". . . has to be the back door—this real busy back door, which is what I missed—over to Jackrabbit Junction."

Jackrabbit Junction: I'd heard that before, but it hadn't sunk in. Now it did. Not lacking in rabbit experience, Chet the Jet. One of the things I'd learned was how those amazing ears of theirs could pick up sound from far, far away, but I was ready.

"And what happens in Jackrabbit Junction?" Suzie said.

"Whatever brought Guy and Stringer together," said Bernie.

We moved away from the mine, but instead of heading back down toward the creek, we walked in the other direction, following a narrow path with the cliff face rising on one side and a steep slope of rocks and scrub dropping off on the other. Up and up we climbed, Bernie, me, and Suzie, then soon me, Bernie, and Suzie. Up, but also in a long curve that led us slowly around to the other side of the mountain, something I didn't realize until I suddenly stepped into shadow, glanced back, and saw the jagged peak blocking the sun.

We paused—others had paused in the same place, easy to tell from the scraps of toilet paper lying around—and took in the view. First, we had a steep, treeless stretch, the trail disappearing in the scree, scree being hiking lingo. At the base of the steep part lay a small lake, kind of football-shaped, and on the other side the trees began, a dark- and light-green forest sloping on and on, eventually out of the mountain's shadow and into bright sunshine. And then a whole chain of other mountains came marching in from the side, and where the base of the last and smallest reached the forest, I could see a thin plume of smoke rising straight up through the trees.

Bernie pointed it out to Suzie; her face was a bit pinkish again. "Jackrabbit Junction," he said. "Actually closer than it looks."

"Then let's get going," Suzie said. "Unless you need a breather."

"Lead the way," said Bernie.

Excuse me? No way would—but what was this? Bernie's hand on my collar? I turned my head right around, looked up at him. He has a look that says "Ch—et?" without actually saying it. That was the look he gave me now. We started down: Suzie, Bernie, me.

Did we go as fast as we did with me up front? Not in my opinion. But at least we didn't get lost, and the sun was still fairly high in the sky when we came to the lake. Was there time for a swim? Maybe a real quick one. And while I was out there—what a feeling!—Suzie took off her boots and socks, rolled up her jeans, and waded in. There was something about her calves, their shape, and the way the water rippled around them, that caught my eye, hard to explain why, exactly. But a very nice sight. I noticed that Bernie, sitting on a log, a cigarette—oh, Bernie—in his hand but the hand frozen in midair—was watching her, too. I paddled to shore, shook off, beads of water shooting everywhere, kind of like the pearls off Leda's necklace when I—but forget that part—and sat beside Bernie.

He puffed at the cigarette and blew out a little cloud of smoke, a faraway look in his eye. "What I'm worried about," he said, "is that Devin has lost his value."

I couldn't get to the bottom of that one, didn't even know where to begin. Suzie stepped out of the water. Bernie spun the cigarette stub into the lake; it sizzled and sank from sight. We got back on the trail.

A very narrow trail at first, with big rocks and roots sticking up—we were in the trees now—but after a while it broadened enough so Bernie and Suzie walked side by side. No huffing and puffing now from either of them, maybe because we were going down; they both breathed deep and evenly, and here was something interesting: a lot of the time they were in the same breathing rhythm. Had I ever noticed that with humans before? Not that I could remember, although during Leda's yoga period hadn't there been a—

Whoa. What was that? I went still, one front paw raised. Voices, yes, voices for sure, somewhere ahead. I sniffed the air, picked up no human smells, but the breeze was blowing the wrong way, flowing down the mountainside. I looked back. Bernie and Suzie came into view, topping a rise and stepping around a boulder in the middle of the trail. They saw me.

"I love when he stands like that," Suzie said.

"Shh," said Bernie, raising his hand palm up. He tilted his head, then whispered, "Do you hear anything?"

Suzie tilted her head. "No."

Not a surprise. They came up to me, taking those sort of slo-mo steps humans take when trying to be quiet. Bernie gazed down the trail, which disappeared around a bend not far away. He tilted his head again, even scrunched up his face a bit—hey! that made him look like Charlie—listening his very hardest. "Still don't hear anything," he said, just a quiet murmur.

Suzie murmured, too, a very nice sound. "Maybe there's nothing to hear."

"Chet heard something," Bernie said.

No doubt about it, and I was hearing more at that very moment, specifically a man saying, "Twelve gauge."

"Like what?" Suzie said.

"Could be lots of things," Bernie said. "Let's go, but nice and quiet."

Bernie was the best, no question about that, now and forever, but this one particular time—not at all important, I'm sure—it couldn't have been a lot of things: a man had clearly said, "Twelve gauge."

We moved on, down the trail, around the bend, around another bend. No more voices, but there were smells: flowers, tree rot, pine needles, peanut butter. Peanut butter was not a favorite of mine, way too sticky under the roof of the mouth and along the back of the throat, although I had no objection to just plain butter, either on toast or right off the butter dish, and English muffins were also—

I topped a crest and there was a clearing in the woods, just steps away. Men were in that clearing, mostly sitting around eating sandwiches. They looked like hikers—real fit hikers—all of them dressed in blue hiking outfits. One of them—a guy with a short haircut—in fact, they all had short haircuts—glanced up and saw me.

"Hey," he said, pointing. "Is that a wolf?"

The others turned fast in my direction. "We call that a dog, city boy," one said.

"Here, fella," said another.

A gray-haired guy—the only gray-haired one in the bunch—stood up and reached into the pocket of his vest. At that moment, Bernie and Suzie came over the rise.

They saw the men and halted beside me. We gazed at them; they gazed at us.

"Hi," Bernie said.

"Hi," said the gray-haired guy.

We walked down into the clearing, me between Bernie and Suzie. She felt tense. Bernie did not, so neither did I.

The men were all on their feet now, some holding their sandwiches, peanut butter and jelly, mostly, but also ham and cheese, tuna, and one BLT.

"Nice dog," said the BLT guy. All at once I felt this urge to move a bit closer to him, but my job was to stay by Bernie.

"Thanks," said Bernie.

"You on a hike?" the gray-haired guy said.

"Yup," said Bernie. "You guys?"

"Uh-huh," the gray-haired guy said. "Where you headed?"

"Jackrabbit Junction," Bernie said.

"Ever been there?"

"Nope," Bernie said. "You?"

"Where you coming from?" said the gray-haired guy.

"Big Bear trailhead."

The gray-haired guy checked his watch. "Must've started early."

"We're making good time," Bernie said.

"Leave a car back there?" the gray-haired guy said.

"Friend dropped us," Bernie said. "He's picking us up in Jackrabbit Junction."

First I'd heard of that. And what friend? But Bernie was Bernie. I was Chet, pure and simple.

"Four-wheel drive?" the gray-haired guy was saying.

"Yup," said Bernie.

"'Cause that first section's kind of rough."

"So I hear."

We gazed at them; they gazed at us. The BLT smell grew stronger and stronger. Other than that, I had no idea what was going down.

"Not much doing in Jackrabbit Junction," the gray-haired guy said. "No restaurants or hotels, nothing like that."

"Heard that, too," Bernie said. "Dinner in Durango's the plan."

"Sounds like a good one," said the gray-haired guy. The others all went back to sitting down, eating their sandwiches. "Have a nice day," the gray-haired guy said.

"Likewise," said Bernie.

"What's your dog's name?" said the BLT guy. He was sitting on his pack now, and I seemed to be standing in front of him. How had that happened?

"Chet," Bernie said.

"I think he's jonesin' for some of my sandwich."

"Just tell him no."

"I don't mind. Can he have it?"

And a little more palaver like that, and then half a BLT on rye was mine. Delish, and gone in two bites; turned out I'd been just about famished.

"Nice dog," said the BLT guy.

And he was nice, too. Bernie gave the gray-haired guy a little wave, almost like a salute. The gray-haired guy gave him one back, just like it. We left the clearing and moved on down the trail.

After not a very long way, the trail took a sharp turn and led us down the side of a ridge wooded with those white-bark trees. Lovely yellow flowers grew all over the place.

"Nice of that guy to share his sandwich with Chet," Suzie said.

"We paid for it," said Bernie.

"What do you mean?"

"The FBI is funded with tax dollars, yours and mine."

"FBI?" Suzie stopped, glanced back up the trail. "How do you know?"

"They just can't hide it," Bernie said.

"Are they on a training mission or something?"

"I doubt it."

"Why?"

"They were too interested in us, especially in how long we

were going to be in the area. Meaning they've got something in mind."

"Like what?"

"No idea," Bernie said. "We just need to be out of the china shop when it happens."

China shop? I'd heard of them but never actually seen one, not that I knew of. As for the FBI, we'd bumped up against them more than once, me and Bernie. All I knew was we always kept it short.

The trail got easier and easier. We moved into sunlight, saw those mountains slanting in from the side. Bernie picked a yellow flower and stuck it in Suzie's hair. The ground began to flatten out and we sped up. Suzie's flower smelled lovely, but I was beginning to pick up other smells as well: wood smoke, also nice, and then not-so-nice ones, like rotten eggs and cat pee. Uh-oh: cat pee to the nth degree. That took me all the way back to K-9 school. I barked my low rumbly bark.

"What?" Suzie said.

"I think something's coming up," Bernie said.

No doubt about that, and I was pretty sure what. First: a little area of grass burned brown, no surprise there. Then I spotted coffee filters, the big size, stained bright colors. We passed through a thick grove of trees and came to a trailer, smoke rising from the chimney and lots of stuff rusting out front: washing machines, bicycles, a tractor.

"Welcome to Jackrabbit Junction," Bernie said.

Oh, and one more thing: I almost left out the septic tank smells.

THIRTY

We walked toward the trailer, a lopsided trailer up on blocks, except for one end which kind of slouched down to the ground. All the windows were open—that was pretty standard—but curtains hung in them so you couldn't see inside. Then one of the curtains twitched and a man's face appeared, lined and scabby but not actually that old.

"Youse on private proppity," he said, or something like that, hard to tell on account of his mouth being pretty much toothless. His eyes went back and forth and back and forth real quick, taking us in over and over. Also pretty standard. "Youse hikers?" he said.

"That's right," Bernie said.

His eyes did more back-and-forthing. Then he hooked his arm out the window—a real skinny arm with a fresh burn mark or two—and pointed around the corner of the trailer. "Road out's thataway."

"Much obliged," Bernie said. "And en route we'd like to pay our respects to Mrs. Rendell, if you can tell us where to find her."

"Huh?"

"Turk's mother," Bernie said. "We want to offer our condolences."

The man stared at us out the window. "You mean 'cause he's dead?"

"Exactly," Bernie said.

His face withdrew, the curtain falling back in place. Bernie took a quick step forward, like he was going to charge in there, but before he could, the curtains opened again and the man stuck his head right out the window, his neck long and scrawny.

"You hiking buddies of Turk?"

Bernie nodded.

"Look like hikers," the man said.

Bernie nodded again.

The man's gaze went to me. "'Cepting for the dog. Dog looks like a po-lice dog."

"He's actually head of the DEA," Bernie said.

The man was silent for what seemed like a long time, enough for me to think, police dog? We were private operators, me and Bernie, meaning we answered to nobody, amigo. Then, quite abruptly, the man started laughing, a harsh and horrible sound, like he was trying to get rid of sharp things caught in his throat. Laughing gave way to hacking, and then a hork or two, and when all that was done, he hooked his arm out again and said, "Quarter of a mile down in the holler, purple double-wide, can't hardly miss it."

We followed a path around the trailer, a path littered with bottles and cans and empty pill containers and scraps of this and that. Trailers were scattered in the woods, some with smoke rising from stovepipe chimneys.

"It stinks in here," Suzie said.

She was right about that—no putting anything past Suzie—but my mind was on other things, specifically jackrabbits. Jackrabbit Junction, so you'd be expecting jackrabbits out the yingyang and so far, not so much as a whiff. What was up with that?

The path split in two, one part leading out of the woods toward some little houses or shacks lining an unpaved street, the other turning into a two-rutted road and slanting down through the trees toward a stream at the bottom, its water kind of orange to my eyes, but Bernie always says I can't be trusted when it comes to color. On the near side of the stream stood a purple double-wide, a satellite dish on the roof, and a big red SUV parked out front.

We went down into the hollow. Bernie knocked on the door. No answer.

"Maybe no one's home," Suzie said.

Maybe, but then how come eggs were frying in there? No missing that smell, and besides I could hear the sizzle. Bernie liked sunny-side up; I wasn't fussy.

Bernie knocked again. "Mrs. Rendell?" he called.

No answer.

He turned to Suzie. "You could be right," he said.

Sometimes life gets frustrating and you've just got to control yourself. I did my very best, barking, but not long or loud, and rising up on my hind legs to paw at that door, but not my hardest, not even close. Hey! The door swung open, taking me completely by surprise, and when that happens, I always get an urge to bark, which I would have done, except that I was already barking from before, if you see what I mean, kind of confusing.

And anyway, not the point. The point was that a short but strong-looking woman stood just back of the doorway, a butcher knife in her hand. Cleon Maxwell, owner of Max's Memphis Ribs, had one a lot like it, not as big.

Bernie raised his hands. "No need for that," he said. "We mean no harm."

"Then how come you bust into my goddamn domicile?" the woman said.

"That was the furthest thing from our intention," Bernie said.

Bernie talking fancy like that often makes bad guys screw up their faces, not quite following, but there was no sign of that on this woman's face: a broad face with deep lines across the forehead, dark angry eyes, and teeth, plenty of them and in not-too-bad shape. Maybe she wasn't a bad guy.

"We came to offer our condolences on your recent loss, Mrs. Rendell," Bernie said.

Her eyes stayed angry but she lowered the butcher knife. "You knew Turk?" she said.

"We did some hiking together."

"What's your name?"

"Bernie."

"He never mentioned any Bernie."

Bernie didn't reply. His face showed nothing.

"On the other hand," she said, "there's plenty he didn't tell me." She stared at Bernie, then at Suzie.

"I'm Suzie," Suzie said. "Bernie's friend. I never met your son, but Bernie's told me about him."

"Told you what?"

"Some things I'd like to discuss with you, Mrs. Rendell," Bernie said. "If we could come inside for a few minutes."

"What things?"

"Things having to do with the manner of his death," Bernie said. "I was one of the last people to see him alive."

There was a long pause. Then the woman said, "All right. And it's Miss Rendell, not Mrs. Never married the asshole. Never married any of the assholes."

We entered the double-wide, passing through the kitchen, where Miss Rendell hung the knife on a hook and turned off the burner under the eggs—sunny-side up, smelling out of this world—without breaking stride, and into a small TV room at the back; a small room but with a very big TV that left not much space for furniture. Suzie sat on the couch, Miss Rendell on the only chair. Bernie wandered over to the window and picked up a trophy that was standing on the sill.

"You won the chemistry prize in high school," he said.

"Junior year," said Miss Rendell. "My last."

"Oh?" said Bernie. "Why was that?"

"Why do you think? We were dirt poor, didn't have a pot to piss in."

Stop right there. What was that? I needed time, lots of it, to think, but as is so often the case when we're on the job there was no time, because Bernie was already talking.

"Did you grow up around here?" he said, or something like that.

"Partly," said Miss Rendell. "If you think it's the armpit of the world now, you should've seen it then."

Pisspots and now armpits? Miss Rendell got more interesting every time she opened her mouth.

"Not following you," Bernie said. "I thought this was one of the most beautiful parts of the West."

"That's because you're from somewhere else," said Miss Rendell. "It's a high-altitude slum. Now can we get back to my son?"

"Sure," said Bernie. "What do you know so far?"

"What the hell kind of question is that?"

"I think Bernie just wants to start in the right place," Suzie said.

Miss Rendell swung around in her direction. "Right place? My son is dead and the county won't even release his body so I can give him a decent burial. There is no right fucking place."

"Understood," Bernie said. "I'd think the same way in your position."

"Just pray that never happens to you," Miss Rendell said.

Bernie was quiet for a moment. Then he said, "I will." Suzie shot him a quick glance. He sat beside her on the couch and cleared his throat. Bernie has several throat clearings; this one was about making a fresh start. I can clear my throat, too, but it doesn't mean anything.

"Did they say why they won't release the body?" Bernie said.

"Because the goddamn medical examiner, Doc Laidlaw—totally senile for years, by the way—hasn't . . ." Her voice thickened for a moment, and I thought tears were on the way, but none came, and she went on, ". . . finished with him."

"When was the last time you heard from the county?" Bernie said.

"Couple days ago," Miss Rendell said. "Maybe they tried since. There's no service here—got to go twenty miles down the road before it clicks in. I was planning on making the drive tomorrow."

"I can save you the trouble," Bernie said. "Doc Laidlaw finished with Turk last night. In court this morning, he submitted a revised finding of death by suicide."

Miss Rendell gripped the arms of her chair real tight, knuckle bones showing right through her skin. "What did you say?"

Bernie said it again.

Now I could see the bones under the skin of her face. Her mouth opened into a round black hole, and she let out a loud and horrible cry that went on until all the breath was out of her; but still no tears. Then Suzie was at Miss Rendell's side with a glass of water. Miss Rendell drank some; most of the rest spilled down her neck, the glass so unsteady in her hand.

"Those monsters," she said.

"What monsters?" Bernie said.

"The judge, the sheriff, those stupid deputies—all of them."

Bernie nodded.

Miss Rendell finished what was in the glass. "Why are they doing this?" she said. "No one who knew Turk will believe it. He was happy and stable and straight up, wouldn't go near my whole—" She cut herself off.

"Go on," Bernie said.

Miss Rendell shook her head.

Suzie turned to Bernie. "Miss Rendell said just what you did."

"About what?" said Miss Rendell.

"About the suicide finding," Bernie said. "They'd have been much smarter calling it an accident, from their point of view."

The lines on Miss Rendell's forehead were getting deeper and deeper. "I don't understand what you're saying. Didn't they arrest some rogue cop? Oh, Christ—does this mean they let him go?"

Bernie nodded. "It wasn't going to hold up."

"How do you know?" said Miss Rendell.

"I'm the one they let go," Bernie said.

Miss Rendell shot right out of her chair, like she'd touched the part of a lamp where the bulb goes when no bulb is in there, which happened to me once, right on the end of the nose. She backed away, hands up to protect herself. I shifted over a bit to get between her and the way to the kitchen, in case that butcher knife was on her mind.

"I didn't do it," Bernie said. "And I'm also a private investigator in good standing, not a rogue cop. I'm up here on a case, and I was the one who found your son's body. There's no doubt in my mind that he was murdered."

"Because you did it?" Miss Rendell's voice was high and wild. "Is that why you're so sure?"

"If I did it, why am I here?"

She gave Bernie a long look, and in the course of that look the expression in her eyes changed a lot, ramping down through fear and rage to anger and worry, to confusion.

"Then who killed my son?" Miss Rendell said.

"That's what I'm trying to find out."

"Who's paying you?"

Bernie has great eyebrows, if I haven't mentioned that already, with a language of their own. Right now they were saying something about being surprised; not them, but Bernie, if you see where I'm going with this. But forget all that. The point was whatever Miss Rendell had said, now gone from my mind, had caught Bernie by surprise.

"No one directly," Bernie said. "But your son's death is mixed up with this other case we're working on." He stopped right there, kind of abruptly, one of his interviewing techniques. We'd had good results from Bernie's interviewing techniques in the past, but at the moment I felt disappointed on account of my curiosity about this other case.

Silence. It went on and on, like something pressing down on the double-wide. At last, Miss Rendell said, "What other case?"

"A missing persons case, which is mostly what we do," Bernie said. "The missing person is a boy named Devin Vereen."

Miss Rendell was very still, her face and body giving away nothing. But Bernie has this saying about how even the way nothing is given can give something—whew, what a thought: Bernie, the one and only! Was this one of those times?

"Name mean anything to you?" Bernie said.

Miss Rendell shook her head. Bernie was watching carefully. He also had a whole thing about how people shake their heads: how many times? too hard? not hard enough? and were they looking you in the eye while the head-shaking was going on? And even more! Just another reason the success of the Little Detective Agency, except for the finances part, should surprise nobody. Meanwhile, Miss Rendell wasn't looking Bernie in the eye.

"Devin went missing during a hike from Big Bear Wilderness Camp," Bernie said. "Turk was the guide."

One thing about humans: they can not age for years and then do it right in front of your eyes. Like Miss Rendell now.

"What are you saying?" she said.

"I'm asking whether you know anything about this missing kid," Bernie said.

"How many times do you want me say it?"

"You haven't actually said it yet."

"I don't know anything about the missing kid. There—I've said it."

"I was hoping for a more believable rendition," Bernie told her.

She didn't like hearing that, whatever it was. "This visit is over," she said, pointing toward the door.

Bernie stayed put. So did Suzie. So did I.

"What you're not getting," Bernie said, "is that we're on the same side."

"No, I'm not getting that," said Miss Rendell. "Not one little bit."

"Your son was murdered," Bernie said. "Do you want the murderer to go free?"

"What the hell do you think?" her voice rising.

Bernie's voice went the other way, but it wasn't gentle. "Then sit down."

Miss Rendell sat down.

"How do you feel about Guy Wenders?" Bernie said.

"Never heard of him," said Miss Rendell.

"You don't have time for this."

"How do you know what I have time for?"

"We'll get to that," Bernie said.

"Is that a threat?" said Miss Rendell. "I don't take to being threatened."

"I'm not the threat," Bernie said.

Miss Rendell gave Bernie a close look, like she was trying to see inside him. Easy as pie for me—although what pies and easiness had to do with each other was a mystery; I'd sampled many of them and gotten nowhere on this—but maybe not for Miss Rendell, because she changed her mind about Guy. "I know Guy," she said. "He's from up this way originally."

"Did you also know that the missing kid is his son?" Bernie said.

Miss Rendell was silent.

Bernie leaned forward a bit, put his hands in a wedge shape, fingertips together. I loved when he did that, wished he'd do it more. "Don't you sense big trouble out there?" he said. "Out there and coming soon?" Miss Rendell didn't speak, but she was scared; I could smell it. "We can help you—maybe not much, but some. First, we need a little cooperation. Did you know Devin is Guy's son?"

Miss Rendell nodded, just the tiniest of movements.

"Where is he?" Bernie said.

Miss Rendell aged a little more. "How would I know that?" she said.

"Maybe you don't," Bernie said. "That just leaves the question of your business. Tell us about it."

"You're talking crazy," Miss Rendell said. "I don't have a business."

"Then what am I smelling?" Bernie said.

That caught my attention, big-time. I waited to hear.

"What the hell are you talking about?" said Miss Rendell.

"Meth," Bernie said. "This whole goddamn settlement smells like one giant meth lab."

Oh, that.

Miss Rendell's head bent slowly forward; she gazed down at the floor.

"I'm guessing," said Bernie, "that you started right out of high school, what with your chemistry background and all. You discovered you were a good businesswoman and things took off. Also, you're smart. Unlike your neighbor by the trail, you stayed away from the product, maintained that nice mouthful of teeth." He paused. "Accurate so far?" he said. "Ballpark, at least?"

Miss Rendell didn't answer or look up.

"After that is where I'm going to need some help," Bernie went on. "What was Turk's role, for example?"

Miss Rendell began to shake. And now came the tears. "He had nothing to do with it," she said. Which was what I thought I heard through the sobs. "He was a good boy." She looked up, her face blotched and streaming. "He loved the outdoors. That was his whole life."

"I believe you," Bernie said.

"I don't give a fuck whether you do or not," she shouted at him.

Bernie nodded like that made sense; it made no sense to me. Miss Rendell wiped her eyes on her sleeve, started pulling herself together, a thing some humans can do, others not, in my experience.

"That leaves the judge and the sheriff," Bernie said. "Or is it the sheriff and the judge? Still not sure which one's in charge."

"Monsters, both of them," said Miss Rendell. She did some more face wiping, also did some sniffling. "But the judge is the smart one."

"When did they start horning in?" Bernie said.

"Almost from the get-go—I found out there are no secrets up here," Miss Rendell said. She took a deep breath and—and gave herself a little shake? What a case this was! "They wanted protection money, of course, ten percent at first, sounded reasonable. Now they're taking just about everything."

"So cleaning up all that cash became an issue," Bernie said. She nodded.

"Some of it went into the camp?"

"One of Guy's clever ideas," Miss Rendell said. "But I never knew much about what they were up to, and never wanted to."

Bernie rose, went to the window. I went with him. We gazed out at the strange-colored stream. Without turning, Bernie said, "I assume you have some escape hatch all set up, somewhere to go, money stashed away, that kind of thing."

"Why?" said Miss Rendell. "What are you telling me?"

"The feds are coming," Bernie said. He turned to her. "And soon."

Miss Rendell rose, not quite steady on her feet. "Thank you," she said.

Suzie stood up.

"And you, too," Miss Rendell said.

Suzie's eyes were locked on Miss Rendell, and they were hard and unfriendly. I didn't quite get that, not coming from Suzie.

Miss Rendell squared her shoulders, met Suzie's gaze. "I have an idea—no guarantees—where the boy might be," she said. "I can drop you on my way."

Sometime later, we were all pulling away from the double-wide in the big red SUV, Miss Rendell driving and Bernie up front with her, me and Suzie in the back. I found I had a bit of egg—the sunny-side up kind—on my face, and licked it off.

THIRTY-ONE

We drove along the unpaved main drag of this town or village or whatever it was; hardly anything you'd call a real building, and what real buildings there were all in crummy shape. Up above the sky was turning purple in such a huge way that Jackrabbit Junction hardly seemed real. Except for the meth business smells: there was no getting away from them.

Miss Rendell checked both sides of the street. No one was around. "Should have done this years ago," she said. "I waited too long, didn't I?"

"I don't know," Bernie said.

"They'll come after me."

"Maybe."

"How can it be maybe? Once the feds get started, they're relentless."

"That's just because they're a bureaucracy," Bernie said. "The memos take on a life of their own." Sometimes Bernie's impossible to understand; that's often when we get our best results. "Your hope has to be," he was saying, "that you're a secondary target. And if you aren't, and they find you, then you make damn sure you become a secondary target. Understand what I'm saying?"

"I make deals?" Miss Rendell said. Wow. She understood all that? Miss Rendell was some kind of perp, no doubt about it, but she turned out to be pretty smart, no taking that away from her.

"Name every goddamn name you can," Bernie said.

Miss Rendell glanced at him. "Thanks," she said.

"No charge," said Bernie.

Whoa. Billing Miss Rendell: I hadn't thought of that. We'd never billed a perp, but why not?

We passed the last of the trailers on the other side of town. The road turned real bad right away, shrank to a narrow track, winding and rutted, mostly going down but up as well, and sometimes we splashed through puddles the size of ponds. "The cornerstone of my business plan, this stupid road," Miss Rendell said.

Bernie laughed. So nice to hear his laugh at a time like this. A tense time, right, leaving in a hurry under that purple sky, now fiery around one edge, black at the other? Not tense for me personally, but the smell of human tension was in the air, and the way Suzie's hand was clutching my back couldn't have been called relaxed.

We came to a steep rise, thick dark woods on both sides, and climbed it in a series of real tough switchbacks, the tires fighting for traction beneath us. At the top, I saw we'd come to a long ridge that curved out in both directions, kind of like open arms. Straight ahead the track went switchbacking down the slope, not quite as steep as the way up. Far, far away against the dark part of the sky I thought I could make out a faint glow.

Miss Rendell pointed that way. "You can't see it, but Durango's right about there." She stopped the car, pointed over toward Bernie's side. "The cutoff back to Big Bear's about at the halfway mark. And over here"—she pointed out her own window at a narrow lane almost completely weeded over—"is what you're looking for."

Bernie peered around her. "Yeah?" he said.

"Twenty or thirty years back," Miss Rendell said, "this developer type from the east waltzed in and built a fancy hunting lodge. Couldn't get the fancy hunters to come here, though, so the place went belly up. What's left is half a mile down that lane."

"And that's where they've got Devin?" Bernie said.

"I told you," said Miss Rendell. "It's only a guess."

Bernie gave her a look, not unfriendly, but I'd never want him to look at me like that. "I'm betting you're a good guesser."

We got out of the car. Bernie tapped the roof. Miss Rendell started down the track. We watched her go.

"You're saying she knows?" Suzie said.

"Yup," said Bernie. "But it doesn't mean she knew all along— she might have just figured it out."

"What makes you think we can trust her?"

"We're not her enemy," Bernie said. "She knows that, too."

He slipped on his backpack; Suzie did the same. The purple was fading fast from the sky.

"Headlamps?" Suzie said.

Bernie shook his head. "We'll just follow Chet."

Of course. Standard procedure, but Suzie couldn't be expected to know that. We turned to the lane. Bernie tramped down some vines and creepers.

"Wish you had your gun," Suzie said.

"It's not the only club in the bag," Bernie told her.

A real puzzler, and maybe for Suzie, too, because she didn't reply. We started down the lane, me first, then Bernie and Suzie side by side.

After a while, I heard her say, very quiet, "Didn't know you were a golfer, Bernie."

I glanced back and saw Bernie was smiling, his teeth so white in the growing darkness. "No talking," he said.

Bernie a golfer? No way, on account of the whole aquifer problem. But once on a case, details of which are all gone from my mind now—except for this—we found ourselves alone on a golf course and Bernie hit one a country mile, the longest kind of mile, I'm pretty sure. That was Bernie: just when you think he's done amazing you, he amazes you again. Hard to believe I haven't gotten that in already, but maybe I slipped up.

We followed the lane, a winding sort of lane with some ups and downs, but mostly downs as the lane took us away from the top of the ridge. Sometimes the undergrowth disappeared and old tire-track ruts appeared, making for easy going, but mostly the lane was all about burrs and nettles and spiky things. I hardly noticed. The noticing part of me was more busy with smells. In a place like this, of course, there were more smells than you could shake a stick at—no time to get to the bottom of that, or even break through at the top—so the trick was to ignore all but the important ones. I smelled two. The first was coffee. The second, and maybe not important—more just interesting that I was picking it up again—was that strange locker-room-laundry-hamper smell. I ramped up the pace. Almost right away, I heard Suzie lose her footing. Bernie made a soft little noise he has, kind of like: *fffft*. It meant slow down. So I did, a bit.

We came over a rise and there lay a clearing, not far away. In the remaining light, still plenty for me, I could see a line of tall trees, and standing in front of them a log house, even bigger than Judge Stringer's back in Big Bear, but in bad shape, with some big gaps between the walls, cracked windows, many with vines growing through them, and a tall chimney leaning so far over it had to fall the very next moment. What had Miss Rendell said? Something about . . . about an old hunting lodge? Yes! Got it! Chet the Jet, totally in the picture.

No cars were parked in front of the old hunting lodge and no sounds came from it, but a light, low and unsteady, shone in an upstairs window. We approached the lodge, real slow, real careful, and were almost at the front door, or rather, doorway, the door itself being gone, when I heard something. I stopped, went still.

Oh, yeah, no doubt. A car, and coming from back down the lane. I turned that way, head up, tail up, completely rigid; but also quiet—Bernie had mentioned something about being quiet, and at times like this I always followed his wishes completely, just about.

Bernie came up beside me and tilted his head. Oh, Bernie, come on. You're not hearing it? But then he did. He motioned quickly to Suzie, then led us to some thick bushes, wild and overgrown, beside the door. We got between them and the lodge and watched the lane through this one tiny gap, all of us crowding in.

A pair of headlights blinked into view, vanished, blinked again, and then shone steady: in our eyes and on the lodge. A car bumped up and parked right beside the bushes that hid us. The headlights went off but those other little ones at the front, name escaping me at the moment, stayed on, casting a pool of light that made for easy viewing, but I'd already seen what was what, namely that this car was a black-and-white, Sheriff Laidlaw in the passenger seat, closest to us, Deputy Mack beside him at the wheel, windows down.

Deputy Mack shut off the engine. It got real quiet. I could hear the sheriff breathing.

"What are you waiting for?" he said. "Go on up there and get them."

"I'm not feelin' too good about this," Mack said.

"What are you?" said the sheriff. "Some kind of pansy? This ain't about feelings. It's about makin' the right move."

"How come this is the right move?" Mack said.

"I'm not walkin' you through it again, shit-for-brains," Sheriff Laidlaw said. "The kid's not an asset anymore. If you don't get that, you're hopeless."

"But—"

"Move!"

Mack got out of the car, tied a bandanna around the lower part of his face, and headed for the lodge, switching on a flashlight as he went in. I caught a glimpse of a wide, lopsided staircase rising into the darkness. The sound of Mack's footsteps faded away.

Bernie can move fast for real short distances, and from behind the bushes to the side of that black-and-white was a real short distance. Zoom. He sprang around the bushes and rushed the car. The sheriff heard him coming and turned; turned just at the same time Bernie was throwing a tremendous punch through the open window, meaning Sheriff Laidlaw was turning his chin right into the blow. Which proved the sheriff was no boxer, on account of boxers knew never to do that, in fact, to roll with the punch, as I'd learned during that period after Leda left when we'd watched lots of fight videos—the Thrilla in Manila! Shut up!

One punch. Bernie clobbered him. The sound was thrilling. Sheriff Laidlaw slumped right over, eyelids fluttering down. Bernie opened the door, fast but quiet, yanked the sheriff out of the car, and dragged him behind the bushes. Did I get in a nip or two along the way? Possibly.

Bernie flipped the sheriff over, stripped off his belt. In what seemed like no time at all, he'd cuffed the sheriff with his own cuffs—behind the back, which was how we did our cuffing at the Little Detective Agency—stuck the sheriff's gun in his own belt, and handed the sheriff's nightstick to Suzie. Her eyes were wide and pearly, like they'd grabbed up the last of the evening light.

"If he makes a sound," Bernie said, speaking real low, "or looks like he's going to, whack him with this."

"I don't know if I can do that, Bernie," Suzie whispered.

Bernie smiled, a quick little smile. "Then just wave it at him." He turned to me. "Ready?"

What a question! We hurried into the lodge, Bernie in a sort of half run he has when we have to be quiet, me in a trot, although I can be quiet at any speed. I pulled slightly in front, which in low-light situations usually gave us better results. We went up the wide, lopsided staircase—no railings, but railings didn't mean much to me, and came to the next floor.

A broad sort of gallery spread into the gloom in both directions. But not quite as gloomy in one of them: faint light glowed from around a distant corner. We headed that way, side by side, silent partners. Hey! I'd heard that expression so many times and now I understood it. And what a great expression it turned out to be! The silent partners crossed the gallery, entered a hall, came to the corner where the light showed, and peeked around it.

Around the corner, the hall narrowed to a corridor that ended at a half-open door, which was where the light was leaking from. And also voices.

One was Mack's: "Hurry it up."

And then the other deputy, Claudie: "We have to tie him up?"

Mack said, "Just do it."

And after that, a new voice, one I'd never heard, the voice of a kid: "Where are you taking me?"

I heard Bernie inhale a sharp little breath and at the same time my fur rose up from the back of my neck to the tip of my tail. We crept along the corridor, quiet and controlled, but I could hear Bernie's pounding heart, and mine, too. What was our plan? I didn't worry about that the slightest bit.

We reached the doorway, most of our view blocked by the door. I saw part of a small room, a gas lantern standing on a table, a backpack lying at the foot of a metal bed frame with just a bare mattress, and sitting on that mattress: a kid, and not just a kid, but the missing kid, Devin. I recognized him from Anya's photo, although his face seemed thinner than I remembered, and he also looked older.

Devin had his eyes on something across the room, where we couldn't see. Claudie, wearing a black Halloween mask, came in view, a roll of duct tape in his hand. Halloween is the only human holiday I can do without. In fact, I hate it. And all of a sudden that hatred surged through me. I saw red, whether I can do that or not.

Claudie tore off a strip of duct tape, and said, "Stick out your hands."

Devin wriggled back against the wall. "Don't," he said.

"Do what I fuckin' tole you," Claudie said and he raised his hand like he was about to clip the boy.

A bit of a blur after that. Bernie hit that door so hard it sagged off its hinges. The looks on the faces of those deputies!

Bernie drew the sheriff's gun. "You move, you die," he said.

For some reason, they both moved. Claudie clutched at Devin, at the same time going for his gun.

BLAM! Bernie fired, a huge sound in the small room. I was

aware of Claudie crying out after that, but then I got busy with Mack.

He'd been sitting in a chair, trying to sip coffee under his bandanna, but now the cup was in midair, coffee slopping over the rim, and he was rising, hand reaching for the gun on his hip. His fingers closed around the butt at about the same moment my mouth closed around his wrist. My jaws are strong. I let Mack know just how strong. He screamed and dropped the gun, tried to wrench his arm free, tried kicking me, tried everything, and ended up flat on his back with me standing over him, teeth at his throat, his bandanna ripped off and possibly a bit bloody. How fiercely I growled, actually thrilling myself, and if I was letting my teeth break through Mack's skin a bit, that real thin skin at the human throat, well, no one's perfect.

"Don't let it kill me," he cried. "Don't let it kill me."

"Him," said Bernie, and then came a hard and heavy thump and Claudie landed beside Mack on the floor. Claudie's shoulder was bleeding, but there was way too much moaning for the amount of blood, in my opinion.

"Real good job, Chet," said Bernie, standing behind me. "That's enough. That's enough, now. Really—plenty and then some. Let's not gild the lily. Okay, that'll do it. Chet? Big guy?"

All right, all right, I got the message, although that lily part was baffling. I let go of Mack, backed up half a step, or just about.

We stood over the deputies, me and Bernie. Devin was on his feet now by the bed, mouth open. Bernie still had the gun, pointed at the floor. Mack's and Claudie's eyes were glued to him.

"Help me find a reason not to shoot you," Bernie said.

At that moment they both pissed themselves, no hiding that kind of detail from me. Mack took a deep breath, twisted his head toward the window, and shouted: "Sheriff! Sheriff!"

"Dream on," Bernie said. Mack went quiet. Claudie kept on moaning, the bleeding down to a slow trickle, hardly noticeable. We'd dealt with plenty of perps tougher than Claudie.

"It's all over," Bernie said. "Either of you smart enough to realize that? Now is where one lucky guy gets to try for a deal, just one and only now."

"What do you want to know?" Claudie said.

Mack turned to him. "Shut your yap."

"Chet?" Bernie said.

I went closer to Mack, stuck my face right in his. He cringed and tried to writhe away.

"Freeze," said Bernie.

Mack froze.

"What I want to know, Claudie," Bernie began, "is who killed Turk—"

"The sheriff, I swear—"

"And who—" Bernie cut himself off. He glanced at Devin.

"You okay, Devin?"

Devin nodded, a very small movement. Did he look okay? I didn't know. He wasn't crying or anything like that, and I saw no marks on him.

"Come over here a sec," Bernie said.

Devin came over. He wore shorts and a T-shirt; his eyes were blue, like Anya's, but not so bright, and there were deep dark patches under them. Was he supposed to be fat? More like a bit pudgy, to my way of thinking, with a nice strong chest. I liked him right away.

"My name's Bernie. This is Chet. Your mom asked us to find you, and now we're going to take you back to her. Okay?"

Devin nodded, a little more vigorously this time.

"First, there's something you can do for us. See that duct tape? Cut off some strips about yo big."

Devin cut off some yo-big strips. I kept watch on Mack and Claudie. So did Bernie. He wanted to do something real bad to them: I could feel it.

Devin came over with the strips. "Good job," Bernie said. He held out the gun. "Ever fired one of these before?"

Devin shook his head.

"There's a first time for everything," Bernie said.

"Jesus Christ," said the deputies, both of them. They were trembling now.

Devin took the gun, real carefully. "Go stand by the door," Bernie told him. "Keep us covered."

Devin stood by the door.

"Maybe better if you just point it down at the floor for now," Bernie said.

Then Bernie got to work with the duct tape. Did we need Devin to cover us? Not at all: covering was one of my specialties. But for some reason I didn't mind, just this once.

Bernie started with Mack, duct-taping his arms behind his back from the shoulders down to the tips of his fingers, and then taping his legs together from above the knees to the ankles. Same thing to Claudie. Claudie made some noises, and Bernie told him to zip it. He zipped it.

After that—and this was one of those nice Bernie touches— he lay them on their sides, back to back, and wound duct tape around their two necks, round and round so they were taped together. You don't see that every day.

He rose. "Thanks, Devin." Bernie took the gun. "There's a very nice woman named Suzie waiting outside. How about you going down with Chet while I say good-bye to these gentlemen?"

"Okay," said Devin.

"But first I want you to look at something." Bernie pointed toward the pool of piss on the floor. "Whenever you think about all this, remember that part, too."

Devin looked. "Okay," he said.

I walked over beside him and wagged my tail. Bernie gave him Mack's flashlight. We went downstairs. I had the boy, right there beside me.

THIRTY-TWO

Devin and I walked out of the old hunting lodge, me keeping real close to him. I led him past the sheriff's cruiser—passenger door open so the inside light was on as well as those little front lights, nice and bright outside—and over to the bushes. The sheriff lay on the ground where we'd left him and Suzie stood nearby, holding the nightstick by the middle, not how it's done.

The sheriff's eyes were open and he was saying something like, ". . . got it all wrong." He shut up when I gave him a long look, my face almost within touching distance of his. The sheriff had pissed himself, too? This was turning out to be quite an evening.

Suzie came toward us. "Devin?" she said.

"Are you Suzie?" he said. "I'm supposed to wait with you."

Suzie gazed at him. The look on her face at that moment: hard to describe. Let's just mention again that Suzie was a gem, and it all came from deep inside her. She held out her free hand, very steady in the space between them. After a bit of a pause, Devin took it. She—how would you put this?—kind of reeled the boy in, slow and gentle. Suzie hugged Devin, not the tight squeezing kind, but just a nice hug. From where I was, I could see his face, eyes open and staring.

"We're going to get you to your mom as fast as we can," Suzie said.

Devin's eyes closed. His arms reached up and circled around Suzie's back.

Bernie came outside, Devin's pack in one hand, the gun in his belt, and a hard look on his face.

"Everything under control?" he said.

Well, of course! Controlling them after the cuffs were on wasn't much of a challenge.

"And you, Bernie?" Suzie said. "What was that shooting?"

"No casualties," Bernie said. "All secure."

The sheriff's eyes shifted.

Bernie gave him a quick glance, the sort of glance you might give to a not-living thing. "Looking at a double murderer here," he said. He popped the trunk of the black-and-white, bent down, grabbed Sheriff Laidlaw, and hauled him to his feet, not gently.

"Whose idea was wiring my car?" Bernie said.

Sheriff Laidlaw did not reply. His mouth made a funny little movement, like . . . like he was thinking of spitting in Bernie's face. I'd seen that once before and won't describe what happened after. But in this case, no spit flew, the sheriff maybe changing his mind.

"Nothing to say?" Bernie said. "Makes sense—you have no cards." He picked up the sheriff's hat, crammed it on his head, and slung the sheriff in the trunk and slammed it shut. Then he turned to Devin. "Did they feed you all right? Hungry or thirsty?"

"I'm a bit thirsty," Devin said.

"Any water, Suzie?" said Bernie.

She moved toward her pack, lying by the bushes. Out of the blue, I was suddenly kind of thirsty myself, but at that moment, from over by those bushes, came wafting that strange locker-room-laundry-hamper scent. I sniffed my way over there, and kept sniffing, the scent growing stronger and stronger. It's possible Bernie spoke, saying something like, "Chet? Chet?" but it's not for sure. Very soon I found myself all the way around the back of the hunting lodge, following the scent toward a falling-down shed, a crooked shape in the darkness. But not complete darkness, on account of the moon, or a slice of it—don't ask me what's going on with that—rising in the night. And what was this? Two sort of chubby little figures seemed to be playing near the shed, bumping into each other, falling down, running around, that kind of thing. It looked like fun. I went closer and saw they were . . . wow! Bears! More specifically bear cubs, which I knew from Animal Planet.

What a time they were having! Who wouldn't have wanted to join in? Once Bernie had said something about what we'd do if we ever stumbled upon bear cubs. Was it play with them? While I was trying to remember, I trotted a bit closer. They heard me, turned, went still. They looked at me. I looked at them and wagged my tail. Friendly little guys, no doubt about it. I took a few more steps and gave the nearest one a friendly bump, the kind that said, you can give me a friendly bump back. And maybe the little guy was about to do that, but before he got the chance, an enormous figure shot straight up behind the bear cubs, and it came to me: *The mother bear will be close by. Do not get between the mother bear and her cubs.*

Yes, this was the mother bear. She had her mouth open: the size of her teeth! And her front paws were raised high: the claws on them! The moonlight gleamed on all those huge sharp things, teeth and claws. But the truth was I didn't happen to be between her and the cubs—I was on the other side of them—so no reason for alarm on her part. I barked to let her know just that.

The message didn't get through. The next moment she roared—a roar unlike any I've ever heard, deep and loud and growly and—I don't want to admit it—scary. I barked my loudest, making my no-reason-for-alarm point as strongly as I could. She roared again, kicking it up another notch to a notch I don't have, also sending waves of locker-room-laundry-hamper scent my way, and then she charged. There are times, hardly any, when booking is the best policy. I booked.

Booked my very fastest, wheeling around and racing back in the direction of the lodge. When I came to the corner, I glanced back and there she was, bounding after me and maybe even closing the distance—how was that possible?—her eyes mad with fury. I picked up the pace, hit a speed of faster than my very fastest, skidded around to the front of the lodge and dashed for the car.

There it was, Devin already sitting in front, Suzie in the back, Bernie standing by the open driver's-side door. I dove right in, landing somewhere in back.

"Chet? What the hell?" And then Bernie saw. He dove in, too, backed the cruiser in a wild fishtailing turn and zoomed down the lane. The mother bear chased us halfway to the track that led out of Jackrabbit Junction.

When we reached the track, Bernie glanced one more time in the rearview mirror and stopped the car.

"Everybody okay?" he said. He glanced back. "Chet? Could you get off Suzie, please?"

"It's all right," Suzie said. "I think he's had a fright."

Whoa. What a suggestion. I moved as far as possible from

Suzie, sat straight and still, got the panting under control. Fright was not part of my world, amigo.

We were back in the spot where Miss Rendell had dropped us—at the top of the crest where the track started zigzagging down toward Durango, its distant glow even more apparent to me than before—but now we had our own wheels, namely this black-and-white. That was how things went down in our business: we rolled with the punches.

"Headed for home?" Suzie said.

"Soon as we finish up," Bernie said.

What did that mean? I wasn't sure, but if Bernie said there was finishing up to do, then that was that. He put the car in gear, and just as he did, lights appeared, bobbing slowly up the track from Jackrabbit Junction.

"Still got that flashlight, Devin?" Bernie said.

Devin handed Bernie the flashlight. Bernie got out of the car, switched on the flashlight, and set it down in the lane, the beam pointing in the direction of the hunting lodge. He got back in the car.

"Civic duty," he said.

"Helping the FBI?" said Suzie.

Bernie laughed. Suzie smiled and touched the back of Bernie's neck through that little gap under the headrest. We started bumping our way down the ridge.

I'd been on bad roads before—and also on no roads at all—but this road was almost worse than no road, if that made any sense. It got no better when we came down off the ridge, pothole after pothole, streams streaming across it every now and then, and once Bernie and I had to get out and drag away a whole tree. But eventually, down lower, it started to smooth out a bit. It seemed almost quiet, and not long after the beginning of the almost-quiet period, Devin spoke up.

"What happened to me?" he said.

It went still in the car. Suzie's eyes seemed very liquid in the darkness.

"How about you tell us what you remember?" Bernie said, his voice not particularly soft and gentle—what I'd expected—but more businesslike. "I'll try to fill in the blanks."

"Okay," said Devin. Then came a long silence. The moon was rising in the sky and stars were shining all over it. Otherwise: darkness everywhere, and rough country gliding by outside my window. After a while, Devin said, "Where do you want me to start?"

"Stiller's Creek," Bernie said. "Where you all camped that last night."

"You want to hear about pitching the tent, getting all set up?"

"Sure."

"Um. We pitched the tent and Turk built a fire and we had these Spam burgers and then it was dark . . . so that's about all."

"You bedded down for the night?"

"Uh-huh," said Devin. There was another long silence. Some silences are just no sound happening. Others are like something heavy is in the room. This was one of those. It got heavier and heavier, and then Devin said, "I . . . uh, didn't feel like sleeping in the tent."

"No?" said Bernie.

"It gets kind of crowded," Devin said. Another silence, but not so long. "And it's nice under the stars."

"Right about that," Bernie said.

"So anyway I took my sleeping bag outside and went to sleep," Devin said. "Turk sleeps under the stars, too—I forgot to mention that. He was over by the fire pit. But he woke me up during the night. And he said, 'Hey, did I want some Coke.' I sat up and he had this Coke. We hadn't had any Coke on the trip—there's no Coke at camp, no sweet drinks at all. So I said yeah."

"Can or bottle?" Bernie said.

"Bottle."

"Did he take the cap off or was it already open?"

"I . . . uh, I'm not sure," Devin said.

"That's okay," said Bernie. "Do you remember that snap-fizz sound you get when the cap snaps off?"

Devin was quiet for a moment or two. Then he said, "I don't think so. Is it, like, important?"

"Not really," Bernie said. "The only important thing now is that you're safe." He gave Devin's shoulder a quick pat. "What happened next?"

"I drank the Coke and went to sleep."

"How did it taste?"

"Like Coke. You know. Great."

"Before you went to sleep," Bernie said, "did you hear any talking?"

"From the tent, you mean?" said Devin.

"Or anywhere?"

Devin shook his head. "The next talking I heard was when I woke up."

"And when was that?"

"I don't know. The blindfold was on."

"Uh-huh," Bernie said.

"I didn't even know what was happening—I thought I was blind. Then I tried to get the blindfold off, but my hands were tied. Then I tried to yell, but there was tape on my mouth. That's when I heard talking. A man said to shut the fuck up."

"Did you recognize his voice?"

"No," Devin said. "But it turned out to be one of those two guys, the meaner one."

"Which one's that?"

"The not quite as big one."

"Mack."

"They never said their names." Devin turned to Bernie. "And I never saw their faces till . . . till you came. Who are they?"

"Criminals," Bernie said.

And soon they'd be breaking rocks in the hot sun. I felt pretty good about that. I squeezed over toward Suzie. She put her arm around me.

". . . he picked me up," Devin was saying. "I kind of struggled, and my shirt got ripped, and I fell and tried to roll away, but he grabbed me and then I felt a sharp thing in my leg and that's all I remember till I woke up again and I was in that room."

"In the hunting lodge."

"Yeah. That place."

"The ripped shirt," Bernie said. "Is it the one you're wearing?"

"Yeah."

Bernie turned. "Is that the rip? At the back of the neck?"

Devin nodded.

"And that's where the name tag goes?"

"My mom sewed it on."

"Check if it's still there."

Devin checked. "It musta got torn off."

"Good thing you're a fighter, Devin."

"Huh?"

"That name tag turned out to be real important."

"You found it?"

Bernie smiled. "A fighter and pretty smart, too."

"Thanks," said Devin in a very small voice. We went bumpity bump over a long washboard stretch, but then came smooth gravel and Bernie stepped on it. "You're taking me to my mom?" Devin said.

"After one quick errand," said Bernie.

"Where is she?"

"At home."

"Can I talk to her?"

"Suzie?" said Bernie.

Suzie flipped open her phone. "No service," she said.

"Should have service soon," Bernie said.

"That's all right," said Devin. "Will my dad be there, too?"

Suzie's arm tightened around me.

"Your dad got involved with some bad people," Bernie said. "That's why this happened."

"Does he know about me?"

"He felt very bad about it," Bernie said.

Devin went quiet for a bit. Then he said, "I want to talk to him."

Bernie stepped on it a little more; we were whipping through the night. "They killed him, Devin," Bernie said.

"My dad's dead?"

Bernie nodded.

Sometimes humans go to pieces. I hate seeing that, and kids going to pieces is the worst. Devin went to pieces. Bernie tried pulling him over, closer to him, but Devin wouldn't be pulled. He went to pieces by himself. We drove faster and faster; I thought we'd lift right off the ground.

"Why? Why?"

Bernie didn't answer at first. But then, after more why-whys, he took a deep breath and said, "Your dad finally stood up to them."

Was that what had happened? Not the way I remembered it, but the whole thing was pretty complicated, and if Bernie said so, then end of story.

Devin started quieting down after that. We came to a crossroads, the crossing road being paved, and made a pit stop. When we returned to the car, Devin climbed into the back with me and Suzie sat in front. We drove down the paved road. Devin said, "So he was brave?"

"Yeah," said Bernie.

Devin leaned against me and fell asleep. Somewhere high above a chopper went *whap-whap-whap*. Not loud; no reaction from Bernie or Suzie; no surprise.

It was still dark when we pulled into the town of Big Bear and parked in Judge Stringer's pebbly driveway. His house was dark, too.

"Here's how this'll work," Bernie said. "Chet and I go up to the house. Devin and Suzie get down out of sight. Suzie counts to ten and beeps the horn, beep-beep. Everybody good?"

Good? Way better than good: what a plan!

Bernie and I got out of the cruiser; he closed the door real softly. We walked up to the house and stood on either side of the door, right against the wall, totally silent; just like in practice.

BEEP-BEEP.

I heard stirring in the house almost right away, and then light flowed out from a window somewhere above us, and I heard the judge's wife.

"Clarence? I think the sheriff's in the driveway."

"Damn it to hell," said the judge, or something like that: he was farther from the window and I couldn't be sure.

Then a bit of quiet, and after that came a soft *pad pad,* moving closer and closer. The door opened.

The judge, standing in the doorway, just out of sight, spoke in one of those urgent loud whispers—so strange: what was the point? But no time for that now.

"Laidlaw?"

Silence.

"Christ almighty," said the judge. He stepped outside, within touching distance of me and Bernie on either side. The judge, wearing pajamas—hey, they were orange—and those slippers with the rawhide laces, wasn't looking sideways. He was peering at the cruiser, his white hair all over the place, his face set in an irritated expression, his eye—the one I could see—angry.

"Laidlaw?"

He took another step. We pounced. The judge twisted around, looked pretty shocked to see us. There was a bit of a struggle. Somehow the judge slipped out of his pajama top, fell free to the ground and started scrambling into the house. I caught him by the pant leg. Weren't pajamas a kind of pants? Case closed.

The judge screamed. No way he could have been in that kind of pain. Then, like his scream had caused it—that confused me for the longest time—lights flashed on, so bright and all around the house and the driveway and the lawn that it was almost day, and dudes, heavily armed dudes wearing blue hiking outfits, came rushing in from every direction and surrounded us. I recognized a couple of them, including the nice one who'd shared his BLT, and the gray-haired one who now faced Bernie and said, "What the hell's going on?"

"We were just about to deliver this prisoner," Bernie said.

The gray-haired dude glanced down at the judge. "But we haven't even arrested him yet," he said.

"What arc you charging him with?" Bernie said.

"A million things," said the gray-haired dude. "Corruption, racketeering, drug dealing, money laundering, blackmail, Christ knows what else—been sitting on this county for months. And now you come to fuck it up."

"Were your eyes open while all that sitting was going on?" Bernie said.

The gray-haired dude turned bright red. "Better have friends in high places, buddy boy. Who the hell are you?"

"Hikers," Bernie said. "We met on the trail—don't you remember?"

The gray-haired dude's face left the red stage, hit purple. A couple of the armed guys stepped forward.

"Take it easy," Bernie said. He handed the gray-haired dude our business card, the new one with the flower. Bernie didn't care for the flower, but it was Suzie's design, so we were living with it for now.

The gray-haired dude scanned the card. "This doesn't tell me a whole hell of a lot."

"Happy to answer any questions," Bernie said. "But they'll have to wait till tomorrow. Meanwhile, you can add kidnapping and conspiracy to commit murder to those charges." He handed over the keys to the cruiser. "The actual murderer's in the trunk. I assume you picked up the deputies."

"Still looking for them."

"They weren't in the hunting lodge?"

"What hunting lodge?"

"You didn't see my flashlight?"

"What flashlight?"

One of the guys toward the back held up the flashlight. "Boss? I didn't know whether to mention this at the time."

Then came more palaver, but after that we were in the Beetle and headed home, Bernie driving, Suzie sleeping beside him—he had his arm around her the whole way—Devin, also sleeping, in the back with me. I was wide awake. Day—the real day—broke all around us as we came down out of the high green country and into the desert. When the most beautiful part of that was fading, I got started on the rawhide lace. It just so happened that I'd ended up with one of the judge's slippers, exactly how being a bit of a mystery.

Anya wasn't inside her house, or in the doorway, or on the front lawn. She was standing right out in the middle of the street. That moment, when Devin ran into her arms and she swept him up, and they cried their eyes out? Well, this job is the best there is, if I haven't mentioned that already.

"Don't know whether to cash the check," Bernie said as we drove away.

I sat up straight.

"Why not?" Suzie said.

"She never leveled with us," Bernie said. "I'm not even sure she—"

"Cash the check, Bernie," Suzie said. "You earned it."

Ah, that Suzie.

But soon came a puzzler: When we stopped for gas and Bernie was at the pumps, Suzie spoke, very quiet, maybe just to herself. "Check means bank account," she said. "Where it wasn't safe to keep money because of the IRS." The check was good? It wasn't good? I got a bit nervous.

Bernie climbed back in the car. "Something on your mind?"

"No." Suzie glanced at him. "Yours?"

He nodded. "I was wondering if he'll tell her the part about holding the automatic while I tied up those deputies."

"What?"

"The safety was on," Bernie said. "As I recall."

When we got home, Mr. Parsons was out on his front lawn, Iggy behind him in the window, jumping up and down. Mr. Parsons stumped over as we got out of the car.

"Saw the news," he said. "Congratulations. So glad you're all back together."

"Thanks for your help," Bernie said.

"A pleasure," said Mr. Parsons. "Iggy slept twenty-four hours solid after Chet left. One bit of neighborhood news—there's this little puppy that's been hanging out in the canyon lately."

"Yeah?" said Bernie.

"Funny thing is," said Mr. Parsons, "he's a perfect miniature of our friend here."

"Chet?"

"The same."

Then they were all looking at me for some reason. I wagged my tail, my go-to move, really, suitable for just about every occasion.

Bernie and Suzie closed the bedroom door and went right to sleep, or pretty soon. I slept under the kitchen table, one of my favorite spots, the table top being a kind of roof and then there was the bonus of the real roof. When I woke up, Suzie was gone and Bernie was showered, shaved, dressed, and drinking coffee; his face looked almost back to normal.

"Hey, big guy." I went over to him. "You did great," he said, and gave me lots of pats. "How about we pay Georgie Malhouf a visit?"

Not long after that, we—how would you put this?—barged, yeah, we barged into Georgie's office without knocking. Georgie was at his desk, in the middle of saying something to Butch, in one of the visitor chairs. They both rose, real surprised.

"Why, Bernie," Georgie said. "We were discussing you this very moment. Butch, didn't I just finish saying that Bernie should be on the receiving end of a nice fat check from Malhouf International?"

"Huh?" said Butch.

"What I want," Bernie said, "is to see some paper I allegedly signed."

"Sure thing, right away," said Georgie. He fumbled in a drawer, handed Bernie a sheet of paper.

Bernie glanced at it, tossed it away. "Not this one. You know what I'm looking for." Georgie gave him another sheet. Bernie scanned it and nodded. "Eat it," he said.

There was pause. Then Georgie said, "Can Butch have some?"

"Butch?" said Bernie.

"Maybe a little," Butch said.

Bernie tore off a thin strip, which Butch ate. Georgie ate the rest. They didn't seem to enjoy it, no surprise to me. Eating paper was pretty pointless, as I've proved to myself more than once.

A few days later, Moondog knocked on our door. He didn't bring Rummy with him, just Rummy's smell.

"Owe you an apology," he said.

Bernie's face was stony. "Some things you can't apologize for."

"Right about that," Moondog said. "I apologize anyhow."

Bernie said nothing.

Moondog shuffled around a bit. "Sheriff killed Turk because he thought you'd get the truth out of him?" he said.

"Something like that," Bernie said.

Moondog reached in his pocket and held out the nugget. "Here," he said.

Bernie took the nugget.

Moondog shuffled around some more. "Don't have to tell me or nothin', but I'd sure like to know where that nugget come from."

Bernie gave him a long look. "Chet found it somewhere in the mine."

Moondog nodded. "What I thought. See, there's stories going way back that hidden deep inside that son of a whore is a chamber with a seam of pure gold yea big."

Not exactly: it was even bigger.

"What I'm thinkin' is you got a real talented dog here. I'm proposin' we go in halves, you and me, lease us some earth-movin' equipment, and get rich as kings."

Bernie thought. Moondog and I waited. "I've made a few investments recently that didn't work out," Bernie said at last.

Tin futures? Hawaiian pants?

"So I'm going to pass on this one."

After Moondog left, we went on a nice long walk. Bernie did some whistling; he was real happy.

"Gotta pick and choose, big guy," he said. "That's what shrewd investing's all about."

Oh, Bernie.

SIMON &
SCHUSTER

Spencer Quinn

DOG ON IT

**If you enjoyed To Fetch A Thief, don't miss Chet's
debut adventure where he sniffs out the culprits of
the disappearance of a 15-year-old girl.**

One day, on her way home from school, Madison
Chambliss disappears off the face of the earth. Begged to
help by the girl's mother, Chet and his human companion,
Bernie, are not convinced it's a kidnapping as there is no
ransom demand. But they are sure of one thing: something
smells funny. And before long, the pair get drawn into a
violent and sinister world that puts both of them in peril …

ISBN 978-1-84739-838-3
PRICE £6.99

**SIMON &
SCHUSTER**

Spencer Quinn

TO FETCH A THIEF

Chet has smelled a lot of unusual things in his years
as trusted companion and partner to P.I. Bernie Little,
but nothing has prepared him for the exotic scents he
encounters when an old-fashioned traveling circus comes
to town. The only problem is that Peanut, the headlining
pachyderm of this particular one-ring circus, has gone
missing – along with her trainer, Uri DeLeath. Stranger
still, no one saw them leave. How does an elephant vanish
without a trace into the dark desert night?

Some very dangerous people would prefer that Chet and
Bernie disappear for good and will go to any lengths
to make that happen. Across the border in Mexcio and
separated from Bernie, Chet must use all his natural
strength and doggy smarts to try and save himself – not to
mention Bernie and a decidedly uncooperative Peanut, too.

ISBN 978-0-85720-852-1
PRICE £7.99

**SIMON &
SCHUSTER**

This book and other **S&S UK** titles are available from your local
bookshop or can be ordered direct from the publisher.

978-1-84739-838-3	Dog On It	£6.99
978-1-84739-837-6	Thereby Hangs a Tail	£6.99
978-0-85720-850-7	The Dog Who Knew Too Much	£7.99
978-0-85720-852-1	To Fetch a Thief	£7.99